Mending Scars

Adrean,
Love is worth
the scars ♡

Nikki
Sparxx

NIKKI SPARXX

Mending Scars
Copyright © 2014 by Nikki Sparxx.

All rights reserved.

ROMANCE THAT *Sparks* YOUR SOUL

For more information
www.facebook.com/NikkiSparxxAuthor

Cover Design: Cover to Cover Designs
www.covertocoverdesigns.com

Photo Credit: Simon Barnes Photography
https://www.facebook.com/HOTSNAPZ

Model: Andrew England

Contents

Mending Scars

Mending Scars

Prologue

Kaiya

It's amazing how scars can still affect you long after they're inflicted. Even though Kaleb's gone, the scars he left continued to resound in the depths of my soul, tormenting me and overshadowing the happiness that Ryker has brought me.

After everything Kaleb had put me through, I still hurt because of his death. I couldn't explain why, but the pang of pain, although small, was undeniable; so was the hollow sliver in my heart for him.

I knew Kamden was hurting, too. I could see the guilt and remorse eating at him every day as he tried to wash them away with liquor, and that made me feel so much worse. I hated that he had to carry such a burden because of me.

Everything was always my fault.

The shooting still haunted me, adding to the nightmares that relentlessly plagued me. Ryker was the only thing that got me through, especially since Kamden was slowly sinking into an all-too-familiar hole of despair. I needed to save him, to salvage and mend the fragments that were left of him, but how could I when I couldn't even save myself?

I didn't think anything else could flip my life upside down again,

1

but I was wrong. So very, very wrong.

Chapter One

Kaiya

I sat up in bed, waking from a nightmare. The air was sucked from my lungs, and sobs racked my body as images of Ryker being shot and the feel of his blood all over my chest and arms assaulted me. My heart pounded furiously against my chest as I screamed through choking tears. "No! Ryker! No!"

"Ky, look at me, baby," a voice heavy with sleep urged. Firm, callused hands cupped my face and forced me to look into mocha-colored eyes filled with worry. *Ryker.*

Sighing in relief, tears trickled down my fevered cheeks as I clasped my hands over his. His thumbs moved beneath my palms as he stroked my skin. "Just another nightmare, Warrior. I'm right here. I'm not going anywhere."

My grip tightened on his inked hands as my eyes ran over his face. My voice was weak and hoarse when I spoke. "It always feels so real."

He brought his lips to my forehead and pressed a soft kiss there. My eyes closed as I enjoyed the tingle he still sent through me. I felt his breath against my face as he sighed, his voice softening with his reply, "I know, baby. I know."

Even though a couple of months had passed, we both still had nightmares about the shooting. When we stayed the night in my own apartment, Kamden often woke us with his or vice versa. I didn't know when or if they would ever stop, but I hoped they eventually would. I didn't want to have nightmares for the rest of my life.

"Same one?" Ryker asked, brushing his lips across my skin again. His hands moved from my face down to my shoulders. My eyes opened and locked on his as he began to softly rub up and down my arms.

I swallowed deeply and cleared my throat. My voice was clogged with ragged emotion. "Yeah."

An exact replay of the events of that night had become my worst nightmare—worse than the ones of Kaleb molesting me over the years, worse than the ones of the *incident*. Seeing Ryker get shot was unbearable, and having to relive it over and over again was agonizing.

My eyes fell to his chest. Bringing my hands up, I placed one over his heart and delicately traced over his scar with my fingers.

I still can't believe how close I was to losing him.

Another flood of tears burned my eyes, but I forced them back.

There's no reason to cry. Ryker's still here. He's still with you. Stop being weak.

Leaning in, I pressed my lips to his scar, letting them linger on his skin before pulling back and looking up at him.

Ryker cupped the back of my head and gently pulled my face to his.

My eyes fluttered shut, my stomach tightening as his mouth met mine. Every touch filled me with bliss, bringing me a happiness I still couldn't believe I had. Ryker was my remedy, the only one capable of washing away the taint from my nightmares, the only one able to take away the pain.

When our lips parted, he lay his forehead against mine. "I love you, Warrior."

My heart warmed, chasing away the ugly, biting cold that crept in from the nightmare.

I don't think I'll ever get tired of hearing him say that.

My response was automatic, instinctive because of how much I felt for him, how real it was. "I love you, too."

Ryker lay us back down and enveloped me in his arms. Draping my leg over his, I nestled into him and released a sigh of contentment. Being like that, warm in his embrace in bed, was my favorite place to be—my own personal heaven from the hell in my mind, keeping my demons at bay.

I yawned as my eyes became heavy. Ryker's fingers softly ran through my hair, and it didn't take long for him to lull me back to sleep.

I loved waking up in Ryker's arms. Even though I absolutely loathed mornings, seeing his handsome face the moment I woke up always made me smile.

He stirred, opening one eye as he gruffly murmured, "Mornin', beautiful."

The grin I had spread wider, making my cheeks feel tight. "Morning, baby."

Pulling me to him, he pressed his lips to mine. I had stopped trying to fight him on that, even though I was mortified by my morning breath. I thought it was sweet that kissing me was still the first thing he wanted to do when he woke up.

We had spent the night at his apartment, where we usually stayed on the weekends. I couldn't be at mine when Kamden drowned himself in alcohol, which was how he spent his Friday and Saturday nights. I had tried to stop him multiple times, but it only escalated things, especially with Ryker being so protective over me. I didn't want to watch the two men that I loved fight, so I let Kamden be—at least for the time being.

I hated watching Kamden burrow himself deeper into his hole. Even though therapy had helped in the beginning, he was slowly sinking into an all-consuming depression. I prayed I could bring him out of it, but I wasn't sure if I'd be able to. I'd still be buried in mine if it wasn't for Ryker.

The brush of his knuckles down my cheek brought me out of my thoughts. "Ready for breakfast?"

"Yeah. I want to check on Kamden first, though." Turning away from him, I reached for my phone on the nightstand. I quickly dialed Kamden's number, but his phone went straight to voicemail.

Damn it.

I pulled the phone away from my ear before getting out of bed. "Went straight to his voicemail. I'm going to go over there and make sure he's okay."

Ryker threw the covers off and slid to the edge of the mattress. "I'll go pick something up." He stood and walked toward me, then wrapped his muscular arms around my waist. My hands wound around his neck as he dipped his head to kiss me again. When he pulled away, I was left in a haze from his kiss, as usual.

God, those lips.

Ryker smirked knowingly when our eyes met. He made me feel like a giddy school girl, even after being together for so many months, which may not have been long for most, but was sort of a record for us. Neither of us were relationship people, and I definitely never thought I would have a love like the one Ryker and I shared. Some things still took some getting used to at times.

I stepped around him, my face heating as I headed for the bathroom. I could hear him chuckling softly as he followed behind me, apparently amused by his effect on me.

When we finished getting ready, Ryker and I left his apartment together. My place was only the next building over, so I walked there while he hopped in his truck and drove out of the parking lot.

I thought moving out of our old complex would help, but it didn't seem like it was. Kamden was still having trouble coping with killing Kaleb, no matter what I said or did. He had even started skipping his therapy sessions.

When I reached my apartment, I slid my key into the lock and twisted the knob. Anxiety knotted my stomach when I entered, worry for Kamden eating at me since he hadn't answered my phone call. "Kam?"

He didn't answer.

Probably passed out, wasted.

I made my way to his room, and the door was wide open. Kamden lay face down, wearing a muscle shirt and a pair of gym shorts. A half-empty bottle of Jack was tipped over on the floor beside the bed. Kamden's arm dangled over the side of the mattress next to it. "Kam?" I slowly crept toward him before sitting beside him.

No response again.

His mouth was wide open and drool dampened the pillowcase.

I gently shook him on the shoulder, but he didn't stir. I jostled him more forcefully, making his upper body shake. He grumbled obscenities and moved slightly, but didn't wake up. I continued to shake him, and he finally jerked awake, sitting up and roughly grabbing me by the forearm.

"Kam! It's just me—it's Kaiya!" My heart pounded as I attempted to pry my arm from his grasp, pulling at his fingers with my own. He squeezed my arm so tightly that I knew I was going to have bruises.

His glazed, bloodshot eyes darted over me before he let go. "Sorry," he muttered, rubbing his hands over his face. I couldn't help but notice his stubble—it looked like he hadn't shaved in days.

I pulled my arm to my chest protectively and rubbed it with my other hand. Glancing down, I could see bruises from Kamden's fingertips already forming.

Shit. Ryker's going to be pissed.

When I looked back up at Kamden, he had his elbows on his knees, cradling his head in his hands. His eyes were closed, and his face was scrunched in discomfort.

"Let me get you some water," I said as I stood. I walked to the kitchen and grabbed a water bottle out of the refrigerator before returning back to Kamden, who was still in the same position.

Sitting back down next to him, I nudged his arm with the water bottle and handed it to him. He took several slow sips before laying back on the bed and groaning.

"You need to stop drinking so much, Kam. I'm worried about you."

"Don't worry about me. I'm fine," he mumbled, draping his arm over his eyes.

I scoffed. "You are not fine. Look at you!" I gestured at him with my hands, even though he couldn't see me.

"Don't fucking start, Ky," he growled in a combination of anger and irritation.

We'd had this conversation before, and I usually let it go because one, I was a coward, and two, I didn't want to fight with him. He had always been there for me, and I wanted to give him his space and let him cope in his own way like he had let me. But this was getting out of hand. "Kam, please talk to me. Don't shut me out."

"Oh, so you can do it to me, but I can't do it to you?" He sat up abruptly and glared at me before pointing his finger in my face. "You're such a fucking hypocrite, Ky."

I flinched, hating the way his words cut through me and impaled my heart. My eyes watered as I meekly replied, "Kam, I-"

He looked away from me, avoiding my gaze. "I think you should go."

I was about to do as he said, but the stubborn side of me said fuck that. I swiped the few tears that had fallen down my cheeks and crossed my arms over my chest. "No."

Kamden's head snapped to me, and his nostrils flared. "Get out, Kaiya."

He may not have been yelling, but there was no mistaking the ire in his low tone. He was pissed off—really pissed off.

I swallowed the lump in my throat, and held my ground, maintaining eye contact as I repeated, "No."

We stared at each other for what felt like forever until he finally sighed and dropped his head, grumbling under his breath.

Uncrossing my arms, I reached one hand toward him and linked our fingers together. "I'm here for you, Kam."

After several seconds, he finally squeezed my hand back, but remained silent, almost as if internally debating whether or not to confide in me.

"Talk to me." My tone was pleading, practically begging him to open up.

"I'm tired of talking—that's all the therapist wants me to do is talk, talk, talk. And for what?" He thrust our joined hands and his other arm forward as he spoke, the volume of his voice increasing with every word. "She doesn't understand shit. She doesn't know our family. She doesn't know what we went through, what you went through, so what's the fucking point?"

He was right—that's why I never went to therapy. A psychiatrist would never understand what I had experienced. But Kam and I had endured everything together and understood what the other had gone through.

"What if I go with you? Would that help?" I spontaneously spoke, then immediately regretted it.

Shit, why did I say that?

He brought his eyes up to mine, and the hope that lay beneath the drunken haze in them tightened my chest. I knew I'd do anything to help him if that glimmer meant I was getting my brother back.

"You'd do that for me?" Even his tone was brighter, optimistic.

Yeah, I'm fucked.

I smiled softly. "Yeah, I would." I squeezed his hand tighter.

"You hate therapists," he remarked with a chuckle.

"I do," I admitted with a shrug. "But I love you. And I'd do anything to help you."

My words caused something amazing to happen—Kamden smiled. The first real one I'd seen since the shooting. Months had gone by since I'd seen his beautiful smile, the one that had gotten me through so many rough times. The one I missed seeing every day.

"I love you too, *sorella.*" Pulling me to him, he embraced me in a hug. I scooted closer on the bed and wrapped my arms around his waist. He smelt like liquor and sweat, but I didn't care. I was taking another step to getting my brother back.

"We'll get through this," I promised.

I wasn't going to fail Kamden, just like he'd never failed me over the years.

Chapter Two

Ryker

Push through the pain—don't be a pussy!

My chest felt as though it was going to rip apart from the aching tension in the muscles around my scar and up into my shoulder. Even though I went to physical therapy for months following the shooting, I still had pain when I did certain exercises—like the one I was doing.

Grunting through it, I did a couple more reps before pushing the bar up and racking it. Sweat coated my skin as I sat up and reached for my water. I chugged back what was left in the bottle as I got up and headed for the water fountain.

After refilling my bottle, I headed back to my bench and grabbed the dumbbells next to my gym bag. I should've picked a lighter weight for my right arm, but that stubborn side of me couldn't swallow his pride. Fifties weren't that heavy anyway.

Settling back on the bench, I planted my feet, then extended my arms out in front of me. Keeping them straight, I brought them out to the sides before bringing them back to their starting position.

I completed a few reps before I cramped up. I dropped both weights, sending them clanging to the floor before sitting up and reaching for my chest.

Fuck, fuck, fuck!

Hissing in pain, I stretched out my right arm and rubbed the muscle above my scar with my other hand. I clenched and unclenched my fist as I waited for the pain to subside.

Once it finally did, I rotated my shoulder several times to try and alleviate the lingering ache and tightness. Grabbing my towel, I wiped the sweat from my face and angrily stood. Frustration flooded me as I snatched my bag off the ground and headed for the kickboxing room.

You're stronger than this. What the fuck is your problem?

I dropped my shit on the floor once I entered the studio. I didn't even bother getting gloves; I still had wraps around my hands from that lame excuse for a workout.

I chose one of the heavier bags and started doing combinations, ignoring the tension in the right side of my chest and shoulder. I put most of my power into my punches with my left arm and my kicks.

I didn't stop until my lungs screamed for air. Both my arms burned as I walked to grab the water bottle I'd dropped next to my bag. I chugged the liquid back, drinking until nothing was left.

Most of my anger had been taken out on the bag, but there was still some lingering frustration as I caught my breath. I needed to compose myself before my next training session, which was in fifteen minutes.

My phone sounded with a text. I swiped my password and the message from Kaiya automatically popped up. My lips curved into a smile as I read her text:

Warrior: Miss you <3

As I typed back my response, I felt the majority of my anger lifting from just thinking about Kaiya.

Me: Miss you too baby

After sending the text, I went back to my office to ice down my injury—or handicap—as I thought of it. The physical therapists said those muscles might never be the same again, but I was determined to prove them wrong.

I was still a little irritated for the rest of the day until Kaiya walked into the kickboxing studio for class. The remaining frustration weighing me down evaporated when I saw her beautiful face and bright, blue eyes.

My Warrior.

She was the first one there, as usual. It had become a routine for Kaiya to get there early so we could talk about our day and have some time to ourselves before class started. When we reached each other, I wrapped my arms around her waist, lifting her feet off the ground as I kissed her.

"How was your day?" I asked when I set her back down.

"Swamped—we have three new projects that we just started working on this week. How about you?"

I shrugged. "It was okay."

She gave me a knowing look, quirking up one eyebrow and crossing her arms over her chest. "Okay?"

I chuckled and shook my head. "Nothing gets past you, huh?"

"Nope, now tell me," she demanded, trying to keep a stern, straight face as a smile fought its way through.

"Nothing big—I just cramped up during my workout. Bothered me for most of the day."

Her eyes went to my chest where my scar was, and her forehead creased in concern. "Are you sure you're okay? Maybe you should go back to the physical therapist."

I definitely did not want to go back to therapy. They'd limit my workouts, and I was already going easy to begin with. Well, for me, at least. "I'm fine. It was more annoying than anything."

That was a lie—my chest and shoulder hurt from earlier; they always did. The bullet had ripped through muscles around my shoulder blade in the back, as well as nerves in my chest that connected up to the top of my shoulder. There was always a dull, constant pain that never went away.

She brought her worried eyes up to mine and linked our fingers together. "Please be careful, baby."

The look she was giving me, combined with the pleading tone of her voice, made me feel terrible. Kaiya was my weakness.

Maybe I should take it easy.

Gently squeezing her hands, I stroked her smooth skin with my thumbs. "I will."

It had only been a couple of weeks since physical therapy had ended and I'd started working out again. Kaiya was apprehensive about the idea, afraid I would injure myself more. I told her not to worry, but that was like telling her not to breathe.

Kaiya's lips curved up slightly, and that small smile twisted up my insides.

Damn, the things she does to me.

I smiled back before leaning down and pressing a kiss to her forehead. My nose brushed her silky hair, and I breathed in her scent before pulling away. She always smelt so good. Students began coming in then, so Ky and I got ready for class. I liked that she still came, even though Kaleb wasn't a threat to her anymore. I wanted her to be able to defend herself in case something happened and I wasn't around. Anything could happen, especially with all the fucked up people in the world. Plus, getting to touch her during the techniques was an added bonus; I couldn't get enough of her.

Once we finished the kickboxing segment, we went straight into self-defense techniques. The students had mentioned in the previous class that they wanted to practice defending against forward punch attacks. "Sometimes, attackers don't try to grab you or subdue you first. Instead they come out swinging. Today, we're going to focus on counters to this type of assault."

After modeling with one of the other instructors, Mark, I had the class split up into their pairs. Kaiya and I went to our usual spot on the mat to get started. She got in her defensive stance and gave me a playful grin as she awaited my instructions. I smiled as I thought of how much progress she'd made since that very first class, when she'd been so tense and nervous. My warrior had come so far. "Ready, baby?"

Her grin spread. "You know it."

I laughed. "Okay, throw a straight punch while coming toward me." Once she did as I instructed, I moved closer to her while simultaneously shifting to face the arm she used to punch with, blocking the incoming hit with both of my arms. "Instinct tells us to back away from an attack, but the best thing to do in this situation is to get in close."

Kaiya's eyebrows furrowed in confusion. She looked so cute when she made that face. "Why?"

"An attacker isn't going to throw just one punch—they'll keep throwing them as they advance on you, and eventually, they will hit you. So you need to disable them before they land one."

She nodded. "Okay. What do you do from here?"

"Grip their forearm with your outside hand, keeping them close to you. Then using your other arm, throw a back elbow to their face and follow it with a forward elbow on the opposite cheek."

I softly modeled each move, careful not to hurt Kaiya. "Grip their shoulder and knee them in the groin before throwing a side kick to the knee closest to you. If the groin hit didn't put them down for the count, the side kick definitely will."

After releasing her, I walked Kaiya through the steps and had her practice a few times before moving on to a slight variation for if she was backed into a wall or car.

"Many attacks happen in parking lots at night. If someone ever pins you to a car and rears back to punch you, you can still use this same technique."

Kaiya quirked up a brow in intrigue. "Really?"

I smiled at her. "Really. I actually think it's more effective. A car can help you do more damage to the asshole attacking you."

I led her to the padded side of the room we used for wall defense techniques. I gently backed her against it as I explained, "Typically, an attacker will push you into a car or wall if one is around, wanting to trap you." Caging her face between my forearms, I leaned in closer to her. "As in every attack, you can't panic, which is what most people do when cornered like this."

Kaiya wasn't afraid of me, but I knew my proximity would kick her heart rate up, just like it did mine. Her eyes focused on my lips, which curved up as I closed the distance between us and kissed her.

Even though I wanted to do more—much more—I broke the kiss and moved back slightly. Kaiya's face reddened as she glanced around, checking if anyone saw us before she met my eyes and gave me a shy smile. I loved that I made her get flustered like that.

"Aren't you supposed to be teaching me something?" she questioned playfully, looking up at me coyly and batting her eyelashes.

"Yeah, but I can't when you keep distracting me," I teased.

Her eyebrows shot up. "Me? I'm not even doing anything."

"Yeah, you are." My eyes ran up and down her body.

Damn, she's so hot. Especially in those tight shorts.

I leaned to the side and craned my head to get a glimpse of her ass.

Fuck, that ass.

Kaiya cleared her throat and stifled a laugh. "Excuse me, but we don't have all night. I'd really like to learn this routine."

This girl.

I straightened and chuckled. "Fine—let's get back to business. After the attacker pushes you against the car, they'll probably hold you there by choking you, pressing down on your chest, or gripping onto your clothes. And they're going to be all up in your space. Remember, you can't panic."

Flattening my hand over her chest, I softly pushed her back into the wall. Then, I brought my other arm back, readying to punch. "When I throw the punch, do the same thing I taught you earlier—block it with both arms."

I slowly threw the punch, and Kaiya turned to block it with her arms. "Good, now grip my forearm and throw the back elbow. I want you to use the momentum of the strike to force me into the wall, pinning me there with your forearm on my throat."

Once Kaiya had me in that position, I continued. My voice was garbled by her arm on my throat. "Now you can throw some elbows, get some knees to the groin, or grab their head and slam it into the car."

We practiced a few more times before I brought the group back together. "I hoped you learned something that will be able to help you if you're ever put in a situation like this. There are several techniques for a straight punch attack, but I felt this was the easiest and most effective. We'll learn others in the future. Any questions?"

I scanned over the class—everyone's faces had a sheen of sweat but held that look of fulfillment from having a good workout. No one raised their hand or commented, so I dismissed the class.

After Kaiya helped me lock up, we headed back to my apartment. I had gotten stuck at a light on the way, so Kaiya's car was parked in her normal spot when I pulled in. We both had keys to the other's apartment, so she was probably already inside.

When I walked in, I threw my keys on the table and shut the door. "Ky?" I called out as I kicked off my shoes.

She didn't answer, but as I went down the hallway towards my room, I could hear water running. A smirk curved over my lips as I thought of Kaiya naked and wet in my shower.

As I entered the bathroom, my eyes went straight to her. Her back was to me as she rinsed her long, dark hair, and water dripped off every inch of her flawless skin. My gaze roamed lower to her sweet ass as I pulled off my muscle shirt and gym shorts.

When I opened the shower door, she turned and gasped, placing a hand over her heart. "Oh my God, Ryker! You scared me!"

Grabbing her hand, I chuckled. "Sorry, baby." I kissed her palm before pulling her into me, immersing myself in the stream of water and pressing our naked bodies together.

Her hands glided up to my shoulders as I nuzzled into the curve of her neck. Gripping her ass, I nipped at her collarbone while lifting her up. Her legs wrapped around me automatically as I backed her into the tile wall.

Kaiya's fingers knotted in my hair as our mouths crashed together. Her lips parted against mine as my tongue slipped inside, finding hers instantly and tangling together. "Fuck, you taste so good. I've wanted to taste you all night."

Kaiya moaned in my mouth as my hands roamed over her wet skin before finding her tits. I played with one of her nipples, squeezing and pulling it, making her whimper louder. "You like that, baby?" I bit her bottom lip before sucking it into my mouth.

"God, yes." Her legs tightened around my hips, and she ground herself against me.

I pushed my cock harder against her clit, making her cry out again. "You want my dick inside you?"

"Yes! Fuck me now, Ryker." Her tone was desperate with lust.

I trailed one of my hands down her stomach between us before grabbing my cock and guiding it to her pussy.

Fuck, she's so wet already.

Teasing her, I rubbed against her and slipped the tip of my dick inside her sweetness before pulling it out.

Kaiya bit my lip when I put just the head of my cock in again. I circled the rim of her pussy, causing her to bite down harder and moan. "Ryker," she breathlessly pleaded as she pulled me closer to her.

I couldn't help myself when she sounded like that—her need and want for me evident in every noise she made. I thrust myself inside, filling her completely as we both groaned out in pleasure.

The water rained down on us as I hammered Kaiya against the tile. My mouth found her nipple, and I toyed with it with my tongue ring as I continued to pound into her. She gripped my hair as I savored her, sucking her tit as her sweet pussy hugged my dick.

She feels so good… fucking perfect.

Kaiya's nails dug into my head as she arched into me. My hands caressed her soft flesh as I drove deeper inside her. I was close to coming, and by the look on her face, she was too.

Her eyes were closed as she bit down on that full, bottom lip.

Fuck, she's so sexy.

Our wet skin slapped together as I increased my pace, thrusting harder into her, bringing us both to the brink.

I wanted to taste her as I made her come, capture the sounds of bliss she made because of me. I grabbed her face and crushed her lips with mine, opening her mouth with my tongue and slipping it inside.

Fuck, so good.

After a few more thrusts, Kaiya cried out, and her pussy tightened around me. I followed, coming inside her as she trembled against me.

Holding Kaiya up, I pressed kisses along her neck as we caught our breath. "I love you," I murmured against her skin.

Turning her head, she grazed her lips against mine. "I love you, too."

Some of her hair clung to her face as she leaned her head against the wall. I pushed the drenched strands back before kissing her again.

Kaiya's legs had loosened, but as our kiss deepened, she tightened them around me again. My dick started to harden inside her.

Damn, she drives me fucking crazy.

I slowly pumped my cock in and out of her, growling against her lips. "You want more, baby? You want me to fuck you again?"

She sucked my tongue into her mouth. Hard. "Yes, please fuck me," she loudly moaned.

I smirked and roughly thrust into her, eliciting a gasp of pleasure from her swollen lips. We stayed there in the shower until long after the water ran cold.

Chapter Three

Kaiya

I awoke with a satisfied smile on my face, even though the annoying blaring of my phone's alarm assaulted my eardrums. Last night in the shower with Ryker was pure heaven. As I reached for my phone, Ryker shifted behind me and captured me in his arms. I barely grabbed my cell before he pulled me back into him and tented the covers around us.

I turned off the alarm and shifted to face him. He gave me a sleepy smile, and his eyes were still half-lidded in sleep. "Mornin, beautiful."

He leaned in and pressed his full lips against mine. After a few seconds, I groaned, "I need to get ready for work." If we didn't stop now, I'd definitely be late.

He grunted but didn't protest. If it were up to him, we would have stayed in bed until noon every day. I would much rather do that, but I'd already taken enough time off work after the shooting.

I gave Ryker another quick kiss and scooted to the edge. He reached for me, then dragged me back into him. I giggled, able to easily fall back into his loving embrace. "I have to get ready," I said, giving him my best responsible stare down.

"Fine, babe. I'll lay back here and watch your sweet ass wiggle its way to the bathroom." He propped his head on his arm and watched me. I couldn't help but smile the entire way.

I turned into the bathroom and my smile vanished as my head darted away from the mirror. Although Kaleb was gone, I saw him whenever I looked at myself. His face haunted me, and I feared it always would. How could I forget it when it was a replica of mine?

After getting ready, I went to say goodbye to Ryker, who had fallen back asleep. His arms were wrapped around my pillow, and his face was buried in it. Butterflies fluttered in my stomach at the endearing sight, and I smiled as I leaned down and kissed his cheek. "I love you," I whispered, not wanting to wake him.

"Love you, too," he murmured in his sleep, not opening his eyes. I quietly walked out of the room, grabbing my purse and keys from the table before exiting the apartment and heading to work.

Work dragged on and on every day since I'd returned about a month ago. I'd gotten spoiled, spending most of the day with Ryker, sleeping in late every morning, and having sex for most of the day in each room of both of our apartments. My phone vibrated next to my keyboard. I expected a text from Ryker when I entered my password, but instead, there was a message from a unknown number. *Weird.*

Unknown: I'd be careful if I were you bitch

I stared at my phone in shock, my eyes glued to the screen for several seconds before warily glancing around. My heart pounded as a million thoughts ran through my head.

What the fuck? Is this some sort of joke? Who would've sent this?

My instincts told me to call Ryker, but I didn't want him to overreact. It was probably some prank. I was about to delete the text, but decided to keep it just in case I got another one.

It's probably nothing, though.

I placed my phone back on my desk and tried to refocus on work, but now I felt like I was being watched.

Stop being paranoid, Ky. Someone is just fucking around with you.

After a few minutes of inputting figures into a spreadsheet, my phone buzzed again. My eyes darted to my phone, and I hesitantly reached for it before stilling my hand over it.

Oh God, get a grip, Kaiya.

I snatched my phone from the desk and swiped the screen. Another text message popped up on the screen, and thankfully it was from Kamden.

Kam: Therapy at 4 today

Shit! I totally forgot!

I normally got off work at four, so I'd have to leave about half an hour earlier to make it to the appointment on time. I typed a quick email to my boss to let him know, then replied back to Kamden.

Me: K see you there :)

Although I was dreading the appointment, I was also somewhat excited. I'd been watching Kamden sink deeper and deeper into the quicksand of depression for months, helpless to stop it. I was ready to stop being weak and help my brother in whatever way possible, and I prayed that going to therapy with him would do just that.

My stomach was jumbled in thick, tight knots as Kamden and I sat in the waiting room of the psychiatrist's office. Paintings of the Boston Harbor, boats, and sunsets hung on the cream-colored walls and a cliché potted fern sat in the corner of the room.

My leg shook nervously as I bit my nails. Just thinking about discussing Kaleb and my past made me sick.

I can't do this. I can't do this.

My phone chimed, interrupting my anxious thoughts, and I dug in my purse looking for it. When I swiped the screen, a text from Ryker popped up.

> **Ryker:** Proud of you :) don't be nervous you'll be fine I love you Warrior

My stomach tightened for a different reason, and a small smile tugged at my lips. I glanced over at Kamden, who had his head leaned back against the wall. Bags laced his closed eyes, making them look sunken in. Stubble dusted the pale skin of his jaw, and I could tell that he'd lost some weight from his cheeks and neck.

My heart clenched as I appraised him—still the familiar face of my brother, yet so different. Aged. Sadder. Dulled. The vibrancy that his smile normally brought was gone.

Looking back at my phone, I took a deep breath and typed back my reply to Ryker.

> **Me:** Thank you I needed that :) I love you too <3

The door next to the receptionist's window opened, causing Kamden to abruptly sit up. The woman who had checked us in stood in the doorway, smiling politely at us. "Kamden Marlow?"

We both got up and walked toward her. She led us to another room with a huge bookshelf, brown leather couch and matching armchair. More paintings of the harbor, boats, and seaside adorned the walls, continuing the ocean theme from the waiting room. Blue and tan pillows decorated the sofa, adding some color to the neutral decor of the office.

"Dr. Lowell will be with you shortly," the receptionist stated as she exited the room and shut the door.

I rounded the couch and sat down. Kamden sat on my right side and picked up a magazine from the coffee table in front of us.

He flipped through it aimlessly as I played a word scramble game on my phone, trying not to focus on where I was sitting at that very moment. I couldn't let my anxiety consume me, not when Kam was depending on me.

About five minutes passed when the psychiatrist walked in, but it felt like hours to me. I was ready to bust out of my skin—I hated therapists

Dr. Lowell looked to be in her forties, with dirty blonde hair pulled back in a low bun. She wore a basic, black business suit with coordinating pumps. Carrying a large legal pad, she smiled as she approached us.

We both stood as she stuck her hand out toward me. "Nice to meet you—you must be Kaiya. Kamden has told me so much about you," she said warmly.

Great.

I looked at my brother out of the corner of my eye. I could have sworn I saw him smirk, but it vanished as quickly as it had appeared.

Dr. Lowell turned her attention to Kam. "Good to see you again, Kamden. Please sit." She gestured to the couch and waited for us to sit before she turned and sat in the armchair directly across from us. "How have you been?"

I waited for my brother to answer, hoping he would be honest and tell the doctor how he'd been struggling. But I couldn't blame him if he didn't—it would be hard for me to address my issues, also.

Kamden leaned forward and rubbed the back of his neck. He exhaled a heavy breath before speaking. "Some days are worse than others."

Dr. Lowell began writing on her note pad as she asked, "Could you elaborate on that?" "Honestly?" Kamden snorted and ran his hands over his dark, buzzed hair before slapping them down on his thighs. "I don't want to."

He was internally shutting down. I did the same thing all the time so I recognized what he was doing. I needed to be stronger for him, for both of us—to help get through the mess we were in.

I placed my hand over his and stroked over it with my thumb. "Kam," I softly urged.

He balled his hand into a fist under mine and sighed deeply. After a few seconds, he turned his palm over and linked our fingers together. Our eyes met, and I gave him an encouraging smile as I squeezed his hand.

He looked away when he spoke. "For so long, I… I wanted to kill

Kaleb for what he did to Ky. Guess I got what I wanted," he said dejectedly as he hung his head.

The room was soundless except for the scribbling of Dr. Lowell's pen on the paper. The silence constricted my chest, making it hard to breathe as I struggled to hold it together. My eyes burned from tears I knew I wouldn't be able to contain much longer. I hated that Kamden was experiencing all these horrible emotions because of me.

"At least I saved her from more abuse from him, right?" His eyes watered, and he swallowed deeply. "I wasn't able to protect her before, but I took care of that. He won't hurt her again."

"Kam." His name sounded disjointed when I spoke as tears dripped down my face. I cleared my throat, hoping my voice would be steady. "Don't blame yourself for what Kaleb did to me—it was never your fault."

He scoffed. "I was supposed to protect you, Ky—that's what big brothers do. I'm a fucking failure. And a murderer."

Rage rushed through my veins at his self-accusation. I jerked his hand, making him look up at me. "You're neither of those things. It wasn't your responsibility to protect me from Kaleb—that was Mom and Dad's job. They're the fucking failures! And you're not a murderer—you killed Kaleb in self-defense to protect us."

He held my gaze as a single tear fell from each eye down his cheeks. "Doesn't matter—I killed my own brother."

He looked away again, hanging his head in shame. No matter what I said, he never believed me. He still blamed himself. I looked to Dr. Lowell, hoping she would chime in and agree with me.

Setting her pen down, she clasped her hands together on top of the legal pad. "Kamden, you can't keep blaming yourself for this. In order to move on, you have to make peace with yourself. You can't dwell on the past."

Easier said than done, lady.

Kamden abruptly wrenched his hand away from mine and threw his arms out in front of him. "How?" he screamed. His voice boomed and was riddled with emotion. "Can you teach me? Because I've been trying to do that, and the only way I get the pain to go away is to drown

26

myself in alcohol." His face was reddened with fury as more tears fell from his eyes. It ripped my heart apart to see him like that, to know I was one of the causes of his suffering. "What kind of person kills their own brother?"

My heart thumped wildly as my own anger took over again. Shaking my head in disagreement, I interrupted his rant to start one of my own. "Stop it, Kam! You wanna know what kind of person you are?" I moved my face to meet his eyes, but he avoided me. I raised my voice to get his attention. "Look at me!"

It took a few moments before he finally brought his gaze to mine. My hardened eyes relaxed some as I held his stare. "You're the kind of person that holds his grown sister when she has a nightmare. You're the kind of person who has held her hand through every bad time, who has never let her give up, who saved her from the hell she lived in. You're the kind of person who has sacrificed everything for her. You—" I choked through a sob before taking a deep breath and softening my voice. "You're the best kind of person there is."

Our eyes met, and his face reflected the emotions that were swarming me: hurt, fear, guilt, sorrow. All I wanted was for him to go back to the way he was before—to be my strong, stable big brother again. Even though I had Ryker, I still needed Kamden—more than he would ever understand.

Kamden silently stared at me as if knowing I had more to say. I took a shaky breath and continued pouring my heart out to him, hoping my words would bring him back from the ledge he was teetering on. "There aren't words to describe what you mean to me, Kam." I gripped both his hands in mine. "I can never repay you for saving me—from Kaleb and myself. You were there every time I needed you, and I still need you. I need my brother back."

Kamden remained silent for several seconds, then spoke so low that I could barely hear him. "I don't think I can be him again."

His words slammed into my heart, splintering some pieces of it. I squeezed Kamden's hands tighter, hoping to hold on to him in more ways than one, to tether him to me. A steady stream of tears flowed down my face as my voice cracked. "Please try, Kam. Don't give up."

He shook his head before looking up at me, scanning over my face. Pulling his hands from mine, he brought them up and wiped the tears from my cheeks with his thumbs. He gave me a small, forced smile. "I'll try, *sorella*. For you."

My lips slowly spread in a full grin as I threw my arms around Kamden's neck and hugged him tightly to me. My voice was soft but threaded with emotion. "We'll get through this, Kam. Together."

He hugged me back. "I hope so."

I knew he didn't completely believe my words, but I would prove them. I wouldn't give up until I saved Kamden from the darkness that had plagued me for so long.

As I was about to leave the psychiatrist's office, I called Nori, wanting to talk to her about the text message and everything going on with Kam. With traffic, I'd have anywhere from thirty to forty minutes until I would get home, so I had time to talk to her.

Nori's cheery voice greeted me, "Hey, girlie."

"Hey. Are you busy?" I chewed my lower lip as I sat in my car in the parking garage.

"Nah, just got home. What's up?"

I sighed and started driving. "I just got done with my first therapy session with Kamden."

Her tone peaked with curiosity and excitement. "How did that go?"

"Better than I'd expected, but we didn't talk about Kaleb much so that's probably why."

"What did you talk about then?"

Pulling out of the garage, I merged into traffic. "Kamden's issues. He blames himself for everything. He thinks he's a terrible person for killing Kaleb. He called himself a failure and a murderer."

"What?" Her voice raised with anger. "How can he think that? It was in self-defense!"

"That's what I said. But he refuses to listen—he's so stubborn," I said in irritation.

"Coming from the queen of stubbornness herself," Nori joked.

"Ha ha, very funny."

Traffic slowed to a crawl.

Ugh, it's going to take me forever to get home.

"There's something else I wanted to talk to you about."

"Oh, really? I hope it's about sex with that hot man of yours."

I laughed. "Sorry to burst your bubble but no. I got this weird text from an unknown number today."

"Weird how?"

"Hold on, I'll forward it to you real quick."

Traffic was stopped at a light, so I was able to pull up the message and send it to Nori. I put the phone back to my ear. "Just sent it."

"Okay, lemme check." She paused for a few seconds. "Creepy. Did you tell Ryker?"

I blew out a frustrated breath. "No—I don't want him to overreact. It's probably nothing, right?"

Nori didn't reply for several seconds. "Yeah, it's probably some punk teenagers or something."

"You don't sound so sure." I said as the cars in front of me moved past the intersection.

"I was just thinking about who would send something like that to you. But I think it was a onetime thing, maybe even a wrong number."

I hope so.

"Yeah, you're probably right. I just wanted to talk to someone about it."

"Well, you picked the right person. If you get another one, let me know, okay? I'm here for you."

"I know. Thank you."

We chatted for a little longer, then made plans for lunch later that week, making the drive a little bearable for a while. As I continued to fight traffic on the way home, I thought about the events of the day, hoping that everything would turn out all right.

Chapter Four

Ryker

Kaiya felt lifeless in my arms.

Please, God no.

I slumped to my knees, cradling her to me as the warmth of her blood soaked through my shirt and coated my arms. My fingers smeared blood over her fair skin as I framed her face in my hands. "Open your eyes, Warrior! Damn it, open your eyes!"

My entire world crumbled down on me as my life lay, dying in my arms, slowly slipping away from me. "Kaiya! Don't do this to me, baby! Come back to me!" My voice was hoarse and full of desperation— desperation I'd never experienced before.

Nothing. No movement, no sound. Was my heart even beating anymore? How could it when it was lying dead in my arms?

The hollow pain inside me seeped into the depths of my soul, searing me with its agony. I buried my face in Kaiya's neck and sobbed. "No! Not her! Take me instead!"

"Kaiya!" I yelled as I sat up in bed. I was covered in sweat as I fought to regain my breath. My heart pounded furiously as I turned my head and glanced over at a sleeping Kaiya.

Just another dream. Thank God.

Laying back down, I propped myself on my elbow and watched Kaiya sleep. Her cheek was on her bicep as she slept facing me. Some hair had fallen into her face, and her lips were slightly parted. *My beautiful Warrior.*

Watching her sleep helped calm me down when I had nightmares. I needed to see her chest rise with breath, see that her heart was beating. Just like hers, my nightmares felt so real; too real.

I brushed the hair back out of Kaiya's face and kissed her forehead softly. She mumbled a sound of contentment and stirred slightly, but didn't wake up. I watched her for a few more minutes before getting out of bed.

Needing air, I went out on the balcony and leaned against the railing. I took a deep breath, enjoying the feel of the crisp, fall air against my heated skin. Images of the nightmare played in my head, and I couldn't believe how much fear a dream could make me feel.

I shook the thoughts from my head, not wanting to think about Kaiya dying. I tried to focus on something else, and my mind veered to Ethan, yet another thing tormenting me.

Normally, I would get pissed off that I even thought of him, but after seeing Kaiya trying to help Kamden over the past few months, I wondered if I should try to make amends with my own brother. Technically, he was the only family I had left.

Before our parents had died, Ethan and I had been close. He was two years older than me, and we both had been on the football, lacrosse, and wrestling teams together throughout junior high and high school.

After the accident, everything had changed. Ethan and I had trouble coping with the loss of Mom and Dad, and when Ethan had turned eighteen a few months after, he left for college and all but disappeared.

I thought I reminded him too much of what he lost. I resembled my dad, who had been our role model since we were little. He would do anything and everything to help us succeed, and had always been there when we'd needed him. Both of our parents had been. Their death left a hole neither of us knew how to fill.

I thought that had changed when I'd left for college. I'd followed Ethan to Boston University, where we both had received scholarships for lacrosse. Our parents' life insurance had helped with the rest of the costs, and Ethan and I were able to get an apartment off campus. Everything seemed to be going back to the way things had been between us, but I'd been wrong.

I had met Molly in my Biology class. She had blonde hair and green eyes, and half the male population at our school was after her. So naturally, I'd wanted her. I'd made it my mission to make her mine.

It had only taken a few weeks before I succeeded—she hadn't given me a challenge like Kaiya had when I pursued her. Looking back, I doubted that she was ever mine to begin with. She wouldn't have cheated with my brother if she had been.

I'd been stupid for not seeing it. Maybe I'd wanted so badly to fill the void from my parents that I'd ignored the signs—the way they snuck glances at each other, how I'd come home sometimes and Molly was already there, how I wasn't able to get a hold of them at times. Plus, I never thought that Ethan would do something like that to me.

After their betrayal, I'd sworn that I'd never let another person in. But Kaiya changed that—she made me feel things I'd never felt before, and showed me what love really was. But deep down, I sometimes wondered— if my own brother was able to hurt me like that, would Kaiya do the same one day?

The sound of the sliding glass door interrupted my thoughts. I looked over my shoulder to see Kaiya, half-asleep trudging toward me. She had her arms wrapped around herself and rubbed her hands up and down her skin. "What are you doing out here, baby?" she mumbled. I turned to face her. Even with her hair all messy from sleeping and no makeup, she was the most gorgeous thing I'd ever seen. I smiled warmly and leaned back against the railing as she pressed against me.

Laying her head on my chest, she wound her arms around me and exhaled.

I pushed a strand of hair behind her ear and kissed the top of her head. Inhaling the sweet smell of her hair, I closed my eyes. "Just needed some air—had a nightmare."

"You should've woken me up. You're always there for me with mine. I wanna be there for yours, too." She propped her chin on my chest to look up at me.

"Okay, Warrior, next time I'll wake you." I chuckled as I looked down at her. I loved holding her, feeling her body warmth with life, not cold with death like in my nightmare.

"Is something else bothering you? You seemed to be deep in thought when I came outside."

I debated for a few seconds before sighing. "I was thinking about Ethan."

Kaiya lifted her head off my chest and pulled back to look at me better. Her face became lined with concern. "What about? Did he call again?"

I shook my head. "No, he didn't call. I was just thinking about you and Kamden, and that maybe I should try to make things right with Ethan."

"Is that what you want?"

"I don't know." I shrugged. "He's the only family I have left, but I'm not sure if I can forgive him for what he did. Even though I have you, and don't care about Molly anymore, he still betrayed me."

Kaiya nodded in understanding. "Whatever you choose to do, I'll support you."

Smiling, I leaned down to kiss her. "Thank you."

A cold breeze blew past us, and Kaiya's skin raised with goose bumps as she shivered. "Let's go back inside. Warm you back up," I said, backing her toward the open sliding door.

Once we were back in bed, I pulled Kaiya into me, bringing her leg over mine and leaving little space between our bodies. I lowered my head to her chest before kissing her scar, just like I did every night. I never wanted to forget its importance or what it signified. I never wanted to take for granted the gift I'd been given. "I love you, Warrior," I whispered against the marred, yet still beautiful skin.

She brought my face up to hers and brushed her lips over mine. "I love you, too."

Kaiya snuggled into me, laying her head on the inside of my bicep and keeping her leg draped over mine. She fell back asleep almost instantly, but thoughts of the shooting and Ethan kept me awake. My mind wouldn't turn off.

I closed my eyes, and lay my head against Kaiya's, trying to shut my brain down. I focused on the sound of her breathing next to me, the smell of her hair, and the feel of her body tangled up with mine, blocking out everything else.

I felt my body relax and my eyes become heavier. Kaiya was my drug, giving me exactly what I needed when I needed it. Sleep finally found me, pulling me under its dark veil.

Chapter Five

Kaiya

A couple weeks had passed before I received another text from an unknown number. I had just arrived at work when my phone buzzed in my purse—I hadn't even had the chance to take it out yet.

Unknown: I'm coming for you

The familiar feeling of fear lacing my veins rushed over me.

Was this text from the same person as last time? Who is it? What should I do?

All the questions ran through my head and combined with my fear and anxiety, making me nauseous. I sped out of my office to the bathroom down the hall, hoping I would make it in time before I threw up.

Bursting through the door of the women's restroom, I darted into the nearest stall and proceeded to vomit my breakfast into the toilet.

Gross. I hate throwing up.

I rinsed my mouth out and splashed some water on my face. Catching a glimpse of myself in the mirror, I thought of Kaleb. I felt sick again as my heart pounded, my anxiety increasing the longer he lingered in my mind.

Closing my eyes, I took a few deep breaths to dispel the queasiness assaulting my stomach and calm my nerves.

Kaleb's gone. Those texts are just some prank. You're safe.

When I composed myself, I headed back to my office. I grabbed some gum from my purse so I wouldn't be stuck with vomit breath for the rest of the day.

As I sat in my office chair, my hands trembled slightly. I clenched them tightly to stop the shaking, but my nerves were shot. There was no denying that I was starting to get scared. I grabbed my phone and forwarded the text to Nori.

Me: FWD: I'm coming for you

Me: Got this a few minutes ago

A few seconds later, she messaged me back.

Nori: WTF Who do you think it's from?

I bit my bottom lip and typed my response.

Me: Idk do you think I should tell Ryker?

Nori: I would do you think it's your mom?

I furrowed my brow.

Could it be her? Would she really sink this low?

I hoped the answer was no—that deep down, my mom still loved me, even if it was just a tiny bit.

I was so excited. I'd just gotten my grade for a huge science project that took me weeks to work on, and I couldn't wait to show Mom and Dad.

At dinner that night, I waited until everyone had plated their food before I brought it up. "You know that project I've been working on? For my biology class?"

"What about it, sweetheart?" Dad responded as he picked at his food. He always seemed to be somewhere else, not really with us.

A smile spread over my face as I excitedly replied, "Well, we got our grades, and I got an A! I was so—"

"That's nice, Kaiya," Mom interrupted. Her tone was dismissive and

uninterested. "How was your day, Kaleb?" She asked brightly, turning her attention to him.

My head hung as I focused on my plate, trying not to cry. Mom never cared about me. She was only concerned about Kaleb and Kamden.

I always tried to sit between Kamden and Dad so I wouldn't have to be near Kaleb. Kamden nudged me and leaned in closer, giving me a beaming grin. "Proud of you, sorella. *Great job."*

A small smile tugged at my lips.

At least someone cares.

Kamden asked me more questions about my day, and I ignored Kaleb and Mom for the rest of dinner.

Maybe she never loved me—she never seemed to care. I sighed and focused back on my phone, dispelling the memory of my mom to type my reply.

Me: Idk maybe

My head hurt thinking about the whole situation. I put my phone down on my desk and pinched the bridge of my nose.

Who would want to do this to me?

I thought about my mom again. We'd never been close, but I was still her daughter. Plus, she didn't have my number, and I knew Kam wouldn't give it to her, so it wasn't likely that it was her.

But then who could it be?

I had a presentation to finish for a new client that afternoon, so I blocked out everything else to focus on it. I had way too much to do that day to spend time worrying about something I had no control over.

Ryker will know what to do... I hope.

Therapy with Kam was not what I wanted to do after the day I'd had. My head had been throbbing since the morning, and it was hard to concentrate on anything other than that stupid text message.

We had just sat down on the couch in Dr. Lowell's office when she opened with her usual question. "How have you been feeling?"

Kamden sighed and rubbed his hands together. "This week's been hard."

"And why is that?" she asked.

He didn't answer for several seconds. "My mom's been calling and leaving me harassing messages."

My head jerked toward him. "What?" I questioned angrily, my voice shrill. "Why didn't you tell me?"

"I didn't want you to worry. You worry about me enough as it is."

My head throbbed more from what Kamden had just told me.

Maybe my mom is sending those texts—trying to harass both of us for what happened with Kaleb.

Dr. Lowell interrupted my thoughts when she asked Kamden, "How do you feel about that?"

Kamden balled his fists. "Upset. Angry. Guilty."

"Don't listen to Mom's bullshit, Kam. She doesn't know what the fuck she's talking about. You have no reason to feel guilty." I blurted out, pissed off about the whole situation.

I am so done with this day.

Kamden didn't reply. He just sat there silently, staring at floor and wringing his hands together.

"Tell me about your mother," Dr. Lowell said, breaking the silence.

Is she fucking serious? This day keeps getting worse and worse.

Kamden's jaw clenched and his hands stilled. I didn't think he was going to speak, but he swallowed deeply, then answered, "My mom has always been different. Definitely not your loving, affectionate type of mom. Well, except with Kaleb. She treated him differently than me and Kaiya." I swallowed the lump that had formed in my throat. Listening to Kamden talk about my mom and Kaleb made my stomach turn—they both had made my life a living hell.

"He'd always been her favorite. Kaleb could do no wrong in her eyes. After I'd stopped Kaleb from... from raping Kaiya, she'd been angry with me for hurting him. She didn't even care about what he'd done to Kaiya, or that he'd been abusing her for years. Hell, she even blamed Kaiya for Kaleb's actions."

My face burned with anger and hurt. Tears blurred my vision as I looked down at my joined hands. I hated being reminded about my past, about everything I had to endure my whole life.

Dr. Lowell quickly scribbled on her paper. "Why do you think she was like that?"

I had to give Kamden credit—if she was asking me all those questions, I would've lost my shit or completely shut down by now.

Kamden shrugged. "I don't know. I'm starting to believe that she might have some type of mental illness like Kaleb—it's the only explanation I can think of to justify her actions. What kind of mother would she be otherwise?"

I'd never considered that before, but I wouldn't know what normal was even if it smacked me in the face. Mental illness sometimes ran in families, so it could be possible that my mom had some type of condition similar to Kaleb.

I could see her having some type of personality disorder, or a combination of different disorders. It wouldn't surprise me. My mother acted bat shit crazy sometimes.

"Kaiya!" my mother yelled from downstairs.

Shit.

Kamden and Kaleb were both at football practice, and I was upstairs doing homework. I stood from my desk and headed out my bedroom door. "What?" I called out as I trudged down the stairs.

She didn't answer, and when I reached the bottom of the stairs, I didn't see her in the living room. "Mom?"

Still no response, so I headed into the kitchen. She was standing in front of the counter, and the overhead cabinet above her was open. As I approached her, I could see her tightly gripping the edge of the counter. "You called me, Mom?"

Her head jerked toward me. "Yes, come take a look at this, Kaiya," she gritted through clenched teeth.

I hesitantly inched toward her, unsure what she was angry about. She grabbed my arm and roughly pulled me next to her in front of the open cabinet. "You put the plates up wrong!"

I looked up at the cabinet—everything looked fine. I'd made sure to neatly stack the plates and keep them from touching the other glasses and dinnerware.

"You don't even see your mistake, do you?" she scoffed in irritation. She squeezed my arm tighter.

"No, I thought that's how they're supposed to be." I replied, trying, but failing to keep my voice steady.

She flung my arm away from her in disgust. "You put the salad plates where the dinner plates go. Dinner plates go on the bottom shelf and salad plates go directly above them on the middle shelf."

"I'm sorry. I'll fix th—"

"Don't bother," she spat. "I'll do it since you couldn't do it right the first time."

She turned away, dismissing me as she set to work, fixing my mistake. I forced back the tears as I walked back to the stairs and up to my room.

"How do you feel about that, Kaiya?" Dr. Lowell's voice broke through my stumble down memory lane.

"About what?" I replied, avoiding her gaze.

I really don't want to talk about this.

"How your mother treated you." She quickly jotted down something on her pad.

I sat back on the couch and crossed my arms over my chest. "She was a bitch." I shrugged. "Still is. If her and my dad had been better parents, things might have been different... better."

Dr. Lowell wrote something else before looking up at me. "Could you elaborate on that?"

Glancing uneasily at Kamden, I rubbed my sweaty palms against my pants. He gave me a small, yet reassuring smile.

You're doing this for him—to help him heal. Suck it up.

I took a deep breath, but my lungs felt constricted. I blew it out shakily. "Yeah, um, maybe my twin wouldn't have molested me for most of my life. He might have gotten the help he needed, and none of this would've happened. He wouldn't be dead right now. Kamden and I wouldn't be sitting here dealing with this bullshit, and I wouldn't be a fucked up mess."

I hadn't noticed I had balled my fists until my palms hurt from my nails digging into them. When I loosened my grip, my hands trembled and my head pulsed again. I felt like the room was closing in on me.

Shit, don't panic. Calm down. Breathe, breathe, breathe.

I shut my eyes as a wave of nausea washed over me.

Don't throw up, don't throw up.

Kamden grabbed my hand. His tone was laced with worry as he questioned, "Ky, are you okay? What's wrong?"

I gripped his hand back as I took several slow breaths to quell my anxiety. My voice cracked as I spoke, "I'm fine."

That was reassuring.

When I opened my eyes, his stormy blue ones scanned over my face with concern. "Are you sure?"

My eyes stung as I battled the tears that wanted to form. I wanted to tell Kamden about the texts, tell him that I hated this and make him take me away from here and never bring me back. But I didn't. Instead, I lied, "Yeah, I'm fine."

Kamden looked unconvinced, but he didn't press me further. Dr. Lowell didn't either. Maybe she knew I wasn't going to talk anymore. And I didn't—I stayed silent for the rest of the therapy session, fighting an impending breakdown.

Chapter Six

Ryker

I knew something was wrong with Kaiya as soon as she walked into the studio. Her body was tense and her face wasn't lit up by that beautiful smile like when she normally saw me.

She forced a smile when our eyes met, but I knew my Warrior—something was off. I walked toward her, and we met in the middle of the room. "What's wrong?"

She didn't answer. Instead, she dropped her bag and fell into me, wrapping her arms around my waist and pressing her head against my chest. Her hands gripped the back of my muscle shirt as she hugged me tightly.

I cupped her face in my hands and forced her to look up at me. "Baby, what's wrong? What happened?"

Her eyes were puffy and red—she'd been crying. Anger and worry built up inside me, and I wanted to punch something, preferably whoever was the cause.

"I had a bad day." Her voice was strained, like she wanted to cry again, but was holding back.

I stroked her cheeks. "Tell me what happened."

Kaiya sighed and proceeded to tell me about therapy with Kamden and the text she'd gotten. My anger amped up at the thought of someone threatening her, especially when there was nothing I could do about it. "Let me see your phone," I seethed, clenching my fists as I tried to remain calm.

Kaiya pulled back to dig through her purse before taking out her phone. After she handed it to me, I clicked the text icon and pulled up the messages from the unknown number.

After reading the messages several times, I gave Kaiya back her cell.

"What should we do?" she asked.

Blowing out a breath of frustration, I roughly ran a hand through my hair.

Fuck.

I didn't know what to do, and Kaiya needed me.

Some fucking boyfriend you are.

When I didn't answer, she continued, "What about the police?"

I scoffed. "They probably wouldn't give us the time of day."

Her voice took on a higher, anxious pitch. "Well, what are we going to do, Ryker?"

Shit.

She sounded so vulnerable and afraid, like when she used to talk about Kaleb. I never wanted her to feel like that again—I was supposed to make her feel safe, protect her. And I was failing.

I pulled her into me and kissed the top of her head. My breath rustled her hair as I spoke. "We'll figure something out. I'm not going to let anything happen to you."

She buried her face in my chest and let out a heavy sigh. Then, the door opened, causing Kaiya to lift her head and turn to look at it.

Some of the students walked in, and Kaiya stepped away from me. She gave me a small smile and hefted her bag over her shoulder before walking toward her usual punching bag.

Once class started, I couldn't get my mind off the texts. Thoughts were running through my head non-stop as I watched Kaiya hit the bag.

Who is it? What do they want? What should I do?

I walked around the room, monitoring the students as I tried to think of a solution for our problem. The police would probably be a dead end—they'd make us fill out a police report that would get forgotten at the bottom of a stack of other reports.

Maybe Kaiya can call her cell phone carrier and see if they can trace the number. That's probably the best option we have right now.

Kaiya seemed to feel better after hitting the bag—her body wasn't as tense and some of the worry lining her face was gone. But once we moved on to the self-defense part of class, I saw it come back when I announced what we would be working on.

"Today, we'll be practicing techniques to get out of a choke that comes from behind. This is a very common M.O. for rapists and muggers."

Kaiya still wasn't comfortable when we did choke maneuvers, but I was concerned that whoever was texting her would come after her at some point. She needed to be prepared in case I wasn't around.

After demonstrating the first technique with Mark and David, I met Kaiya at our usual spot. "I know you hate chokes, but I want you to be ready for any situation, especially since someone is threatening you."

"I know. Let's get this over with." She exhaled heavily.

"Come behind me." When I felt her at my back, I continued, "Now, put your dominant arm around my neck and squeeze my throat with your bicep. Use your other hand to secure the choke by grasping right below your wrist."

I squatted some so she could reach my neck. When she had the choke in place, I instructed, "When put in this position, the escape is actually pretty simple. First, you're going to move your inside leg around and behind your attacker like this." Kaiya had me in the hold with her right arm, so I moved my left leg around her right one, shifting my body to face her as I planted my foot behind her. My dick pressed against her hips. I had to shake the dirty thoughts that formed in my head so I could concentrate on the move.

Focus. She's yours—you can have her later.

"Feel how my body's fitted to yours? My elbow is right against your stomach, so I'm going to use that to my advantage. Throw an elbow strike to the stomach, then follow through using your body to push them over."

I lightly elbowed her, then pushed against her, turning my body into her and using my momentum to knock her over my thigh to the ground.

I helped Kaiya up, then pretended to brush some non-existent dust off her ass, trying to get her to loosen up. She giggled and swatted my hand away, giving me a look of amused disapproval.

"What? You had something on your ass." I laughed.

She rolled her eyes. "Sure." She was trying so hard not to smile, but it broke through after several seconds.

"Ready to try, Warrior?"

Her smile faded some as she stiffened slightly and nodded.

"I'm going to come up behind you and put you in the choke, okay?" I made sure to meet her eyes and get her approval before walking behind her. I hated how tense she was, especially considering that it was me—I felt like she didn't trust me.

Rubbing her shoulders, I attempted to help her loosen up. "Easy, baby, it's only me. You know I would never hurt you."

She relaxed some and shook out her arms. "I know, I know. It's not you—it's me. Some habits are hard to break."

I knew it would take her time to get over her trust issues, but it still made me feel like shit that after everything we'd been through, she still didn't trust me. I told myself that it would take longer to reverse all those years of fear and trust issues, and I was determined to break through every wall by earning her trust.

I let go of her shoulders. "I'm going to put you in the choke now." I slipped my arm around her neck and secured the hold with my other hand. "Bring your left leg around behind my right one, squatting slightly into a horse stance."

Once she was in the correct position, I continued, "Now elbow me and continue to push while turning your body into mine. Use as much force as possible to knock me backward over your knee."

It took Kaiya a few times to knock me over, so we practiced until she became more comfortable with executing the move before I ended class.

Everyone joined together on the mats. "I hope that learning this technique will be helpful to you if you ever need it. Remember to practice at home so that the movements become reflexive and automatic. Have a good night, everyone."

After I locked up, Kaiya and I picked up some Chinese takeout for dinner, then headed back to her place. When she opened the door, she called out, "Kam? We're home."

Kaiya slipped off her shoes and threw her keys and purse on the table as I shut the door. "Kam?" Kaiya repeated louder.

I set the bag of takeout on the table while Kaiya searched the apartment for Kamden. She entered the dining room with a perplexed look on her face. "He's not here. He's usually home by now."

She went to her purse and pulled her phone out. After dialing his number, she put the phone to her ear and paced back and forth between the living and dining room. She chewed on her bottom lip as she waited for Kamden to answer.

Her face fell as she lowered the phone. "No answer. I hope he's okay. I wonder why he didn't call or text me."

I took out the various boxes of food and placed them on the table. "I'm sure he's fine. Kamden can take care of himself."

"Yeah, you're right," she halfheartedly agreed as she stared down at her phone in her hands. "I'm going to send him a text, anyway."

Her thumbs quickly swiped over her screen as she typed her message. Once she was finished, she went into the kitchen to grab some plates before coming back and setting the table.

Throughout dinner, Kaiya barely touched her food or spoke. I could tell she was still preoccupied about Kamden. "Don't worry, babe. He's probably out drinking or something."

Her eyes snapped up to mine, then narrowed in anger. "That doesn't make me feel any better. He's an alcoholic."

I reached across the table and placed my hand over hers. "I didn't mean to upset you, I'm just saying that he's probably at a bar, and can't hear his phone because of the loud music."

Ignoring my comment, she grabbed her phone off the table and angrily swiped the screen. She put the phone to her ear and stood from the table before storming into the living room.

After several seconds, she pulled the phone away from her ear and cursed, "Damn it, where is he?"

I stood from the table and walked over to her. I rubbed my hands up and down her arms. "Don't worry, baby. I'm sure he'll be home soon."

She sighed in frustration, then changed the subject. "Let's clean up this mess." She gestured to the dining room table.

After we put the dishes in the dishwasher and packed up the leftover food, we headed to Kaiya's room to get ready for bed.

Once we showered and changed, Kaiya insisted that she wait up until Kamden came home. We went back out to the living room and curled up on the couch with one of her extra blankets.

Kaiya was laying with her back on me in between my legs. She leaned her head back against my chest and let out another deep sigh.

I tried to keep her mind occupied by asking, "Tell me more about therapy today."

Shit, this probably isn't the best topic.

She turned over, propping her chin on her hands atop my abdomen as she looked up at me. I expected her to get upset and not want to talk about it, but she didn't. She seemed relieved to have the chance to get it off her chest. "We talked about my mom."

"What about her?" Kaiya's mom was a crazy bitch, and I didn't see how talking about her would help Ky or Kamden.

"Kamden said she'd been leaving him messages and harassing him. Then, Dr. Lowell asked him how he felt about that and wanted to hear both of our opinions about her."

No wonder she was so stressed when she walked into class— Kaiya's mom was a tough subject for both of them. Add in the threatening text message and her day seemed pretty shitty. "I'm sorry— sounds like you had a bad day."

She chortled. "Bad is an understatement. To top it off, I've had a fucking headache all day. This therapy shit sucks."

I laughed and rubbed her back. "I think it's great that you're doing

50

it for Kamden. I'm really proud of you."

She smiled warmly and pushed up to kiss me. My hands moved down to grip her ass as I slipped my tongue in her mouth. I pressed her down into my hardening cock, making her gasp and break the kiss. "We can't—what if Kamden comes in?"

I smirked and squeezed her ass. "So?"

She smacked me on the shoulder and scoffed. "Ryker!"

I laughed. "Okay, okay. I'll behave."

Kaiya scooted down and lay her head back in the center of my chest. We talked a little longer before we both drifted off to sleep.

Loud, drunken laughter and the door hitting the wall woke both Kaiya and me. Kamden and some girl stumbled into the living room—both of them were wasted. They could barely stand, and their eyes were bloodshot and red.

Kaiya got up and furiously strode toward Kamden, who was oblivious to us. She placed her hands on her hips and stared up at him when she reached the drunken couple. His glazed eyes focused on her as he directed his attention away from the blonde that was all over him.

"Where have you been, Kam? I've been worried sick about you!" Kaiya's voice was clouded by sleep, but there was no masking the anger in it.

Kamden's eyes narrowed as he slurred, "None of your fucking business."

Kaiya was about to speak again as Kamden walked around her with the girl in tow. "You are my fucking business, Kamden! I just want to help you!" Kaiya yelled as she followed him. She grabbed his arm. "Talk to me, Kam."

"I don't want to fucking talk anymore!" Kamden roared as he wrenched his arm from Kaiya's grasp. "Leave me alone, Kaiya!"

Rage lit up my veins, sending my heart pummeling against my chest as I watched him push her away into the wall.

Fucking bastard!

Shock and hurt filled Kaiya's face as I rushed over to them. I reared back to punch Kamden in his fucking jaw for touching my girl. I didn't give a fuck that he was her brother.

Kaiya's voice was barely above a whisper as she stopped me, gripping my forearm with both hands. "Don't. Just let him be."

Kamden's face morphed from anger to sadness as realization sank in. He let go of the blonde, who almost fell from the loss of his support, and approached Kaiya with open arms. "Ky, I'm so sorry. I didn't me——"

Kaiya turned away from him, burying her face in my chest. I wrapped my arms around her and shook my head at Kamden. He had another thing coming if he thought I was going to let him near her after what he just did.

Kamden backed away as he apologized again, "I'm sorry, *sorella*. So sorry."

Kaiya softly cried into my bare chest, and I clenched my fists to temper my anger. Kamden was so fucking lucky that Kaiya was in between us, or I would've beat the shit out of him.

Kamden turned and went into his room. He slammed the door, leaving the drunk girl leaning against the wall in the hallway. I lifted Kaiya into my arms and carried her to her bedroom, only concerned about her well-being. I couldn't care less about Kamden's booty call.

Once I shut the door, I heard banging. The girl yelled, "What the fuck, Kamden? You said you'd show me a good time."

Ignoring her, I lay Kaiya in bed before climbing in next to her. I covered us with her comforter and wiped the tears from her face. "Don't cry, baby. He didn't mean it."

Her bottom lip quivered. "I know. I just feel like I'm losing him. How can I save him?"

"You can't save someone who doesn't want to be saved."

She closed her eyes. "I can't lose him—he's the only family I have left."

I caressed her cheek. "You have me, too, Warrior. Always."

Her vibrant blue eyes opened and locked on mine. "I love you."

I brushed my lips over hers before leaning down to her chest. I gently kissed her scar, then moved back up to her lips again. "I love you," I murmured against them.

Enclosing Kaiya in my arms, it didn't take long for us to fall back asleep, exhausted from the events of the night.

Chapter Seven

Kaiya

My eyes burned as I stared at the computer screen at work. They were still puffy and swollen from crying the night b ore. Kamden pushing me had been replaying in my mind since I woke up. Plus, I still had the same fucking headache, and I'd thrown up again this morning when I'd gotten out of bed.

I rubbed my eyes as I swiveled away from the screen. My phone buzzed on my desk, and I thought about ignoring it, not wanting to deal with another text from the unknown number.

Don't live in fear—you wasted most of your life doing that.

I grabbed the phone and keyed in my password. A message from Kamden popped up on the screen.

Thank God.

Kamden: I'm sorry sorella

My stomach tightened uncomfortably thinking about what happened. Kamden had never laid a hand on me before, and it was like a piece of my heart broke when he pushed me into the wall.

I gnawed on my bottom lip as I thought about what to text back. I was hurt and upset, but not to the point where I didn't want to talk to him and resolve everything.

Me: It's ok I know you didn't mean it

I set my phone down and tried to concentrate on my projects, but with everything on my mind, it was virtually impossible. I was lucky that I hadn't been fired for my lack of work since I'd returned from my leave of absence, but my boss had been understanding of my situation, which I was extremely grateful for.

I had just typed some figures into one of my new account's spreadsheet when my phone vibrated again. A new text popped up on my screen, and fear strangled the air from my lungs.

Unknown: Soon you will pay for what you did

My heart thundered in my chest as I stared down at my phone. I exited out of the message and went through my phone log to call Ryker. I clicked on his name and was about to press call when I stopped.

Ryker was already worked up about the texts, especially since he couldn't do anything about them. I didn't want to worry him when there was nothing he could do—that would only frustrate and upset him more. And I didn't want both of us stressed out over the situation. Plus, I still needed to call my phone company and see if there was anything they could do on their end, and I wanted to be able to give Ryker answers.

I went back to my home screen and opened my texts. I tapped Nori's name and started typing a message.

Me: Wanna grab some lunch today

It only took a few seconds for her to respond back with her answer. Nori worked about ten minutes away from my office, so we decided to meet at a small cafe about halfway between our buildings.

I took a cab to the cafe to save time, and Nori was already there, waiting for me outside.

We rushed in, clutching our coats around us as a gust of wind attacked us. The door practically slammed behind us from the force of the wind blowing outside.

I unbuttoned my coat. "Why didn't you wait inside for me? It's freezing outside."

Nori shrugged. "I don't mind the wind, unlike you. You freeze when its fifty degrees outside and a small breeze brushes past you."

I rolled my eyes. "I'm not that bad." I really was.

Nori gave me a seriously look, arching an eyebrow with a playful smirk. We both laughed after I failed to fight a smile. Nori and I always had a good time together, and it was nice to forget about everything that relentlessly weighed down on me, if only for a brief time.

Once we were seated, I took off my jacket and set it beside me in the booth. Nori did the same as she asked, "So, what's new?"

I groaned and Nori chuckled. "That bad, huh?"

Exhaling a heavy breath, I nodded. I proceed to ramble about the therapy sessions with Kamden, the confrontation the night before, and the text I had received this morning.

Nori sat in stunned silence, both her eyes and mouth wide open as she took everything in. "Wow, I, uh-"

Just then, the waitress walked up, interrupting our conversation. "Hi, my name is Amy and I'll be your server today. What can I get you to drink?"

Once she left with our orders, I urged Nori, "Well?"

She looked at a loss for words, which was definitely unusual for her. After a few seconds, she finally spoke. "Damn, girl—I don't know what to say."

I snorted. "That's a fucking first."

Nori flipped me the finger and laughed. "Hey, you threw a lot at me at once. Give me some time to process."

"Yeah, its some heavy shit. I've been so stressed out that I've been throwing up every morning and have never-ending headaches."

"Wait, what? You've been throwing up every morning? For how long?" Nori asked with her eyebrows raised.

"Um…" I thought back to when I got the first text. "A few weeks maybe. Why?"

"Do you think you might be pregnant?" Nori blurted out.

I laughed loudly. "Are you joking?" When she didn't join in my

57

laughter, I stopped and met her gaze. "Wait, you're serious."

It wasn't a question. The look on Nori's face told me she wasn't joking—she was dead serious. "I can't be pregnant. I'm on the…"

Oh shit. When was the last time I went for my shot? The last I remember was before the shooting. Fuck.

Nori smiled sympathetically. "Would it be that bad if you were?"

Would it?

I never planned to have kids because I didn't think I was in the right emotional state to be able to raise any that weren't totally fucked up. I rubbed my palms on my pants. "No, but I'm sure it's just stress."

Nori gave me a knowing look. "Maybe you should take a pregnancy test—just to be safe."

I sighed. "Fine, I will. But I really think it's only stress."

The waitress came back with our drinks and wrote down our lunch order. When she left, Nori said in disbelief, "I can't believe Kamden pushed you."

I sadly shook my head, then stared down at my hands in my lap. "Me neither. He's gotten really bad. I don't know what to do to help him."

"Just keep doing what you're doing. Don't give up on him."

I looked up and made eye contact. "I won't." I could never give up on Kamden after everything he'd done for me.

Nori changed the subject. "So, what does Ryker think about the text messages?"

I took a drink of my water. "He's beyond pissed. Especially since he can't do anything about it."

"What about the police? Have you thought about going to them?"

"Yeah, but Ryker said they won't do anything." I stirred the straw around in my drink before taking another sip.

Nori shrugged. "Maybe, maybe not. I think it's worth a shot. What if they could help?"

She had a point. Ryker didn't know for sure whether or not the police would be able to help, and the messages weren't stopping like I wanted. "You're right. I'll look into it."

Amy came with our food, and we started eating. In between bites,

Nori said, "Tell me something good. I'm tired of all this negative bullshit."

"Tell me about it." I laughed. "I don't have much to tell you, except that everything with Ryker is amazing. I keep waiting to wake up from this dream."

"Aww, that's so sweet," she crooned with a smile. "I'm so happy that you finally found someone that treats you how you're supposed to be treated."

My lips curved up. "Yeah, I'm pretty lucky."

Nori took another bite of her sandwich. "At least you have him to help you through all this."

I nodded as I swirled my spoon in my soup. "Yeah, I'd definitely go crazy with all this if I didn't have him."

That's an understatement.

Ryker was my anchor, keeping me from drifting out and getting lost in the sea of despair that still tried to tow me under constantly.

Once Nori and I finished eating, we paid our bill and left. We both gave each other a hurried hug goodbye as we hailed down taxis, and I promised to keep Nori updated on everything.

As I reluctantly trudged up to my office, I thought about what Nori had said about going to the police. Ryker worked today, so I could head down to the station on my way home without him knowing. I didn't want him to worry more than he already was.

The rest of the day was uneventful—I got absolutely nothing done at work. My mind was consumed with thoughts of Kamden, the text messages, and, of course, me being pregnant.

You're not pregnant. It's just stress.

I told myself that if I kept throwing up over the next few days, that I would take a pregnancy test.

But I'm not pregnant.

Yeah, keep telling yourself that.

I took the elevator to the parking garage, then got in my car and drove to the police station. I was so nervous that they'd laugh in my face and tell me to grow up, but Nori was right—I'd regret not going to them.

Taking a deep breath, I got out of my car and walked to the entrance. Another man was walking up at the same time as me and opened the door. "Thank you," I said as I hurried inside and to the front desk.

The cop barely acknowledged me, not even glancing up from his computer. "Can I help you?" he asked, the irritation apparent in his tone.

Maybe this isn't such a good idea.

"Hi, I, um, wanted to speak to someone about some threatening text messages I've been getting from a blocked number."

He looked at me like I was stupid as he handed me a clipboard with a paper. "Fill out this police report, and we'll look into it."

I'm sure you'll get right on it.

"Okay, thank you."

Even though I doubted that they were going to do anything to help me, I filled out the form. When I finished, I took it back to the desk and handed it to the police officer. He gave me a fake smile as he said, "We'll be in touch."

Yeah, sure you will, asshole.

"Thank you so much." I smiled sweetly, returning his fakeness tenfold.

Dick.

As I drove home, my mind warred as I debated whether or not to tell Ryker. With the police seeming to be of no help like he said, and no other options, I didn't really see the point in worrying Ryker when nothing could be done.

I'll just deal with it myself. No sense in both of us stressing out.

When I got home, Kamden was sitting on the couch. He stood and came toward me as he asked, "Hey, can we talk?"

I set my purse down. "Yeah, sure." I slipped off my heels and padded over to the couch before sitting down. I patted the cushion next to me as I looked up at him.

Kamden sat down and rubbed his hands anxiously on his jeans as he avoided eye contact with me. "Look, I'm... I'm really sorry for last night. I wasn't thinking straight."

I placed my hand over his on his thigh and smiled softly. "I know."

He met my eyes. "I would never hurt you—that's the last thing I'd want to do. I don't want to be anything like *him.*"

That last word was laced with so much disgust. I squeezed his hand. "You're not, Kam. Nothing like him."

"How could I do that to you?" he angrily asked. I knew he was more asking himself than me, so I didn't answer. He looked away. "What's happened to me?"

I happened. This was all because of me and Kaleb. Kam would have been so much better off without us.

"We're all having trouble dealing with the shooting, Kam. It's o—"

He abruptly stood and narrowed his eyes at me. "Don't tell me it's okay, Kaiya. You have no idea what I'm feeling. No fucking idea." He took a deep breath as his eyes watered. "You didn't pull the trigger—you didn't take your brother's life."

Rising off the couch, I reached my hand out to touch his shoulder. "Kam, I—"

"Don't," he growled as he whipped away from me and stalked down the hall toward his room. I heard the door slam a few seconds later.

Damn it.

I flopped back on the couch and clutched my head in my hands.

What the fuck am I going to do?

Chapter Eight

Ryker

Kaiya hadn't been acting like herself since the whole incident with Kamden a couple of weeks ago. She tried to pretend like everything was okay, but I knew her well enough to know when she was putting on her armor.

My stubborn Warrior.

Even though she hadn't gotten any more texts, I wanted to be on the safe side and continue to teach techniques that would be helpful in case something happened. Plus, the phone company had told her that the number couldn't be traced because it was from one of those disposable burner phones, so there really wasn't anything they could do. At least I was doing something by teaching her what I could.

"Today, we're going to work on rear hair pull defense. Having long hair is a disadvantage in a fight scenario since it can be used against you. But there are some easy techniques to turn the tables."

After explaining the move a few times with Mark and David, everyone split up and got to work. I paired up with Kaiya and turned around as I instructed, "Grab my hair."

"Where? You barely have any." She chuckled.

"Run your hand up my head until you can grip something."

Her fingers went up the back of my head and almost to the top when she finally grabbed a good chunk and tugged lightly. "Good, now pull harder."

As she jerked my head back, I put my hands on top of hers and secured them in place. "First thing you want to do is grab their hand and trap it on your head—it may seem like the opposite of what you should be doing, but this keeps you from having your neck snapped and makes it harder for them to jerk you around."

"Next, bring your elbows to shield your face in case your attacker tries to slam you into something." I pivoted into her. "Then, turn into your attacker and duck under their arm." I squatted under her arm and went to the outside, forcing Kaiya to bend over as her arm twisted unnaturally. "Now, you have them in an arm lock. If they haven't let go by now, then you can throw a side kick to the ribs, a roundhouse to the stomach, or if you really want to do damage, throw a sidekick to the knee. I guarantee that'll put them out."

I let go of her arm. "Pretty simple, right?"

She rubbed her elbow. "Almost seems too good to be true. I can't believe it's that easy."

I laughed. "Well you just felt how much it hurt. Sometimes it doesn't take that much effort to inflict pain." I stepped behind Kaiya as I spoke. "Your turn."

I grabbed Kaiya's ponytail and wrapped my hand around it once before tugging. "Bring your hands up."

She clasped her hands over mine and pushed down against her head. "Now get in a horse stance and pivot inward as you duck under my arm."

Kaiya wrenched my arm around, bringing it up as my body was forced to bend over. "Good, throw a sidekick into my ribs."

I let go as she kicked my side. I shrugged the shoulder of the arm that was just twisted and shook it out.

Good thing it wasn't my other arm—I'd be in some serious pain.

"Great job, Warrior. Let's practice again, a little faster this time."

Kaiya turned around, and I gripped her ponytail and pulled. She made a noise that sounded like a gasp and a low moan put together.

My dick twitched.

Holy shit, did she just moan?

I snaked my other hand around her waist and brought her against me, pressing that ass into my growing cock. I leaned next to her ear and murmured, "You like that, baby?"

She nodded and cleared her throat. Her voice was throaty with arousal when she responded, "Yeah, I do. Maybe we can practice more at home."

Fuck me.

I pulled her hair tighter and fought the urge to suck on her earlobe. She moaned again as I rubbed my erection against her. "Ryker."

Focus—your students are still in here.

I looked around to make sure no one was paying attention to us before yanking her ponytail one more time and growling in her ear. "I want to fuck you so bad right now. Just slip those shorts over and slide into you from behind."

I could see her biting her lip as she stifled a whimper.

Fuck, so hot… damn it, concentrate! Hair pull defense.

My voice cracked as I put some distance between us and asked, "What are you supposed to do now?"

Kaiya didn't answer or move. "Ky?"

"Huh? What?" Her voice was still coated with lust.

I chuckled and pulled her hair again. "What do you do now?"

"Oh, um, this?" She brought her hands up to cover mine and secured them in place.

"Good, and then?"

She ducked under my arm and twisted it, forcing me to bend over as she kicked me in the stomach with a roundhouse.

"Great job, baby," I praised when she let go. We practiced one more time before I dismissed class.

After everyone left, I asked Kaiya if she wanted to stay and practice sparring. Those text messages were still in the back of my mind, and the thought of her being attacked made me sick to my stomach. I needed to do whatever I could since I wasn't able to prevent another text or track down whoever was sending them.

I wanted her to be as prepared as possible for any attack, and that meant conditioning her body and developing her muscle memory. Doing combos on the bag helped with that, but sparring was the best way to get comfortable with fighting and defending yourself.

I locked up the gym before meeting back up with Kaiya in the kickboxing room. She had already started putting on her gear when I walked in. "Ready, Warrior?"

"Born ready, baby," she said, bouncing up and down on the balls of her feet.

I chuckled as I grabbed a helmet from the equipment bin and strapped it on. I stood across from Kaiya on the mat and got in my defensive stance. "I'm going to go a little hard on you because I want you to be ready for anything."

She brought her gloves up in front of her face. "Let's do this."

I smiled—Kaiya loved sparring, and had gotten really good over the past few months. She was becoming more natural and fluid when she fought and executed more combos than in the beginning.

She was a better defensive fighter than offensive, so I advanced toward her and threw a jab, which she easily blocked.

That's my girl.

She countered with a ridge hand, one of her favorite moves, but I knocked her hand away. She followed up with a roundhouse to my thigh. "Good leg check, babe."

We exchanged several hits and kicks before I decided to up the ante. Grabbing Kaiya by the arms, I backed her into the padded wall and pinned her against it.

She tried to wriggle out of my grasp, forgetting her basic defense maneuvers she should've been using, like knees and elbows. Most people tended to forget their training when put in a high stress situation like the one I was subjecting Kaiya to. Mix that with adrenaline, and panic resulted. That was why it was so important to train your body to automatically react. And the only way to do that was to practice those specific scenarios.

Kaiya was breathing heavily, and her tits quickly rose and fell against my chest. Feeling her sweaty skin and body on mine combined with our sexual tension leftover from class made my cock harden.

Adrenaline rushed through my veins from sparring, making my heart rate increase. I forgot about the exercise. All I could think about was being inside Kaiya and filling her with my cock. I ripped my gloves and helmet off before trailing my hands down her arms to her hips. Leaning into her, I gruffly spoke, "I know I should be concentrating on training you, but feeling you against me like this makes me fucking crazy, baby."

I pressed my dick against her and was rewarded with a moan from that sexy mouth.

Fuck, I have to have her. Now.

She rushed to take her gloves off as I slipped her helmet off. Hooking my arm under Kaiya's thigh, I lifted her leg up as I pulled my dick out with my other hand. After moving her shorts and panties over, I rubbed my cock against her wet clit and sucked on her bottom lip.

I roughly thrust into her pussy, making her gasp in pleasure. Then, I lifted her other leg and picked her up. She wrapped her legs around me as I pressed her against the wall and slammed myself deeper into her.

Grasping her wrists with my hands, I brought her arms up and pinned them above her head. My mouth greedily claimed hers as I drove harder into her.

I loved the sounds Kaiya made when I fucked her. Those needy whimpers and moans were like the perfect soundtrack when we had sex—a masterpiece only I was capable of creating with her. Just for us.

Slowing my pace, I dragged my cock out of her before inching myself back in, stretching her pussy as I filled her. Her walls perfectly hugged my dick as I continued to stroke in and out of her.

Kaiya's head fell back against the padding as she cried out it pleasure. Her legs quivered around me as I sped up, hammering my cock further inside her.

My grip tightened on Kaiya's wrists when I came, filling her sweet pussy with my cum. Letting go, I wrapped my arms around her and held her to me as we caught our breath.

Kaiya's lips curved up when I set her down. "So, is that the proper technique for how to escape being pinned against a wall? Because I don't think it's very effective."

"Ha ha, very funny." I smacked her ass. "I can't help myself with you sometimes."

Grabbing me by the straps on my muscle shirt, she pulled me to her. She stood on her tiptoes to kiss me. "Maybe we should practice it again. I don't think I have all the steps down right."

I smirked as I gripped the undersides of her thighs and lifted her. She wrapped her legs around my waist again as I pinned her against the wall. "Sure, baby, I can show you again. I can show you over and over again until you get it." I guided my dick to her pussy and rubbed the tip against her wetness.

She tugged on my bottom lip with her teeth before making a sound between a growl and a moan. "Yes, show me again."

And I did. I sank my cock inside her and showed her over and over again.

Chapter Nine

Kaiya

I stared down at the sink of my office's restroom while I brushed my teeth. I had been consistently throwing up in the mornings at work, so much so that I had to bring a toothbrush to combat my vomit mouth.

I was still getting texts from the unknown number, and things with Kamden were rocky at best, so I continued to contribute my nausea to that. But it was getting harder and harder to deny what Nori had suggested at lunch two weeks ago.

I rinsed my mouth before staring at myself in the mirror.

Maybe you're pregnant.

Shit.

I decided I would pick up a pregnancy test from the store on my way home from work, just to be safe. If I was pregnant, I wanted to get the proper medical care, and if I wasn't, I needed to get back on the shot.

Begrudgingly, I dragged myself back to my office and slumped in my chair. I was so exhausted lately, and still had to suffer through constant headaches on top of everything else.

My office phone beeped. I groaned before picking up the receiver and putting it up to my ear. "Yes?"

Our receptionist, Amanda, answered, "Miss Marlow, there's someone on the phone for you."

Great.

I was definitely not in the talking mood. "Can you take a message, please? I'm not feeling well."

"Sure, Miss Marlow. I'll leave it in your box."

"Thank you, Amanda." I hung up and sighed, then directed my attention to my computer screen. Opening a spreadsheet from my files, I began inputting numbers, trying to take my mind off everything hanging over me.

A few minutes later, my cell phone vibrated on the desk.

Unknown: Too busy to take my call?

My heart felt like it stopped beating as fear hooked itself deep in my stomach.

They know where I work? Holy shit.

Darting my hand out to grab my office phone, I knocked it off the receiver, then scrambled to pick it up. I pushed the button for the receptionist's desk and Amanda answered, "Yes, Miss Marlow?"

I tried to keep my voice steady. "Amanda, who just called for me?"

"I don't know, ma'am. When I tried to take a message, they said that they'd call back and hung up."

Fuck.

"Was it a man or a woman?"

"It was a man. Why? Is something wrong?"

I swallowed the lump in my throat. "No, everything's fine, Amanda. Thank you."

I hung up before she could respond. Panic clawed at me, constricting my chest like it used to when I thought about Kaleb. My head throbbed, and I struggled to breathe. Clenching my eyes shut, I tried to pull myself free of the demons inside me.

Breathe, breathe, breathe.

Inhaling and exhaling deeply, I blanked my mind, then refilled it with thoughts of Ryker—my light in all the darkness that always tried to smother me.

I played his voice in my head.

I love you, Warrior. I'll never let anything happen to you.

The tightness in my chest faded.

Ryker will keep you safe.

Opening my eyes, I stared at my phone.

Maybe I should get a new number.

That would stop the texts, but the person knew where I worked and could call my office incessantly to harass me that way.

Fuck.

I decided I was going to tell Ryker everything—this phone call took things to a more serious level that I wasn't capable of handling by myself. I needed him.

I sent him a text asking to meet me on my lunch break at the police station so that we could follow up on my report. He didn't see the point until I'd told him about the strange call I'd just received.

Ryker was there when I pulled into the lot of the station. When I parked next to his truck, he got out and came around to my driver's side to meet me. "Hey." He leaned down and kissed me.

I linked our fingers together. "Hey."

He gave me a forced smile before leading me inside and up to the front desk. He cleared his throat to get the attention of the officer behind the desk, who had his back to us.

The officer swiveled around in his chair. It was the same asshole that had taken my report. "Can I help you?"

Ryker released my hand and placed them on top of the counter. "Yeah, my girlfriend said she filed a report a couple of weeks ago and we wanted to check the status. She's been getting threatening text messages and calls."

The officer stood. "Have you received a call from the station?"

"No." I moved to stand next to Ryker. "But—"

He rudely interrupted me. "Then, we're still working on it."

Ryker's body tensed as he tightly gripped the counter. "Well, it doesn't look like you're doing anything but sitting here on your fat ass eating donuts."

The officer's lip curled up. "Sir, I'm going to have to ask you to leave."

Ryker raised his voice. "My girlfriend is being harassed by some lunatic, and something needs to be done about it!"

Two other officers came from the hallway to our left. They eyed Ryker warily, then directed their attention to the asshole behind the desk. "Rick, you okay out here?"

Rick gave us a smug smirk and crossed his arms over his chest. "I asked this guy to leave, but he's refusing."

The two officers loosely placed their hands on their gun holsters, giving Ryker an unspoken warning.

"Ryker, let's go." I grabbed his forearm and tugged him toward the exit.

His muscles tensed beneath my hand. "I'm not leaving until I get some answers," he gritted out.

"If you don't leave right now, I'll be forced to arrest you for failure to obey a police order." Rick threatened.

I pulled on his arm again. "Ryker."

He wrenched his arm away. "Fine. Let's go."

I rushed to keep up with him as he stormed out. When we got to where we were parked, he punched the door of his truck and roared angrily. "God, that was such fucking bullshit!"

He paced back and forth beside our vehicles. "If you get anymore threats, I'm going to come back up here and force them to do something. I don't care if I get arrested."

Fear slithered through me. That was exactly what I was afraid of.

Ryker stopped and our eyes met. "Don't worry. I'll take care of everything from now on. Next time you get a call or text, you let me know immediately, okay?"

I swallowed the lump in my throat. "Okay," I lied. There was no way I was going to tell him anything else and risk him getting arrested. I decided to keep everything to myself like I'd originally planned. Ryker was too hot-headed when it came to me. I was going to have to deal with it myself.

When I returned to work, my head painfully throbbed throughout the remainder of the day, making me feel like my skull was going to explode. Knots formed in my stomach, elevating my nausea, and I did the best I could to block everything out by immersing myself in all the presentations and documents I was so behind on.

When it was time for me to clock out, I was caught up on my work. I was exhausted, but also relieved to have been able to zone out for a while without worrying about Kamden, the man harassing me, or my possible pregnancy. Not to mention the new worry of Ryker getting arrested.

As I hopped in my car, my next destination caused me to think about how Ryker might react if I was pregnant.

Will he be angry? Happy? Disappointed?

Closing my eyes, I rubbed my temples as I sat in my car. There was so much shit going on that I couldn't even began to analyze how Ryker would feel. I couldn't even decipher my feelings because my mind and emotions were so jumbled.

Taking a deep breath, I started my car. I told myself not to worry when I wasn't sure yet. I had enough to stress over without adding something on top that might not even be an issue. I'd deal with it once I was positive.

I stopped at a drug store on the way home from work to pick up a pregnancy test. Standing in the aisle, I stared at the shelves of all the various pregnancy tests and started to get a little overwhelmed.

Which one do I choose?

I dug my phone out of the bottom of my purse and called Nori. "Hey girl, what's up?"

"Guess where I am," I said as I scanned over the boxes.

She chuckled a little. "Alaska."

I snorted. "I'm staring at the million pregnancy tests they have available. How the fuck am I supposed to choose one when there's so many different options?"

Nori's laughter echoed through the phone. "Just pick one, Ky. They're all the same."

"But I want to pick the best one. Not some cheap one that might

73

not be accurate."

"Well, then you're going to have to read the boxes and see which one is the most accurate."

I groaned before sarcastically replying, "Thanks for the help."

"Sorry, babe. Call me as soon as you find out. I want to know whether or not I'm going to be an auntie!" Nori squealed.

Her enthusiasm brightened my mood, getting a small laugh out of me. "I will. Bye."

I put my phone back in my purse and grabbed one of the tests off the shelf. I read the back, then did the same with a different box. I went through about five or six before I finally decided on the one that I thought was the best.

Looking down at it, I sighed before walking to the register. "Here goes nothing."

I stared at the pink pregnancy test in my hands.

Just open it and pee on the damn thing, Kaiya.

Blowing out a long breath, I ripped open the box and took out one of the tests. I had read the directions about a hundred times—one more time wouldn't hurt.

I sat on the toilet and positioned the stick as indicated.

Great, now I can't pee.

My leg bounced nervously as I tried to get myself to go to the bathroom.

Waterfalls. Showers. Oceans. Rivers.

I still couldn't go, so I got up with a huff and turned on the sink, then sat back on the toilet. I closed my eyes and concentrated on the sound of the water as I repositioned the pregnancy test under me.

After several seconds, I finally started peeing.

Thank God.

When I finished, I put the test on the counter and washed my hands. Then, I set the timer on my phone and waited.

And waited.

And waited.

I paced the bathroom and chewed on my bottom lip as I waited for the designated amount of time. The minutes seemed to last a lifetime as I waited for the answer that would change my life.

The timer went off, and I froze. My heart pounded, ready to burst from my chest as I slowly inched toward the sink. My mouth went dry as I approached, and my stomach twisted in anticipation.

What if it's positive? I can't be a mother.

But what if it's negative?

My heart sank into my stomach as I considered that I might not be pregnant.

Do I really want to be? Am I ready?

Is Ryker ready?

I rested my hands on my flat belly and rubbed it. A smile formed on my face as I thought about having a little Ryker inside me.

I grabbed the test off the counter and looked at the result window. Two pink lines.

Two pink lines.

I'm pregnant. Holy shit, I'm pregnant!

My mind ran a mile a minute as I stared at myself in the mirror.

I can't be a mom. I'm too fucked up.

Kaleb's face took over my reflection. I shut my eyes and gripped the edge of the sink as my heart began to pound.

He ruined you. You can barely take care of yourself let alone a baby.

My face felt flushed, and my breathing quickened as anxiety crept in.

Calm down, Kaiya. Breathe, breathe, breathe.

I slowly inhaled and exhaled, attempting to push Kaleb out of my mind as I thought about the life growing inside me—something I never pictured having because of my past and the scars inflicted from the abuse I endured.

You can do this.

Kaleb's voice played in my head. "You're too weak to raise a baby. It's going to end up fucked up like you."

No!

"You're a failure. You destroy the lives of everyone around you. You'll do the same with your baby."

Closing my eyes, I covered my ears with my hands. "No! No! No!"

"Maybe they'll look like me." His sinister laughter echoed in my head. "Then, you'll have to deal with my face for the rest of your life."

Tears leaked from my closed eyes as I tried to fight from the abyss Kaleb always pulled me in. "No!" I screamed, on the brink of losing control.

Calm down. Let go of the past and embrace the future. You've been given a gift—don't take it for granted.

I opened my eyes and released another deep breath, facing the source of all my demons in the mirror.

"My child will be nothing like you." I stated resolutely. "You hear me? Nothing like you!"

My face came back into focus as Kaleb's slipped away. Easing my grip off the counter, I stepped back and stood taller.

Time to move on.. You have to take care of your baby—give them a better life than you had.

Tears filled my eyes as I stared down at my stomach and placed my hands over my belly. "Hi, little one. I'm your mommy."

Mommy—I'm going to be a mommy.

Thoughts about how Ryker would react filled my head again. After everything that had happened with Molly, I doubted that he wanted to have a baby. We'd been together for less than a year, and having a baby together would be the ultimate commitment. There was no denying the love we had for each other, but I wasn't sure that either one of us were ready to be parents.

I looked down at the test on the counter again, and my stomach flip-flopped. In a matter of minutes, my life had been changed. I was left feeling more conflicted than I'd ever been before. Feelings of joy and excitement combated with worry and uncertainty. I had no idea what Ryker would think, but I prayed that he would be happy—I needed him now more than ever. And so did our child.

Chapter Ten

Ryker

When I got home from work, the apartment was filled with the smell of steak and spices. I threw my keys on the table and made my way to the kitchen, where Kaiya was pulling a tray of roasted vegetables out of the oven. "Hey, baby."

Kaiya set the pan on the stove as she turned to look at me. She gave me a nervous smile. "Hey. How was the rest of your day?"

I was still irritated from what had happened at the police station earlier that day, but working out had let me relieve some of the tension and aggression. "Better."

"Good. I don't want you to worry about that anymore. I have a relaxing evening planned for us."

I loved coming home on days like this. We didn't always have time to have a home-cooked meal, and I always felt special when Kaiya made me dinner.

I walked over and pulled her into my arms. "Whatever you say, baby. How was the rest of your day?"

She ran her hands up my chest and around my neck. "Interesting." Bringing my head down, she pressed her soft lips to mine.

Mmmmm.

The timer on the oven beeped, interrupting our kiss. Kaiya stepped back from me and slipped on her oven mitt as she said, "Dinner's almost ready. I made your favorite—Filet Mignon with roasted veggies and baked sweet potatoes."

I quirked my eyebrow curiously. "What's the occasion?"

She gave me a mischievous smile. "It's a surprise."

Bending over, she opened the oven and grabbed another cookie sheet with sweet potatoes on it. I lightly smacked her on the ass as I moved past her. "Guess I'll go get cleaned up for this surprise."

I took a quick shower and threw on some clothes before going back into the kitchen

Kaiya was in the adjoining dining room, setting the table with our plates of food and silverware. "Need any help?" I asked as I leaned against the door-frame.

"No, I think I have everything," she replied as she bunched her lips to the side.

I went to the table and pulled her chair out for her. Once she sat down, I kissed her cheek. "Thank you."

I rounded the table and sat down across from her. "This looks amazing, babe."

"Thanks." She smiled brightly.

"How was work?" I asked as I started cutting my steak.

Kaiya frowned. "Exhausting. I finally caught up on everything, though. I've been so behind. How was yours?"

"Pretty good. Every client met their goals for the week, and all my classes went well."

Kaiya took a bite of her sweet potato. "That's great. Has your shoulder been bothering you?"

"I've been taking it easy like you wanted so it's been fine." I ate a piece of my steak. "This is delicious, babe. You cooked it perfectly."

Kaiya blushed and a smile curved her lips. "Thank you."

We continued talking as we ate, but once I had finished my food, I noticed Kaiya had barely eaten anything. "You okay, Warrior? You didn't eat very much."

She gave me a small smile. "Yeah, I've just been feeling a little sick lately."

My eyebrows furrowed in concern. That was news to me. "Really? Sick how?"

"I've been throwing up and having bad headaches for the past month or so."

That didn't sound good at all. A lump formed in my throat that I quickly swallowed.

Don't freak out. It's probably just the flu or something.

"Maybe you should go to the doctor."

"Yeah, I'm going to call and make an appointment tomorrow. I'm going to have to make several appointments."

Now I was getting really worried. "Why? What's wrong?" My chest constricted as I thought about Kaiya having some serious illness that she hadn't told me about.

Her lips curved up in a wide smile. "I'm pregnant."

My stomach clenched as my heart pounded wildly.

Did she just say what I think she said?

I cleared the huge lump that formed in my throat. "What?" I finally managed to croak.

Her eyes watered even though her face was beaming with happiness. "I'm pregnant. We're going to have a baby, Ryker!"

We're going to have a baby.

I couldn't stop the huge smile that spread over my face as I rushed over to Kaiya.

She stood once I reached her and threw her arms around my neck. I picked her up and spun her around before setting her back down again. I cupped her face in my hands and looked in her eyes. "You're pregnant?"

She nodded excitedly. "I took a test when I got home. I've been throwing up at work in the mornings, but I thought it was from stress. Nori asked if I could be pregnant, and I remembered that the last time I got my shot was before the shooting. It completely slipped my mind."

I was letting everything sink in as a million thoughts raced through my mind.

Is it a boy or a girl? Will I be a good dad? Are we ready for this?

"Are you upset?" Kaiya nervously asked. She bit her bottom lip as she stared up at me.

I stroked her cheeks with my thumbs. "Upset? Why would I be upset, baby?"

Tears filled her eyes again. "Well, we've never talked about kids before. I don't even know if you want a baby with me, and you thought I was on birth control, and—"

I pressed a finger to her lips, cutting her off. "Stop. I'm not upset." I looked down at her stomach, then back up to meet her eyes. "I love you, Ky. We've never talked about kids before, but that doesn't mean that I don't want to have them with you."

She brought her hands up to cover mine and gripped them tightly. "Really?"

"Really, baby. You've made me so happy with what you just told me."

Letting go of her face, I knelt down and lifted her shirt to look at her stomach. I thought about the baby growing inside her and my smile stretched wider.

My baby.

I leaned forward and softly kissed her belly. Ky rested her hands on my head as I pressed more kisses all over her abdomen.

I'm going to be a dad.

I scooped her up and cradled her in my arms. "This calls for a celebration!" I started walking down the hall to my room.

Kaiya giggled and wrapped her hands around my neck. She raised an eyebrow and gave me a flirty smile. "What did you have in mind?"

I smirked. "It's a surprise."

Chapter Eleven

Kaiya

Ryker gently laid me down on the bed and straddled me. As his eyes met mine, the amount of love I saw in them caused my heart to swell and my stomach to knot. Tears pooled on the rims of my eyelids as he leaned down, propping himself on his forearms on each side of my head. Cupping my face in his hands, he softly feathered his lips over mine before murmuring against them, "I love you, Warrior."

My response came out in a breathless whisper. "I love you, too."

Ryker pressed another kiss on my lips before moving down my body. He lifted my shirt and stared down at my stomach in admiration. A sweet smile curved his full lips as he brought his face down to my belly and tenderly kissed it.

His hands framed my stomach as he ran his thumbs over my skin. "Hey, kid. I'm your dad."

Tears trickled down my cheeks even though happiness streamed through me. My adoration for him must have been apparent all over my face because I felt it deep in the darkest recesses of my soul, bringing new life to the pieces of me that had long been dead inside.

Ryker kept looking at my abdomen as he talked to our baby. "I'm going to do my best to take care of you and your mom. I love both of you so much." He glanced up at me and softly grinned. "I don't know if I'll be a good dad, but I do know that you're getting the perfect mom."

Those warm chocolate eyes captured mine as more of his sweet words poured out. "She's the most beautiful, caring, and selfless person I know. I don't deserve her, but I'm so lucky that she's mine."

He lowered his head back down and pressed his lips on my belly again, then trailed his mouth up to my breasts, searing my skin with heat and kindling a blazing fire in my core.

Ryker inched my shirt up as his lips continued their journey along my skin. They brushed over my collarbone and up my neck as he tugged my shirt over my head and tossed it to the floor.

His mouth barely grazed mine as his hands caressed my bare skin, fueling the inferno overtaking me. A shaky breath shuddered through my body as Ryker sparked every nerve alive with his touch.

He unhooked my bra and tossed it aside before pulling off his shirt. The rest of our clothes came off in a blur, and then his warm, inked skin finally met mine.

The way he felt on top of me, fitted between my legs, was absolutely perfect. Ryker had gradually been able to erase my insecurities and trepidations about sex, helping me heal from the abuse I'd sustained. And now, because of him, I truly understood how beautiful sex was; how it was one of the best ways to express your love for someone, giving every part of yourself to them in the most intimate way possible.

I could feel Ryker's love for me in every caress of his skin, every press of his lips, and it was the most incredible feeling I'd ever experienced.

Ryker laced his tongue with mine, flooding my mouth with his intoxicating taste. Passion was evident in every brush of our lips as we slowly savored one another.

His cock nudged my entrance as he rocked against me. I couldn't help but moan as he repeatedly stroked my clit with his thick, hardened shaft.

As he slowly inched inside me, a gasp escaped my lips. I loved how he completely filled me, molding our bodies together flawlessly as we made love.

Clasping my face in his hands, Ryker leisurely pumped his hips against me, prolonging every sensation with each deliberate thrust as he brought me closer to ecstasy. He whispered huskily against my lips, "I love you."

"I love you," I responded in a throaty moan as I threaded my hands in his hair.

He nipped my jaw as he drove deeper into me. His rough hands left my face to caress my skin as he trailed them down my body, sending a shiver through me. I arched against him, so close to unraveling from his divine touch.

"So perfect, baby. So fucking perfect," Ryker growled against my neck.

Our lips met again, and after a few more deep thrusts, I cried out in bliss as Ryker brought me to heaven; the only heaven I had ever known.

My body quivered as Ryker continued his strokes, intensifying my orgasm as it spread through my limbs. He stilled and groaned in my mouth as he followed me into euphoria.

He rested his sweaty forehead against mine as we regained our breath. Pressing another sweet kiss to my lips, he rolled off me and pulled me into him. He traced circles on my stomach as he propped himself up on his elbow. "So, we're having a baby, huh?"

I giggled and stared up at him. "Yeah, we are."

Our eyes met, and he smiled. He brought his lips to mine, and soon, we were lost in the beautiful haze our bodies created once again.

I called my gynecologist's office as soon as they opened the next morning to make an appointment. They were able to fit me in that afternoon, so I sent a text to Ryker to let him know.

Me: The dr can see us today at 430 :)

Ryker: Great baby I'll pick you up

Me: Ok :) I love you

Ryker: Love you too Warrior

Ryker had the day off, so he had dropped me off at work. I had meetings all day, along with a couple of presentations that were interspersed in between. I was so eager to find out more about the baby that I knew work was going to drag on and on until the appointment. My head kept snapping back and forth to the clock on the wall throughout the day as I waited and waited until four o'clock finally came around.

When Ryker picked me up, I could see the excitement all over his face, especially in his huge smile and shining eyes. Once I got in the truck, he asked. "How was your day, babe?"

"Long," I groaned in displeasure. "I've been so anxious all day for the appointment."

"Me too," he replied as he put the truck in drive and merged onto the street. "Where's this place at?"

I gave Ryker directions to my doctor's office, which was only a few blocks away from my work. We parked in the parking garage across the street before heading to the elevator. Ryker threaded our fingers together. "You nervous?"

I looked up at him. "A little. I have no clue what I'm doing. I know nothing about being a mom."

He stroked the back of my hand with his thumb and gave me a reassuring smile. "We'll figure it out together, Warrior."

Some of the tension and unease filling me were alleviated with Ryker's words. He always knew exactly what to say when I needed it most.

Once we checked in and I filled out the extensive paperwork, Ryker and I waited in the waiting room to be called back. Thankfully, it only took a few minutes for the nurse to come for me. "Kaiya Marlow?"

Ryker and I both stood, but the nurse stopped him. "We only need Kaiya for this part." She smiled politely. "I promise I'll bring her right back."

Ryker glanced at me reluctantly. "Okay."

I gave him a reassuring smile and squeezed his hand before following the nurse to the nurse's station. She handed me a plastic cup and lid that had a label with my name on it. "We need a urine sample. When you're done, please place it on the shelf above the toilet."

She directed me to the bathroom, and I went in and did my business. I left the sample where indicated on the shelf and washed my hands before exiting.

The nurse, who was wearing a name tag that read 'Sophie', took my blood pressure, height, and weight before walking me back to the waiting room. "We'll call you back for the rest of the exam shortly."

I sat back down next to Ryker, who was flipping through a fitness magazine. He glanced up at me. "Everything okay?"

"Yeah, they just did some routine stuff—height, weight, blood pressure."

We waited another fifteen minutes when Sophie came back out to get us. She led us to a room, and handed me one of those exam gowns that barely covered anything. "I'll give you a few minutes to change, then I'll be back to take your blood sample."

I quickly changed into the unattractive paper gown and hopped on the exam table. Ryker sat in a chair next to me right as a knock sounded on the door.

"Ready?" Sophie asked.

That was fast.

"Yes," I replied.

Sophie opened the door and came in with some small vials and a huge needle. I gulped.

Fuck.

Sophie laid out all the equipment on the counter before sterilizing my arm with an alcohol-soaked cotton ball. I began to feel hot, and my heart pounded as she tightly secured a band around my bicep and prepped the needle.

Ryker linked our fingers together and tugged on my hand. I looked toward him and squeezed tightly. He brought my hand up to his mouth and kissed the back of it. "Did I ever tell you about the time I got my first tattoo?"

I tried to remember if he had mentioned it. "No… I don't think so."

"Well, I had just turned eighteen. Tribal tattoos were popular, and almost everyone had one, so naturally, I wanted to get one, too." He paused and looked at his right arm, which had a huge tribal that wrapped from his shoulder down to below his elbow. My eyes followed his gaze to the ink on his arm as he continued talking. "My boys and I went together to this tattoo shop in downtown Boston to each get a different tribal piece."

My eyes went back to his as he continued speaking. "When I sat on the table, my heart was pounding and adrenaline surged through my veins. Once that needle pierced my skin, I was hooked."

"Doesn't it hurt?"

What a dumb question. Of course it hurts, genius.

He chuckled. "Yeah, it hurts, but the rush you get from it is awesome. Everything about it is addicting, even the pain."

"I've always been too scared to get one. I hate needles," I replied.

"All done."

I looked away from Ryker to Sophie, who was cleaning up the counter. I glanced down and saw a Band-Aid already applied to my inner elbow. "I didn't even feel it."

"You had a good distraction." She chuckled as she motioned to Ryker before opening the door. "Dr. Wallace will be with you shortly."

My eyes went to Ryker, who had an adorable, lopsided grin on his face. He shrugged. "I didn't want you to panic."

My insides somersaulted and a smile spread over my lips.

He is so sweet sometimes.

"Thank you, babe."

After a few minutes, my doctor knocked and entered. "Hi, Kaiya. How have you been?"

"I've been good. Busy, but good."

"Great," she replied as she looked at the iPad in her hands. After several seconds, she looked up and smiled. "I have your results."

Ryker stood next to me and squeezed my hand. My heart thudded wildly and my stomach twisted in anticipation as we waited for the answer that would change our lives.

Dr. Wallace's smile stretched wider. "Congratulations! You're having a baby!"

Tears welled in my eyes as I looked up at Ryker. He wrapped his arms around me and hugged me tightly to him as he kissed the top of my head.

Hearing the confirmation from Dr. Wallace was so much more fulfilling than seeing it on a plastic stick. I couldn't remember a time when I felt so happy. "We're having a baby, Ryker." I softly murmured into his neck.

Pulling back, Ryker cradled my face in his hands and softly kissed me. He stroked my cheeks with his thumbs and looked deep into my eyes.

He didn't need any words to express how he felt. I wasn't sure there were even words to describe the emotions we were experiencing at that moment. Pure love and joy reflected in those beautiful brown eyes that always captured me. I would never get tired of seeing him look at me like that.

Dr. Wallace cleared her throat, gaining both of our attentions. She gave us an apologetic smile. "I'm sorry to interrupt, but we have a lot to discuss."

She came and sat down in an office chair across from the exam table and wheeled it closer to us. "Let's go over your medical history, then we'll get to your exam and hear your baby's heartbeat."

Your baby.

The grin I had on my face widened.

She used a stylus to tap the screen of her iPad several times, quickly scanning over it with her eyes. "It says here that you're a twin, which means that you have a higher chance of having twins yourself."

And just like that, my stomach sank.

No.

"We can check that during your first sonogram."

Ryker rubbed my back and gave me a sympathetic look. It wasn't that I wouldn't be happy with two babies, but just the thought of having twins after what I went through with Kaleb gave me anxiety.

They wouldn't be like Kaleb and me—don't worry over nothing.

Easier said than done. My mind was preoccupied as we went through the rest of my medical history. After answering several questions, Dr. Wallace asked one that I didn't have the answer to. "When was the date of your last period?"

I swallowed nervously. "Well, my periods have never been regular. I was on the shot, but I can't even remember when I came in for it the last time, or my last period."

Dr. Wallace peered back down at the tablet in her hands. "According to our records, the last time you received your contraceptive was in June."

Shit, that's over six months ago. I can't believe it slipped my mind for that long.

Dr. Wallace continued. "We'll need to do an ultrasound to determine how far along you are. Let me see if there's an ultrasound tech still here."

She swiveled in her chair and placed the iPad on the counter before reaching for the phone. "Rachel, can you please check if there's an ultrasound tech available."

A few moments later, she spoke into the phone again. "Thank you. Please send them to room nine."

Turning back to face us, she stated, "Let's get you all checked out. Lay back, please."

Ugh, I hate this part.

A few seconds after she finished with my exam, a knock sounded on the door.

"Just in time," Dr. Wallace said as she took off her gloves and washed her hands. "Come in."

A woman opened the door and entered with a large cart. "Hi, I'm Jen. I'll be your ultrasound tech today." She smiled at us. "Ready to see your baby?"

"Yes," Ryker and I said simultaneously.

"Great! Lay back down and lift the top part of your gown up."

Jen wheeled the cart next to me and grabbed a tube. "This is going to be cold, okay?"

I nodded. Jen squirted the gel on my stomach before placing the ultrasound wand on it. Immediately, the computer screen on the cart came to life, but it took a few seconds before she found the right spot. "There's your baby," she practically cooed.

Both Ryker and I stared in awe at the screen with our tiny baby on it.

Our baby.

Looking up at him, I briefly wondered if he had done all this with Molly, and if he felt the same way with her as he did with me. I quickly pushed the thoughts aside, not wanting to ruin the moment of seeing my future child for the first time.

Dr. Wallace studied the screen. Jen glanced at her before stating, "I'd say she's about twelve or thirteen weeks along."

Dr. Wallace nodded. "I think so, too." She directed her attention to me. "Only one fetus—no twins."

Thank God.

"Would you like a picture?" Jen asked.

I nodded enthusiastically. "Yes, please."

After she pressed a few buttons on the computer, a small sonogram picture printed out. She took the wand off my stomach and cleaned me up before handing me the photo. "Here you go—the first picture of your baby."

I glanced down at the sonogram in my hands, then up at Ryker. He was staring at the image with so much love all over his face that it made my heart skip a beat.

He darted his eyes to mine and gave me a sweet smile. I couldn't stop my own from forming over my lips because of his. I handed the picture to him as Jen said, "It was nice meeting you. Good luck with your pregnancy."

My head turned to see her wheeling the cart out the door. "It was nice to meet you, too. Thank you so much!"

Dr. Wallace sat back down in her chair. "Do you have any questions for me?"

91

I looked up at Ryker, then back at my doctor. "This is all so new and overwhelming, but my mind is blank right now."

Dr. Wallace laughed warmly. "That's understandable. This is your first child, and not everyone knows what to ask. That's why we have a packet with everything you need to know to take home. We can go over it before you leave."

Some tension left me, and I sighed in relief. "Thank you. I feel so much better."

Dr. Wallace's eyes lit up as her eyebrows rose. "Oh, I almost forgot! Let's listen to your baby's heartbeat." She stood and grabbed a handheld machine and another tube of gel from one of the cabinets. It had a wand similar to the ultrasound machine at the end, only smaller. "This is a fetal doppler."

Dr. Wallace squeezed more gel on my belly and placed the wand on my stomach. Static and swooshing filled the room as she moved the sensor around my stomach. "Where are you, little one?"

She traced my lower abdomen before a noise that sounded like a horse galloping mixed with the other sounds. "There you are."

I looked from my stomach to Dr. Wallace. "That's the heartbeat? It's so fast."

"That's perfectly normal. The heartbeat of a fetus ranges anywhere between one hundred twenty and one hundred eighty beats per minute."

I continued listening to the beautiful sound. Ryker squeezed my hand and gave me a huge grin. It was amazing hearing something that he and I created together, something so pure and perfect.

Dr. Wallace left the wand there a little longer before pulling it off, and I immediately missed the sound once it stopped. I could've listened to it all day if she let me.

Before we left, Dr. Wallace went over some of the packet of with us, answered what questions we had, and scheduled my next appointment for four weeks later.

As we walked out, Ryker held the door for me and asked, "Crazy, huh? We're having a baby."

I laughed. "Yeah. Who would've thought?"

He linked our hands as we walked to the elevator. "Not me. You turned my life upside-down." He pressed the down button with one of his free fingers then poked my stomach.

I feigned offense. "Hey, you're the one who wouldn't leave me alone." I playfully yanked my hand from him, but he pulled me into him and closed his huge arms around me, trapping my body against his.

"I'm glad I didn't." Our eyes met as he looked down at me. He reached his hand up and brushed his knuckles down my cheek, making my knees weak and causing my face to instantly heat.

Ryker's proximity always made my heart race. My voice was unsteady as I spoke. "Oh, yeah? Why?"

The right corner of his mouth curved up in a sexy grin as he leaned, barely brushing those heavenly lips against mine. "Because I wouldn't have found my family if I hadn't."

My heart fluttered from his words. *Family.* The only family I'd ever truly had was Kamden, and to hear Ryker say that I was his family made me feel… amazing.

His hand pressed against my stomach as he closed the sliver of a gap between our mouths and kissed me. The elevator sounded, and Ryker pushed me through the doors and against the wall.

I didn't know if anyone was in there, and frankly, I didn't care. When Ryker's lips were on mine, all I was concerned about was consuming as much of him as I possibly could. The building could catch on fire and I'd be oblivious to it.

My hands framed his face as his tongue slipped past my lips. His fingers threaded through my hair until he reached the back of my head and gripped tightly, devouring me right there in the elevator. And I loved every second of it.

When the elevator sounded again, Ryker broke away from me, leaving me breathless and flushed. My lips tingled when I gave him a flirty smile as we exited.

I called Nori as soon as we got in the truck. The excitement was evident in her voice as she answered the phone. "So? What's the verdict?"

I paused for dramatic effect. "They said I'm about twelve weeks pregnant. I'm due August 2."

Nori squealed like a five year old into the phone, "Shut up! Oh my God, I'm so happy for you, Ky!"

Ryker started driving, then placed his hand on my leg and rubbed it affectionately. "Thank you. I think I'm still in shock."

"How did Ryker take it? Is he excited?"

I grinned as I looked over at him. "Very. The smile still hasn't come off his face."

"Aww, that's so sweet." She paused before squealing again. "I'm going to be an auntie!"

We chatted for a few minutes about my appointment hanging up.

"She's excited, huh?" Ryker asked as he turned at a stoplight.

"Yeah, she is. Already planning a baby shower and everything." I chuckled.

"How do you think Kamden will react?"

Shit.

I hadn't thought about that. Given his current state, I couldn't even speculate what his response to the news would be. "I don't know. I think he'll be happy, but I'm not positive."

Ryker squeezed my thigh. "I'm sure he will be. Don't worry about it, Warrior."

I looked out the window and sighed. I hoped that he was right.

Chapter Twelve

Ryker

Kaiya was nervous about telling Kamden about the baby the whole drive home. She was worried he would blow up at her for being irresponsible, and to be honest, I was concerned about how he would react, too. He had become pretty hot-headed since the shooting.

When we walked in, the smell of fresh, baked bread greeted us. Kaiya gave me a confused look as she tossed her keys on the table and took off her coat. "Kam?"

"In here," he yelled back.

I followed Kaiya into the kitchen, where Kamden was cooking. He turned his head toward us and smiled as he stirred a pot on the stove. "Hey."

"Hey, yourself," Kaiya replied as she quirked up an eyebrow. "What are you doing?"

He set the spoon he was stirring with on the counter before facing us. "I know I haven't been the easiest person to deal with lately." He rubbed the back of his neck sheepishly as he looked at Ky. "I wanted to start making up for how I've been acting. I shouldn't have taken my issues out on you, and I'm sorry."

Kaiya didn't say anything in response. Instead, she rushed to Kamden and threw her arms around his waist. A loving smile spread over his lips as he wrapped his arms around her and hugged her tightly. "I'm going to try and stop drinking, too. Haven't had a drink since Saturday."

"That's amazing, Kam. I'm so proud of you."

My mouth curved up involuntarily as I watched them. Kaiya loved Kamden so much, and watching him sink into a downward spiral had been tearing her apart inside.

The timer on the stove went off, and Kamden let go of Kaiya. "Don't want the bread to burn."

He grabbed an oven mitt and opened the oven before pulling out a tray with French bread on it. He set the tray on the stove and said, "It's nothing elaborate, but I did make the meatballs from scratch."

"It's perfect, Kam. You really didn't have to do this," Kaiya said.

"I wanted to, *sorella*. Now go sit down. It's almost ready."

Kaiya walked to the cabinets. "Let me set the table at least."

Kamden blocked her path and gave her a stern look. "Out," he ordered as he fought a smile.

"Fine." Kaiya laughed. She grabbed my hand as she walked by me and tugged me into the dining room.

Kamden came with plates a minute or so after we sat down. He set one down in front of each of us, then went back into the kitchen.

When he came back and set everything on the table, he sat down across from us and gestured to the food. "Go ahead. Dig in."

Kaiya and I served ourselves, then waited for Kamden to do the same before we started eating.

Kamden stopped and rose from his seat. "Forgot drinks."

He came back with three water bottles and handed us each one. He unscrewed his bottle and took a drink as he sat back down. "How's everything with you guys?

Kaiya glanced over at me and smiled. "Well, uh, we have some exciting news."

Kamden took a bite of his spaghetti. "Oh, yeah? What?"

Kaiya joined our hands under the table, but directed her attention to her brother. "I'm pregnant." Her voice was shaky and unsure.

Kamden choked on the water he'd just drank and quickly cleared his throat. "What?"

She squeezed my hand. "I'm pregnant. We just found out today. Isn't that great?" Kaiya asked nervously.

His eyes darted back and forth between us before they settled on Kaiya. "Are you sure you're ready for this, Ky?"

Kaiya's face fell and her shoulders sagged. "Yes. Ryker and I love each other. Aren't you happy?"

His eyes softened. "I'm concerned, *sorella*. That's all. If you're happy, I'm happy."

"I am." She looked down at her stomach and smiled. "We got to hear the baby's heartbeat and everything. Wanna see the sonogram?"

"Of course—let me see my future niece or nephew," Kamden replied enthusiastically.

Kaiya started to stand, but I stopped her. "I'll get it, baby. You relax."

I went to Kaiya's purse and dug around for the sonogram. II found it in one of the inner pockets of her purse. A smile came over my face as I looked down at the little bean shaped image.

I'm going to be a dad.

A fullness in my chest filled me. I'd never felt anything like it before—I was in love with a little bean. And then I remembered, I had felt that way before. I closed my eyes as my stomach dropped.

What if he's not mine?

Doubt replaced the joy. I glanced over at Ky and Kamden, who were laughing at the table. Her eyes found mine from across the room, and they told me everything I needed to know.

Fuck all the doubts.

Molly had never looked at me that way, even at our best times. Kaiya's love for me was always written all over her face. There was no reason I should be doubting her.

Our eyes remained locked as I walked back to the dining room. I leaned down and kissed Kaiya before handing her the sonogram. She excitedly gave it to Kamden. He scanned over the picture as a grin tipped up his lips. "Is it a boy or a girl?"

"We won't find that out until between eighteen and twenty weeks. I'm only about twelve or thirteen weeks now," Kaiya answered.

Kaiya told Kamden about what we had learned at her appointment throughout dinner. Once we were finished, she started collecting the dishes from the table as Kamden asked, "What are you doing?"

"I'm cleaning up—you did enough tonight," Kaiya replied as she stacked the plates and began putting the dirty silverware on top of them.

"I don't think so—you need to rest." Kamden took the dishes from her.

Kaiya rolled her eyes. "I'm pregnant, not dying."

Kamden chuckled. "Enjoy it while it lasts. Once you pop out that baby, you'll get all your old chores back."

"Seriously, go rest, Warrior. You've been stressing yourself out too much." I stood and rubbed her arms. "It's not good for the baby."

She sighed. "Fine. I'm gonna go lay down. You coming?"

I kissed her on the forehead. "I'll be right there."

Kaiya turned and walked away. You could see the exhaustion in every weary step she took—she was so stubborn sometimes.

Kamden had taken most of the dishes off the table, but I grabbed the remaining bowls with the leftover spaghetti and salad in them and carried them into the kitchen.

I set the bowls on the counter as Kamden began loading the dishwasher. "Thanks."

"No problem." I leaned back against the counter. "I just wanted to say that I think it's great what you're doing. I know it means a lot to Kaiya."

"Yeah. I can't keep hurting her like I have been. That night I pushed her" —he shook his head and scowled— "was an eye-opener. I hadn't realized how bad I was."

Before I could comment, Kamden looked up at me and changed the subject by asking, "You're going to take care of my sister and the baby, right?"

I could hear the warning in his tone. I stood tall and crossed my arms over my chest. "Of course. I love her." And I wasn't a punk bitch who ran away from their responsibilities.

Kamden looked me up and down. "You better."

I never understood why Kamden and I'd never gotten along. Maybe older brothers were always assholes to their sister's boyfriends, or felt they had some kind of territory to mark, but he had another thing coming if he thought I was going to let him intimidate me.

I stepped up to him. "Look, let's get this straight. I don't give a fuck what you think. Kaiya and our baby are the only things that matter to me. Get your own shit together and let me worry about Kaiya."

His jaw clenched as we stared each other down.

"Ryker?" Kaiya called out from her room.

I kept my eyes locked on Kamden's as I replied, "Coming, babe." I held his stare and said, "I'm going to take care of Kaiya and the baby. You handle your business and I'll handle mine."

I brushed past him to go down the hall. I heard dishes roughly clanging together as I entered Kaiya's room and shut the door.

She was lying down on the bed, propped up with pillows under her back as she read a book. She glanced up at me and smiled as she closed it and set it on the nightstand. "Hey."

"Hey." I flopped onto the bed and scooted next to her. I pulled her body into mine, and she curved up against me and rested her head on my chest. "Big day today, huh?" I asked.

I played with her hair as she traced my abs through my shirt. "Yeah, I was just thinking about what we're going to do when the baby comes."

"Like what?" She moved so that she could look up at me. "Like whose apartment we're going to live in, everything we need to get for him or her, stuff like that."

I hadn't thought about where we were going to live once the baby was born—I was still processing the fact that we we're even having one. "Definitely not here." I was not living with Kamden.

Kaiya chuckled. "Well, your apartment is too small—we need a nursery for the baby."

"We can get a bigger apartment or maybe even a house."

Her eyes lit up. "Really?"

I ran my fingers through her hair. "Yeah." I smiled. "Get our own place, start a family."

Kaiya smiled sweetly and looked at me dreamily. "That sounds perfect."

I had to admit that it did. Settling down hadn't ever appealed to me, but Kaiya always found a way to change my mind about things.

"Yeah, it does." I kissed the top of her head. "So are you happy about Kamden?"

The sigh she made was full of relief. "Yes. I hope he can pull through this. I want him to be a part of the baby's life, but not if he's going to be angry and drunk all the time."

That's not going to happen. I wouldn't let Kamden near our baby if he didn't get his shit together, Kaiya's brother or not. "I'm sure he will. He's stubborn like you, so I don't think he'll give up."

She smacked my chest and scoffed. "I'm not stubborn."

My chest rumbled with laughter. "Sure, baby, whatever you say."

Kaiya softly giggled, then suddenly stopped and became serious. "Do you think I'll be a good mom?"

I looked in her eyes and cupped her cheek. "The best. I couldn't have asked for a better woman to have my kids."

She placed her hand over my mine and her eyes watered. "I'm just worried that because I'm so fucked up that I'll screw their life up, too." She hung her head and avoided my eyes.

I framed her face in my hands, forcing her to look at me again. "Hey. You're not fucked up, Warrior. You may be scarred, but you're not broken. You're the most incredible person I've ever met. You've changed my whole life, made me better." I paused and stroked her cheeks softly. "You're going to be an amazing mother, Ky."

A few tears slipped down her face. I wiped them away as she leaned up and softly kissed my lips. She pulled back, and the corner of her mouth slightly lifted. "I think you're biased but thank you."

I lightly chuckled. "No, I'm not—you are. You think what Kaleb did to you made you weak, but in reality, it did the opposite. He tried to break you, but he didn't. He only made you stronger."

"He didn't make me stronger." Her eyes held mine. "You did."

I smiled and caressed her cheeks. "I only built on what was already there. You may have had some splinters and cracks, but your foundation was still strong."

She turned into one of my hands and kissed my palm. "I don't know where I'd be without you. Thank you for everything you've done for me." She looked down at her stomach and placed her hands on it. "Especially blessing me with this."

Leaning my forehead against hers, I followed her gaze. "You're the one blessing me, Warrior. You carrying my baby is just…" I put my hands over hers. "Amazing."

We stayed like that for several seconds before Kaiya spoke. "Did you say kids?"

I pulled my head back from hers. "Huh?"

She grinned playfully. "A minute ago—you said that you couldn't have asked for a better woman to have your kids."

I raised an eyebrow. "Yeah?"

"Plural, meaning more than one?"

I chuckled. "Yes. I want you to have my kids, plural."

She tucked some of her hair behind her ear. "You know, I never planned to have kids."

"Well, sorry to have ruined your plans," I teased.

She stared into my eyes. "You didn't ruin anything. I wasn't living before. I always blocked out the world and the ugliness it contained." She gave me a shy smile. "You changed that—you showed me how beautiful life can be."

My eyes ran over her face. "Same here. After my parents died, life wasn't the same. And then, everything that happened with Ethan and Molly solidified what I thought—life's a bitch, and then you die. But then I met you, and you reminded me that life is a gift." I brushed my knuckles down her cheek. "You are my gift."

Leaning in, I gently kissed her lips and pulled her against me. My heart raced every time that sweet mouth of hers met mine. Kaiya was my high, the addiction I couldn't satisfy. No matter how much I had of her, it wasn't enough; I still wanted more.

My hands went to her ass as I pushed my hardening cock against her. She softly moaned in my mouth and threaded her fingers through my hair.

A knock on the door broke us apart. I buried my face in one of Kaiya's pillows and let out a groan of frustration.

Damn it, we should have stayed at my place.

I peeked up at Kaiya to see her lips twitching as she fought a smile. She mouthed sorry before saying, "Come in."

Kamden stuck his head in the room. "Hey, I rented a couple of movies for us to watch. I was just about to put the first one in." He raised his eyebrows expectantly, like a kid asking for ice cream.

I knew Kaiya would say yes before she even spoke. The endearing look on her face said it all. "Okay, we'll be right there."

"Awesome, I'll make some popcorn," Kamden replied before turning around and going back down the hallway.

Kaiya yawned as she sat up on the edge of the bed. "I don't know if I'll even make it through the first movie. I'm so tired."

She came around to my side as I stood up. "Are you sure you want to stay up? Maybe you should get some sleep—it's been a long day."

"No, it's okay. I want to spend some time with Kam, especially since he's trying to work through his issues."

I draped my arm around her and kissed her temple. "Okay, Warrior. Whatever you want."

We headed out the door toward the living room. Even though I would much rather be in bed alone with Kaiya, I still enjoyed doing homey stuff with her.

We sat down as the sound of popping and the smell of popcorn filled the air. Kaiya snuggled close to me and leaned her head on my shoulder, then yawned again.

Yeah, she'll be asleep in half an hour, tops.

I put my arm around her as Kamden brought the popcorn in two bowls and handed us one. Kaiya started munching on the snack as Kamden started the movie.

Kaiya made it about twenty minutes before she started dozing off. Her head would slip off my shoulder and she would jolt awake and start fighting sleep again.

Kamden laughed. "Tired, *sorella?*"

"No," Kaiya lied. "I was just resting my eyes."

I snorted, causing Kaiya to glare at me as she sat up.

So stubborn.

She finally gave in to sleep halfway through the movie. I gently cradled her in my lap before rising off the couch. "I'm gonna take her to bed. It's been a long day."

I heard the movie turn off as I walked down the hall to Kaiya's room. I shut the door with my foot and laid her down on the bed. She didn't move an inch, even when I covered her and kissed her lips—she was completely out.

I took off my jeans and shirt, then slid into bed next to her. Wrapping my arms around her waist, I placed one of my hands on her stomach and smiled.

My baby.

The smile was still on my face when I fell asleep.

At work the following day, my mind was still swarming with thoughts about the baby. Most were good, but every now and then, a negative one slipped in there.

What if the baby's not mine?

I pushed the thought away, not wanting to ruin the happiness I felt. I hated that what had happened in my past was making me question Kaiya, but I couldn't help having doubts given my experience with Molly.

I wasn't upset over Molly and Ethan anymore, but what they did had left a mark on me, a scar I would never forget. But now that I was going to be a dad and start a family of my own with Kaiya, I was starting to see that there were more important things than holding grudges.

Ethan had also been in and out of my mind all morning. Seeing Kamden trying to make an effort to rebuild his relationship with Kaiya made me think more about doing the same. Ethan was my blood, and I didn't think my parents would want us to be the way we were.

I still had his number in my phone; I could never bring myself to delete it. I'd told myself it was so I would know not to answer his calls or texts, but I think deep down, I didn't want to completely let him go.

I scrolled through my contacts until I came to Ethan's. I pressed the text message icon, and began typing my message to him.

Me: You free for lunch today? Wanted to talk

I set my phone on my desk and looked over my client invoices for the month. A few minutes later, my phone buzzed, and I was surprised by how nervous I was. I hadn't spoken to my brother since before the shooting, and the times before that weren't on the best of terms.

Grabbing my phone, I clicked on the text icon and pulled up Ethan's message.

Ethan: R u serious or is this a joke?

The corner of my lip curved up. I couldn't blame him for not trusting me, especially with how hostile I'd been every time he'd tried to contact me.

Me: I'm serious do u want to meet up or not?

Ethan: When and where?

I told Ethan to meet me at one o'clock at a deli not too far from the gym. Once sending the text, my nerves skyrocketed. The meeting could either completely destroy what little remained of our relationship or get us on the path to mending it. I tried to tell myself that I didn't care either way, but deep down, I was hoping we could make amends.

I was a few minutes early, but Ethan was already seated at a table. When he saw me, he stiffly waved his hand and gave me a tight-lipped smile.

I walked toward him, disliking the unease settling in my gut. I was starting to second-guess my decision.

Why am I doing this? What are we going to talk about? How can I ever trust him again?

When I reached the table, I sat down.

"Hey," Ethan nervously greeted.

This is awkward already.

"Hey."

Ethan anxiously tapped his finger on the table. "So, how have you been?"

"Fine," I clipped. I wasn't ready to share personal details about my life just yet—baby steps. "How about you?"

"Good. Everything's good. Tristan is getting big." He smiled broadly.

Thinking about Tristan used to piss me off so much. He used to remind me of what I had lost and the betrayal committed against me by my own brother. It still irked me a little, only because there was still animosity between Ethan and me, but I didn't have anything against the kid.

I visualized having my own son, and a small grin tipped my lips. "That's good."

Ethan leaned back in his seat and scanned over my face. "Why did you invite me here, Ryker?"

The million dollar question. I cleared my throat. "A lot has happened since I last saw you, and they've made me realize some things." I paused and rubbed my hands together. "Life is-"

A tiny brunette interrupted me. "Hi, my name is Brooke, and I'll be your waitress today. Can I get you something to drink?"

After she left to get our drinks, Ethan's eyes met mine. "You were saying?"

I sighed. "Life's too short to hold grudges and take things for granted. You're my only brother, and I wanted to try and make amends. Mom and Dad would've wanted that."

We silently stared at one another until our waitress came back with our drinks. "Are you ready to order?"

"We need a few minutes," Ethan responded without breaking eye contact. Brooke said something I didn't make out and walked away, leaving us alone again.

After a minute or so, Ethan smiled. "I'd like that. Believe it or not, I miss your arrogant ass."

I snorted as our waitress came back up to our table. She raised her eyebrows at us. "Ready?"

We scanned the lunch specials, and settled on sandwiches. When she walked away, Ethan asked, "Does this change of heart have anything to do with the woman you were with when I came to the gym?"

I smiled as I thought about Kaiya. "Yeah. She's made a big difference in my life."

"Tell me about her," Ethan urged.

I took a drink of my water. "Kaiya is… something else." I chuckled. "I've never met anyone like her. She's shown me what real love is."

"Sounds pretty serious." Ethan raised his eyebrows.

"Yeah, we are. We just found out she's pregnant." The grin on my face spread wider.

"That's great! Having a child is one of the most fulfilling things you'll ever experience. Tristan is the best thing that's ever happened to me."

As if realizing he said something wrong, Ethan's smile fell. "Look, I'm really sorry about what I did to you. Neither one of us planned to. We just fell in love. I don't regret it, but I do regret hurting you in the process."

A year ago, what Ethan had just said would've sent me into a furious rage. What they did had disrespected my relationship with my brother. It still annoyed me, but didn't piss me off like it used to. "I know. Let's just try to move on—put the past behind us."

Ethan nodded. "Sounds like a plan."

Once our food came, we started talking about our lives—work, daily life, likes and dislikes, basically trying to get reacquainted. So much had changed since college.

While we waited for our tab, Ethan suggested, "Maybe we should all go out to dinner—me, you, Molly, Kaiya, and Tristan. Get to know each other better."

I was not ready for that. Reconciling with Ethan was one thing, but Molly was a different story. "I'm not sure about that just yet. Let me think about it."

"Too much, too fast, huh? I understand. Let me know when you're ready."

I nodded. "This was good. Maybe we can do it again next week—start off with that."

Ethan stuck his hand out across the table. "Deal."

I looked at it hesitantly before grabbing his hand with my own. "Deal."

Ethan shook my hand firmly and smiled. He reminded me so much of my mom with his green eyes and light brown hair.

Maybe this'll work out.

Our waitress came with our tab, and I took my wallet from my back pocket. Ethan protested as he placed his card on the table. "Let me."

"It's cool. I got it." I slipped a ten on the on the receipt for my part of the lunch. I wasn't ready to take anything from him.

Ethan chuckled and shrugged. "Suit yourself."

We made plans to get together for lunch the following week—same time, same place. As I drove back to work, I felt like some weight had been lifted off me from trying to work things out with Ethan. I just hoped that he didn't end up screwing me over again.

Chapter Thirteen

Kaiya

The day following our appointment, Ryker texted me questions he wanted me to ask my doctor about attending class. He'd read some of the packets Dr. Wallace had given us before going to work and had thought of a few questions when he got to the section on exercise. The fact that he took the time to read any of it warmed my heart—I didn't think most guys would even bother.

I'd found out that I could continue kickboxing until I was about seven or eight months along, but I wouldn't be able to keep doing the self-defense techniques the same. I wasn't allowed to throw anyone or be thrown, spar, or take any type of hits to the stomach whatsoever.

I wasn't surprised when Dr. Wallace informed me of my limitations. I'd already assumed that I would just have to watch class if I wanted to continue learning the various self-defense maneuvers before she confirmed it.

I was disappointed, especially since I was still receiving the harassing texts from the blocked number. I wanted to keep practicing, but I knew I had to think about the health of my baby first.

When I walked into the studio, Ryker smiled broadly as he strode toward me. "I have some good news."

"Oh yeah? What?" I replied, tiptoeing up to kiss him.

He rubbed his hands up and down my sides. "I did some research and found some self-defense maneuvers you can do."

A hopeful grin teased my lips. "Really?" My voice brightened from the dull tone I'd had after talking to my doctor.

"Yeah." He nodded. "The techniques come from jujitsu martial arts. They're referred to as small circle hapkido techniques."

My eyebrows furrowed. "What makes the moves different from the ones you usually teach in class?"

Ryker gripped my hands in his and held them in between us. "Small circle hapkido focuses primarily on wrist and hand locks and maneuvers, which disable your attacker with just simple, fluid movements focusing on various pressure points in the hands and wrist."

He took my right hand in both of his and massaged it. "There are so many vulnerable spots that take just a little force to cause substantial pain." He squeezed the area between my thumb and index finger, right next to the base of my thumb. "Like here. It was interesting to read about."

I was still skeptical. "Hmm, are you sure? I don't want anything happening to the baby."

The corner of his lip curved up in a small smirk. "I called your doctor and described the techniques. She said they were fine."

I quirked my eyebrow up in surprise. "You called Dr. Wallace?"

He nodded. "I didn't want to do anything that would endanger you or the baby."

My heart melted. "That was sweet of you, baby. Thank you."

Ryker reached out his hand and placed it on my stomach. "Anything for you, Warrior."

I stood on my tiptoes to kiss him. His hands traveled around my sides to my back, pulling me against him. I broke the kiss and smiled. "I love you."

He brushed his fingertips down my cheek. "I love you, too."

The other instructors walked in, so I went to my bag and put my gear on as Ryker approached them to discuss the class.

Once we finished working on the bags, Ryker gathered us on the mats. "Today, we're going to start a series of self-defense techniques that are different from what we normally practice, but just as effective, if not more."

He motioned for Mark to come to him and grabbed his hand. "We're going to focus on maneuvers that concentrate on the hands and wrists to disable your attacker." He gripped two of Mark's fingers and pushed them back, causing Mark to wince in pain and squirm in discomfort. "As you can see, I'm putting very little effort into causing Mark pain already."

Ryker twisted Mark's hand while keeping his fingers bent back. Mark fell to his knees and tapped out almost instantly. Ryker let go and addressed the class. "Simple, but extremely effective. Even those that don't know any punches, kicks, or other self-defense maneuvers could still defend themselves using these techniques."

"Looks easy—too easy," one of the students voiced.

Ryker smirked. "Looks can be deceiving. Let me show you the first technique before you make your mind up."

After Ryker demonstrated, he came over and stuck his arm out. "Grab my wrist."

I gripped his thick wrist like he instructed. "Most of the small circle techniques defend against some type of grab." Using his other hand, he reached over and grabbed my hand, right at the base of my fingers. "So if someone grabs your wrist, there are various ways to get out of it without exerting too much force."

He squeezed and started prying my hand off his wrist. "Secure your hand over the top of theirs and apply pressure. Then, pull their hand off and turn it as you bring it up to your chest. Their palm should face away from you." The side of my hand was twisted uncomfortably as Ryker held it against his collarbone. "From here, bring your other hand up and grasp the inside of their elbow." He pressed his fingers against my inner elbow and pulled it back. "Then, apply pressure while pulling and pushing down on the joint."

Ryker had forced me to bend over to compensate for the pain and unnatural position he'd put me in. "Once you have them in this position, you can easily snap their arm, get some kicks to their stomach or groin, or even some knees to the face."

He loosened his grip but held onto my arm. Moving his hands up my forearm to my elbow, he started massaging the strained joint. "You okay?"

"Yeah, I'm good." I pulled my arm away and started bending and moving my elbow to get rid of the remaining tension. "My turn?"

One side of Ryker's mouth lifted. "Yeah, Warrior." He grabbed my slender wrist with one of his large, inked hands. "Go ahead."

The move was pretty simple to execute, so I didn't need much guidance from Ryker. Like some of the other students, I was skeptical about how easy the small circle techniques seemed and wondered if the moves were as effective as Ryker said.

But as soon as I brought Ryker's hand up to my chest and saw his face straining from the pain, my doubts faded. While the move was uncomfortable for me, it didn't hurt too much because I was flexible. However, Ryker, and most men for that matter, weren't typically limber. At all.

Ryker tapped out as soon once I started pulling back on his elbow. I let him go and giggled. "I can't believe it's that easy."

Ryker rotated his shoulder and bent his elbow several times. "I told you. Simple, but effective."

"But what if the person tries to hit you while you're attempting the move?"

Ryker stepped toward me. "That's a good question. With any technique that I teach you, there's always that possibility. You have to stay aware of what your attacker is doing and counter if needed. How an attack will progress can't be predicted, and that's why I teach so many different maneuvers so that you're as prepared as possible for whatever is thrown at you."

I nodded. "That makes sense. It sucks not knowing what they're going to do, though."

"I know, baby. What's good is that most attackers aren't trained like you are, so you have that advantage. Plus, when someone is in pain, that's typically all they focus on. They don't even think about anything else like fighting back. All that's on their mind is how to stop the pain."

Ryker had me practice a few more times and threw in some punches for me to block as I tried to execute the move. While it was more difficult, I instinctively reacted and countered. The move took longer, but I was still able to complete it.

Once class ended, many of the students gave Ryker a lot of positive feedback on the new technique. They were excited to learn more, which thrilled him. He'd been worried about how small circle hapkido would be received by the class.

As we walked into the parking lot, my phone started ringing. I grabbed it out of my purse and automatically answered it without looking at the screen. "Hello?"

There was no response, so I repeated myself. "Hello?"

Heavy breathing sounded through the phone. My stomach tightened as I pulled the phone away and looked at the caller ID on my screen. It was an unknown number.

I immediately hung up and shoved my phone back into my purse.

"Who was it?" Ryker asked as we reached my car.

I swallowed the lump that had formed in my throat. "Wrong number."

"Weird." He leaned in to kiss me. "I'll see you at home."

I hugged him tightly for a few seconds after our kiss before letting go. "Okay."

"Drive safe." He smiled as he backed away in the direction his truck.

I quickly opened the door and got in the car. My hands trembled as I locked the doors and fumbled to get the keys in the ignition.

I dropped my keys on the floorboard. "Shit."

Breathe, Kaiya. Calm down.

I rested my head against the steering wheel and took deep breaths before reaching down for my keys. My hands were still shaking as I put the key in and started the engine.

I told myself that everything would be fine, but I knew better. Things were always too good to be true, and I wondered when this would come crashing down on me, just like everything else always did.

Kamden bounced his leg anxiously as we sat waiting for Dr. Lowell to come in for his weekly session. He was opening up more during therapy, which seemed to be helping with his drinking since he wasn't looking for a way out anymore. He was facing his issues and not trying to wash them away with alcohol.

Even though Kamden had been sober for about two weeks, he was more irritable than ever. He was strung so tight that I was afraid he would snap at any moment, but thankfully he hadn't yet. I hoped that it would start becoming easier for him soon so that he could stop his self-loathing and finally start healing. I could only imagine what he was going through.

Once Dr. Lowell came in and got settled, she opened with her standard greeting of asking us how we were doing. Kamden drummed his thumbs against his knees as he answered, "Still sober—going on two weeks now."

"That's great, Kamden." Dr. Lowell replied proudly. "How do you feel about that?"

Kamden looked down at the floor and rubbed his palms together. "I want to drink so bad. I want to get rid of this guilt eating at me; take away the pain. I've come so close to giving in."

Dr. Lowell scribbled on her notepad. "What's stopped you?"

Kamden sat up and fixed his gaze on the window. "I deserve it—the pain, the guilt. I deserve to feel every bit of it, not be a coward and hide from it."

His words stung my heart—I hated that he felt that way. He didn't deserve any of what he was experiencing, especially when it was because he had been protecting me.

Dr. Lowell set her pen down. "I know it's hard right now, and things will probably get worse before they get better. But, they will get better. Time heals all wounds."

Did she really just say that?

I hated that stupid saying. "Is that what they tell you to say to everyone? That's such generic bullshit. I can be the first to tell you that it doesn't. Time just allows scars to form over your wounds that you never forget." I crossed my arms over my chest and huffed in frustration. I didn't care if I looked like a bratty child.

I hate therapists.

Out of the corner of my eye, I saw a smirk tilt Kamden's lips. "Kaiya is an expert on wounds."

Dr. Lowell directed her attention to me. "It's not just time that heals your wounds. It's a combination of various things. Support from your loved ones is a big part of it, too. You being here with Kamden is an example of that. Believe or not, you are helping so much with his healing process just by being here."

I didn't believe that, but then Kamden looked at me and gave me a small, but genuine smile. "She's right, *sorella*. You're the main reason that I'm doing this."

I stared into his eyes—those familiar, stormy eyes that had kept me from completely losing it when my demons tried to pull me under. Reaching out, I placed my hand on his thigh. "I'm going to be there for you, Kam, just like you were for me. No one else ever has been."

Silence settled over the room as Kam placed his hand over mine. After several seconds, Dr. Lowell broke it by saying, "The bond you two have is very strong. The love between you is apparent. I want to know more about how your relationship developed into what it is today. Tell me more about your family life when you were younger."

I stiffened apprehensively and tightened my grip on Kamden's leg. My eyes widened as they locked on his, and his jaw tensed as he swallowed deeply and rubbed my hand.

I darted my gaze to Dr. Lowell. "How is that relevant?"

She held my stare. "No matter how much you hate your past and family, they're still a part of what made you who you are today. The source of most issues stems back to a specific part of someone's past. You need to face them in order to move on."

When neither one of us said anything, she directed her attention to Kamden and continued, "We've discussed your mother and brother extensively. Tell me more about your father."

Kamden stilled his hand over mine. "Our dad left shortly after Kaleb was committed. I think that broke the last thread he was tied to us by."

Dr. Lowell wrote on her notepad. "Was your father involved in your lives before that?"

Kamden shook his head and tightened his grip on my hand. "He was there, but not really there, you know? My mom didn't make life easy, and I can't imagine what he had to deal with being married to her. I think it was too much for him."

Thinking about my father, or lack thereof, made me angry. I pulled my hand away from Kamden and crossed my arms over my chest again. I felt that my dad should've protected me from my mom and Kaleb, prevented any of what they'd done to me from ever happening. He was a complete failure as a father in my eyes.

"Kaiya, do you have anything that you would like to add?" Dr. Lowell inquired.

My eyes watered. I shifted uncomfortably in my seat and avoided her gaze. I didn't want to have another meltdown like when we talked about my mother, and typically anything involving my past triggered my outbursts. "I agree with what Kamden said—he described our father pretty accurately."

"How does that make you feel?"

Damn it. This woman does not know when to quit. Fucking therapists.

Giving in, I sighed. "Angry. I think so much could've been prevented had he been more involved."

"Do you think this had any effect on your relationship with Kamden?"

I glanced at Kamden before meeting Dr. Lowell's eyes. "No. I kept everything to myself before everything happened with Kaleb. Our relationship didn't develop until after that." Looking over at my brother, I smiled softly. "He's kept me from falling apart ever since."

Kamden grinned and put his arm around my shoulders before pulling me into him. He kissed the top of my head and squeezed me tightly. He whispered softly against my hair, "Thank you for not giving up on me, *sorella.*"

Winding my arms around him, I returned his embrace. "I could never give up on you, Kam. Ever."

Dr. Lowell spoke, "The support you give one another will be what pulls you through. I have no doubt in my mind that you will overcome this. Both of you."

I'd always thought that, but deep down, I was afraid that I wouldn't be enough to get Kamden through. I didn't consider myself to be the best person to lean on because of how unstable I was, so hearing Dr. Lowell say what she had just said was very reassuring.

I pulled away from Kamden and looked up at him.

We can do this. We will do this.

Ryker and I drove around one of the nicer, older neighborhoods in Cambridge, hoping to find a house to buy. We'd started looking the day after we found out about the baby, and a couple of weeks had passed without finding one that we really liked.

"Oh my God, Ryker. Look at that house!" I gasped in excitement as I pointed out my window.

Ryker slowed down and peered out toward where my finger was pointing. "Which one?"

"The white one with the big trees. It has a for sale sign out front."

Ryker pulled over and parked right in front of the beautiful home. A Victorian style house complete with a wraparound porch sat on a nicely manicured lawn with two huge magnolia trees in the front.

I stepped out of the car and stared in awe at the gorgeous home in front of me.

It's perfect.

Ryker came and draped his arm over my shoulder. "You like it, Warrior?"

I couldn't take my eyes off the house. "I love it."

He chuckled as he led me to the For Sale sign on the yard. Taking out my phone, I keyed in the number and called the realtor listed.

"Thank you for calling Cambridge Realty, this is Tanya, how may I help you?"

"Hi, I'm calling about one of your properties for sale. I'd like to set up an appointment to see it."

Her voice brightened. "Great! What's the address?"

I looked at the number on the house. "9603 Briarwood Lane."

"Oh, I love that property. It just went on the market last week." She paused for a few seconds. "I can show tomorrow at two. Will that work for you?"

"Hold on a second, please." I pulled the phone away from my ear and directed my attention to Ryker. "She can show us tomorrow at two."

He nodded. "Works for me."

I smiled and put the phone back to my ear. "We'll take it."

"Great! I have you down. Let me get some information from you before we hang up. I also want to get your email to send you the detailed listing for the house so you can look over everything before the showing."

I gave Tanya all of my contact information and thanked her before hanging up. I looked at Ryker. "She's going to send me the listing for the house tonight."

He reached out his hand toward me. "I bet it's expensive. It's a really nice place."

I took his outstretched hand, and he led me back to the car. "Yeah, I hope it's in our price range."

He opened the car for me. "Me too, Warrior."

After he shut the door, I stared out the window at what I hoped would be our new home. It reminded of the home I used to dream of having when I was little, a safe haven where I wouldn't have to deal with Kaleb or my mother.

Maybe my dreams are finally coming true.

A small smile formed over my lips as we drove away, and I couldn't wait for tomorrow to come.

Butterflies of excitement swarmed my stomach as we drove back to my dream house. I could barely contain my anticipation, fidgeting in my seat as I stared out the window.

"Excited?" Ryker chuckled, patting my thigh affectionately.

"You have no idea," I responded, still not taking my eyes off the passing scenery in the neighborhood. The landscaping of every house was like out of a movie scene, with beautiful trees, colorful gardens, and perfect grass.

I'd read over the listing several times last night before going to bed. The house was about fifteen thousand more than we had been pre-approved for through our lender, but we were hoping that the sellers would accept a counter offer.

I practically jumped out of the car when we pulled up. I felt like I was about to bust out of my skin because of the excitement coursing through me.

"Wait for me," Ryker laughed as he shut the door to car. He reached for my hand and led me up the walkway toward the house.

When we walked up the steps to the porch, I could see the front door open through the closed screen. A woman stood inside near the staircase to the second floor. She smiled broadly when she saw us. "Welcome!" She opened the screen door. "My name is Tanya. It's so great to meet you. Please, come on in."

I fell more in love with the house when we stepped inside. Hardwood floors spread beneath our feet. A fireplace crackled in the living room to our right, and the dining room sat to our left.

We introduced ourselves before Tanya started the tour. She gestured to the living room. "Let's start in here."

As Tanya led us through the house, she explained every intricate detail, from the crown molding to the vaulted ceilings. The home had been built in the late 1800s, but the interior had been completely remodeled within the last few years.

All of the bedrooms but the master were upstairs, along with a game room and two full bathrooms. In addition to the living room and dining room downstairs, there was also a half bathroom, a study, and the most amazing kitchen I'd ever seen. Perfect for us to build our life and start a family.

Tanya showed us the backyard last. Another magnolia tree sat in the back corner of the spacious lawn. A large deck led down to a stone-tiled patio and pool area. I pictured our children running around playing as Ryker and I chased them. I was completely in love.

Tanya turned toward us with a smile on her face. "So? What do you think?"

I looked up at Ryker hopefully. His eyes searched mine and he held my hands in his. "What's the verdict, Warrior?"

I squeezed his hands. "I love it. This is the one I want." I knew we should shop around and look at other houses, but my heart was set on this one. It was everything I'd ever dreamed of, and never thought I would have. This house was the setting of my happily ever after.

Ryker grinned before directing his attention to Tanya. "Where do we sign?

My joy faded when I remembered that we didn't have enough to cover the estimated costs. I directed my attention to Tanya. "We were only approved for fifteen thousand less than the list price."

"That's okay," she smiled. She took out her Blackberry and used a stylus to tap the screen several times. "I can give the owners your offer, then call you and let you know their answer."

My happiness started to return, but I didn't want to get my hopes up. "That would be great."

We went back inside the house and Tanya walked us to the front door. She shook Ryker's hand, then mine. "Thank you for coming. I'll call you as soon as I hear from the seller."

"I hope they accept the offer." I told Ryker as I fastened my seat belt when we got in the car.

"Me too, babe." He put the car in drive and made a U-turn. "We have to think positive."

My eyes ran over Ryker's face as he drove and my lips spread widely. I was still in slight disbelief over everything that had happened since Ryker and I met—he had definitely turned my life upside-down, but I'd never been happier.

The following Friday at work, I finally received a call from Tanya. I quickly swiped my phone off my desk and hurried to answer it. "Hello?"

"Kaiya? Hi, this is Tanya with Cambridge Realty."

"Hi, Tanya, how are you?"

"Good, thanks." She paused. "I heard back from the seller."

I felt like I had jumping beans in my stomach from the anticipation that had been building within me over the past week. "Good news, I hope."

"Well, I have good news and bad news. The seller rejected your offer, but did propose a counter offer. They're willing to drop the price five thousand, and cover the closing costs."

My heart sank into my stomach as I felt the sting of tears forming in my eyes. That was still ten thousand more than what we could afford.

"We can't afford that." My voice was meek, the sadness evident in every syllable.

"I'm sorry. Truly, I am. You and Ryker seem like great people." Her tone was genuine and sympathetic—she'd probably hug me if we were talking in person.

I took a deep breath to keep my tears at bay, not wanting to cry until I got off the phone. "Thank you. I really appreciate your time."

"No problem. Would you like me to look for other properties within your price range for you to consider?"

No, I want that house.

"Yes, please. That would be great." I sniffled.

"Great. I'll compile a list and email you next week."

"Thank you."

The tears started flowing as soon as I hung up.

I should have known things were too good to be true.

After several minutes of sobbing, I grabbed a few tissues from the box on my desk and wiped my wet cheeks and snotty nose. I needed to calm down so I didn't stress myself out more.

It's just a house. Your dream house, but still only a house. You'll find another one. Hopefully.

I was depressed for the remainder of the day, wearing a frown and slumping in my seat as a worked. I stayed in my office to eat my lunch, wanting to be alone. I'd done that a lot in the past before Ryker and I had met, but I'd been trying to be more social the past few months, so I ate in the break room.

A couple of my coworkers popped in from time to time to get documents signed or drop off reports, and I had to force a smile so they wouldn't pry. I couldn't wait to get off and go home, although I dreaded having to tell Ryker the news—I didn't want to relive the disappointment over again.

My stomach was jumbled with thick knots when I walked in the door to our apartment. Ryker was sitting on the couch on his laptop, but closed it when he saw me. "Hey, baby. How was your day?"

My voice trembled. "Not good."

Ryker set the laptop on the coffee table and stood up. "What's wrong? Did something happen at work?"

I shook my head as he approached, fighting tears. "No. Tanya called—the seller declined our offer."

Our eyes met. "I'm sorry, Warrior." Ryker's forehead creased, and his brows furrowed as he rubbed my arms.

I sadly smiled at him. "It's not your fault."

He wrapped me in his warm embrace. I buried my face in chest, unable to hold back the tears as I sobbed.

Damn pregnancy hormones.

After a few seconds, I pulled away and wiped my eyes. "I'm sorry. I think the baby is making me overemotional."

Ryker rubbed my back. "Don't be sorry. I know you loved that house."

"I did," I sniffled. "But there's no reason to be crying over it. There are other houses out there."

"That's true." His mouth curved up to one side. "We'll find one that's right for us."

My heart still weighed down my stomach.

But I want that one.

"Yeah, you're right." I forced a smile before laying my head against his chest and hugging him tightly. "We will."

Chapter Fourteen

Ryker

Ethan and I had been meeting weekly for lunch since the first time we'd met at the deli, and our relationship was slowly building back to how it used to be before our parents died—joking around, hanging out; normal shit brothers do.

After a month or so, I'd finally decided that it was time to take the next step and meet Tristan. I still wasn't comfortable seeing Molly, and I wasn't sure that I ever would be. She'd caused the rift between my brother and me, and we'd lost many years because of it. If I never saw her again it would be too soon.

We planned to catch a Red Sox game one Saturday. Ethan and I had never played baseball, but our dad had taken us to many games when we were kids, and Ethan wanted to continue the tradition with his own son.

They were already waiting at the gate when I walked up to the stadium entrance. As I approached them, Ethan waved me down. "I got the tickets already," he said when I reached him. He handed me one. "They're pretty good seats."

"Awesome." I looked at the ticket, then back up at Ethan. He picked up Tristan, who looked just like his dad when he was little.

Tristan looked me up and down. "My daddy told me you're his brother."

"Yep, that I am. Nice to meet you, little man."

"He says that you got mad at him, but now you're friends again."

I raised an eyebrow at Ethan, who looked away. "Yeah, I think we're friends again."

"Do you like hot dogs?" Tristan asked, changing the topic.

I laughed. "Yeah, with lots of ketchup."

"Good, then we can be friends, too." Tristan looked up at his dad. "Can we go inside now, Daddy?"

Thank God for a five-year-old's short attention span.

We definitely didn't need to be getting into the details of what had caused the problems between Ethan and me.

Ethan lightly chuckled. "Sure, buddy." He set Tristan down and grabbed his hand. "Let's go."

I followed behind them as we entered the stadium. Our seats were in the middle section, facing the stretch between third base and home plate. When we sat down, Tristan sat himself between his dad and me. Ethan smiled as his son looked up at me and said, "Did you know they call this place the Green Monster?"

A grin curved my lips. "Oh, yeah?"

He kicked his feet as he looked out at the field. "Yeah. But there's not really any monster. They just call it that because it's big and green."

My smile spread wider. "Good, because I'm afraid of monsters."

Tristan giggled. "Monsters aren't real, silly. Don't be scared."

I laughed and messed up his cap. Vendors were walking up and down the aisles as more people filled in the seats surrounding us. Ethan looked at me and asked, "Hey, you want a beer?"

"Yeah, thanks."

Ethan stood as he waved the vendor down and got two beers. He handed me one as he sat back down. I tipped the cup to him. "Thanks, bro."

Tristan tugged on Ethan's shirt sleeve. "Daddy, I want fries—the ones with all the stuff on them. And a hot dog, too."

"Don't forget the ketchup," I added.

Ethan took a drink and set it in the cup-holder. "Okay, buddy. Let's go." They both stood before Ethan looked at me. "You want anything?"

"Nah, I'm good, thanks." I took a sip from my beer.

Ethan picked up Tristan and nodded. "We'll be right back."

They pushed through the growing crowd of people toward the concession areas. I watched the players warm up on the field as I thought about how much my life had changed over the past couple of months. Six months ago, I never would've believed that I'd be at a Red Sox game with my brother and his kid, let alone be expecting one of my own.

If it's even mine.

Damn it, don't think like that.

I tried to push the thought away, but it always lingered in the back my mind. Every single time. There was no reason for me to question Kaiya, but I couldn't shake the doubt that hung over me. The scars from my past still affected me; I'd probably never forget the pain they resulted from.

When Ethan and Tristan came back and sat down with their huge order of chili cheese fries and a hot dog, Ethan gestured to the food. "Help yourself. We won't finish them all."

Tristan stabbed a clump of fries with his fork. "Yeah, Uncle Ryker, they're so good. Have some."

I laughed as he stuffed the food in his mouth, making his cheeks bulge out as he attempted to chew. Ethan's mouth twitched as he fought a smile while halfheartedly scolding, "Tristan, don't put so much food in your mouth. You could choke."

Tristan continued chewing his food before looking up at Ethan. "Sorry, Daddy." He rubbed his stomach in circles before patting it. "They're just so good."

A loving smile spread over Ethan's face. "I know. Just be careful, son."

Tristan continued eating as Ethan directed his attention to me.

"So, how's everything?"

"Pretty good—we've been looking for a house."

Ethan's eyebrows rose in interest. "Really? How's that going?"

"We found the perfect house, but we don't have enough—the seller denied our offer."

Ethan's face fell slightly. "I'm sorry, bro."

I shrugged. "It's okay—not your fault. They gave us a good counter, even offered to cover the closing costs, but it was still about ten thousand too much." I sighed, feeling defeated. "I just feel so bad that I can't give Kaiya the dream house that she deserves."

Ethan reached behind Tristan and patted me on the back. "You'll find something—don't worry about it."

I nodded. "Yeah." I took another drink from my beer before changing the subject. I hated thinking about the devastated look on Kaiya's face when we found out we couldn't afford the house. "How's everything with you?"

"Work has been great. I've been selling a ton of prime property above market value."

Ethan sold commercial real estate in and around Boston, which had proved to be a profitable career for him. He lived in a luxury condo in the Wellesley area of Boston and earned enough where Molly didn't have to work.

"And…" Ethan's eyes lit up as a wide grin spread over his lips. "Molly's pregnant."

"That's great, bro." I swallowed the lump that inexplicably formed in my throat. "Congratulations."

I didn't understand the uncomfortable twisting in my gut. I should've been happy for my brother, but I guess I wasn't completely over what had happened yet. Whenever Molly's name was mentioned, it caused anger to rush through my veins.

Ethan broke through my thoughts. "She's not as far along as Kaiya, though. Molly's only seven weeks. How many weeks is Kaiya now?"

I thought for a minute, trying to push aside the negative reaction I was having to Ethan's news. "She's about eighteen weeks. We find out the sex of the baby at her next appointment."

Ethan smiled knowingly. "You want a boy, right?"

I shrugged. "When we first found out, all I could think about was that I wanted it to be a boy." I chuckled and shook my head. "But lately, the thought of having a little Kaiya running around has been going through my mind a lot."

"That would probably be better than having another Ryker terrorizing everyone," he joked as he shoved my shoulder.

I bit my lip and clenched my eyes shut as a sharp pain shot up my neck and through my chest.

Ethan's humorous tone flipped to concern. "Hey, are you okay? I didn't think I hit you that hard."

I exhaled through my nose as I grit my teeth. "You didn't. I just have an injury that I haven't fully recovered from yet." I slowly rotated my shoulder and winced again. "You hit it in just the right spot."

"Injury? What injury?" Ethan asked in confusion.

I opened my eyes as the pain subsided. I could see Tristan out of the corner of my eye, oblivious to us as he munched on his hot dog. I sat up straight and moved my shoulder again to work out the remaining stiffness and lingering pain. I turned to meet my brother's perplexed eyes. "I was shot."

Ethan's eyebrows practically sprang up into his hairline. "What? When? And by who?" His voice rose angrily with each question.

"About six months ago. Kaiya had been shot at by her brother, and I blocked her and took most of the impact from the bullet." I rubbed my hands together anxiously as I remembered the shooting. The anguish of almost losing Kaiya felt fresh when I thought about that night. "But it still went through me and into her. I… I thought I'd lost her. The doctors said it was only inches from piercing her heart."

"Wow." Ethan's mouth hung open as he stared at me. "That's crazy," he said in disbelief.

I nodded and took a sip from my cup. "Yeah."

Our eyes locked. "Why didn't you call me?"

I held his gaze silently for several seconds before responding, "The only thing I was concerned about when I was in there was Kaiya. You didn't even cross my mind."

A flash of hurt crossed over Ethan's face before he forced half a smile and covered his heart. "Ouch, bro."

"Just being honest." I shrugged. "I learned to block out most of the pain and anger, but to do that I also had to block out the source."

He nodded in understanding before breaking eye contact. "How is it now?" He gestured to my shoulder with his head.

I followed his gaze. "Ripped some the muscles in my shoulder and chest and fucked up the nerves."

"It still hurts?"

"Always. The pain dulls, but never completely goes away."

His eyes came back to mine. "That sucks. I'm sorry."

I glanced away to look at Tristan, who was back to eating his fries. I quickly grabbed one and ate it before licking my thumb and index finger. I laughed as Tristan looked up at me and narrowed his eyes. "Hey!"

Darting my hand out, I snatched another fry from him and stuck it in my mouth. Tristan giggled as I looked up and away, pretending that I hadn't done anything.

"Daddy, Uncle Ryker keeps eating my fries," he tattled playfully.

My eyes widened in mock shock as I looked back at Tristan and tried to keep a straight face. "I didn't do anything."

"Tristan, you need to share," Ethan said in a parental tone.

"You sound just like Dad." I chuckled. I imitated my father. "Ryker, don't touch that. Get off your brother. Put that down. Go to time-out."

Ethan roared with laughter, and I did the same. Tristan stared at us like we were crazy as we continued laughing like hyenas.

"Daddy, are you okay?" Tristan asked in a confused voice.

Our laughter subsided. Ethan patted Tristan on the back. "Yeah, buddy, I'm fine."

More people began filling the seats around us. I took another drink of my beer and settled back into my chair. One of Boston's mascots started dancing around on the field, getting Tristan's attention. "Daddy, look!" He pointed enthusiastically in the direction of the oversized, cartoon red sock.

"I see it, buddy."

Tristan stood on his seat. "I can't see, Daddy. Lift me up."

Ethan picked up Tristan, then stood and set him on his shoulders. I smiled as I watched them laugh and talk about the performance on the field. My grin spread as I pictured myself one day doing the same with my own son.

Tristan crashed out about halfway through the sixth inning. How he was able to sleep through all the cheering and commotion was beyond me, but he stayed asleep until we left the stadium.

Once we got through the mob of fans celebrating the Red Sox victory, and made it to Ethan's SUV, I stopped and faced him. "This was great. We should do it again."

He disabled the car alarm and opened the door to the back seat. "Definitely." He carefully set Tristan in his car seat and strapped him in before quietly shutting the door. "Just let me know when."

We clasped hands and hugged. "Will do, brother. See ya later."

"Sure thing. Drive safe," Ethan called out as I walked away.

When I got home, Kaiya was sitting on the couch with her Kindle.

I tossed my keys on the table. "Hey, Warrior."

She closed her case and set the device on the end table next to the couch. "Hey. How was the game?"

I sat down next to her and pulled her legs into my lap. "It was good. Sox won nine to six."

"That's good. How was it meeting Tristan?"

I smiled. "He's a good kid. Looks just like Ethan."

She looked down and placed her hands on her stomach. Her belly was starting to look noticeable. "I hope our baby looks like you."

I followed her gaze and put my hands over hers. "I'd want our little girl to look just like her momma with gorgeous, blue eyes."

She scrunched her nose in displeasure. "I don't want them to look like me."

I didn't ask why because I already knew the answer. Kaiya had always battled with her appearance because of Kaleb. Having a kid that looked like her would remind her of him.

I tilted her chin up to look at me. "Our baby will be beautiful no matter who they look like."

She gave me a soft smile and nodded. After a few seconds of silence, she asked, "Speaking of babies, have you thought of any names you like?"

Honestly, I hadn't really thought about it. "No. Have you?"

"Of course. I've been thinking about names since we found out."

I chuckled. "Well, let me hear them."

Kaiya's smile spread over her face. "For a girl, I like the names Jocelyn, Harper, and Piper."

"And if we have a boy?"

"For a boy, I like the names Hayden, Asher, and Noah."

One name stuck out to me. "I like Hayden."

She brought her eyes to mine. "Yeah?"

I brushed my knuckles down her cheek. "Yeah, Warrior. I do."

"And if it's a girl?"

"Piper is cute. Harper is too. But we're having a boy so it doesn't matter," I joked.

Kaiya softly laughed. "Is that a fact?"

"Yep, boys run in my family."

Those full lips curved up at the corners. "A little Ryker wouldn't be so bad."

"Neither would a little Kaiya."

She shook her head. "You'd have your hands full with two of me. You wouldn't know what to do."

"Hey, I have a way with women. I'm sure I'd be fine." I smirked.

Kaiya rolled her eyes and changed the subject. "You hungry?"

"Yeah, baby. You want me to go grab something?" I asked as I rubbed her legs.

She bunched her lips together to one side. "Let's order in—take-out or pizza?"

I rubbed her stomach. "Whatever you and the baby want."

"I have a craving for Pad Thai. Extra spicy."

"Pad Thai it is." I pulled out my phone. "Which place?"

"Sugar and Spice. I like theirs the best."

I called the restaurant after Googling it. In the middle of placing our order, Kaiya tugged on my shirt sleeve and whispered. "Ooh, get some veggie dumplings, too."

I tickled her sides and she squirmed out of my grasp. "Can I also get an order of the veggie dumplings?" I paused as they confirmed my order. "That'll be it. Great, thanks."

I hung up the phone. "They said about thirty to forty-five minutes." I settled back onto the couch and started rubbing Kaiya's legs again. "How was your day, baby?"

She laid back on the couch. "Amazing. Nori and I went to this relaxing spa and got mani-pedis." She wiggled her toes and spread her fingers out in front of her. "You like the color?"

I looked down at her hot pink nails. "Yeah, babe." I could care less what color her nails were, but I complimented her choice anyway. "Looks great on you."

She gave me a shy smile as her cheeks turned a little red. "Thank you."

Kaiya's phone started ringing in front of me on the coffee table. She quickly swiped it and answered hesitantly after looking at the screen. "Hello?"

Her eyes darted to me, then quickly away as she repeated louder, "Hello?"

She tensed slightly before hanging up.

Strange. I wonder who that was.

I gave her a questioning look. "Who was that?"

She swallowed deeply and avoided my eyes. "Wrong number."

I couldn't stop the doubt that crept and settled in my stomach.

What if she's seeing someone else? This isn't the first time she's gotten a call from a "wrong number."

I shoved the thought away. "Everything okay?" I asked in concern.

"Yeah," she replied with a clipped nod. "Just tired."

Something seemed off to me, but I didn't want to prod her. Work and the pregnancy always wore her out. "Well, lay back and relax, baby."

Resting her hands on her little bulge, she laid back down and sighed. I couldn't help but repeatedly glance at her phone sitting right beside her, wondering who had just called her.

After a few seconds, the screen lit up. "You got a text," I said as I cocked my head toward it.

Her eyes went from me to her phone, then back again. "It's probably Nori. I'll check it later."

Something was definitely going on. My suspicions about her cheating seemed more valid with each passing second. So many calls from wrong numbers, her leaving the room or turning the phone away when she gets a text, not to mention that one time when I answered a call from an unknown number and they hung up.

Maybe she's still getting those texts from the unknown number. Would she really keep that from me?

"You're not still getting texts from the unknown number, are you? You'd tell me, right?"

She nodded stiffly. "Of course I would." She sounded unsure.

Well, then what is she hiding?

"You sure?"

Our eyes locked and she gave me that look that always knotted my stomach; the one that showed her love for me deep in those blue eyes. "Yeah, I'm sure." She grabbed my hand. "Can we drop this? You just got home. I haven't seen you all day, and I want to spend some time with you."

The distrust building within me started crumbling as Kaiya smiled her beautiful smile at me. She rubbed the back of my hand. "I missed you."

I looked at her for a second before turning my palm up and linking our fingers together. "Yeah, I missed you, too."

Kaiya pulled herself up and sat in my lap. She draped her free arm around my neck and placed our joined hands on her stomach.

Exhaling, she laid her head on my shoulder and snuggled into my neck. "I love you."

No, she doesn't. She's probably cheating just like Molly did.

Stop being paranoid.

I didn't have much proof to warrant my suspicions yet, and I hoped my past wasn't coming back to haunt me. I'd probably lose my shit completely if I was cheated on again.

Pushing the doubts from my mind, I leaned my head against hers and ignored the remaining knots in my gut. "I love you, too, Warrior."

Chapter Fifteen

Kaiya

Come on, fit!

I sucked in my stomach as I tried to button my jeans for the third time, and just like all my previous attempts, I had no such luck.

Letting go of the waist of my pants, I released a sigh.

No more skinny jeans for me.

I was almost twenty weeks, and had recently started showing. I hadn't gained much weight until a couple of weeks prior—the doctor said it was probably due to stress and all the morning sickness I'd had during my first trimester.

I'd been able to fit into all of my pants up until now. I frowned at my protruding belly.

I feel so fat.

I rubbed my baby bump. A smile replaced the frown as I thought about my son or daughter inside. The weight gain was more than worth it. Not to mention I had to get new clothes. Hello, shopping spree!

"Babe, have you seen my belt?" Ryker called from down the hall.

I could hear his footsteps approaching me as I answered, "I think it's in the closet."

His arms wrapped around my waist as he pressed against me from behind and placed his hands on my bare stomach. I was only wearing my bra and unbuttoned jeans. Leaning back into him, I tipped my head back on his chest. "My pants don't fit anymore." I pouted.

He chuckled before moving his hands down beneath the waist of my jeans. His fingers traced the delicate skin, slipping under my panties and sending a small shiver through me. "I guess you don't need them on anymore then," he whispered huskily in my ear.

My voice wavered slightly as desire began to wash over me. Ryker's touch always turned me into a sex-crazed fiend. "No, I guess I don't."

His fingers slipped into the loops of my jeans. Slowly, he shimmied them down my legs before his hands traveled back up and grasped my hips.

I pushed my ass back into him, wanting to feel his hardened erection against me. He gripped my hips tighter and growled as he pressed his cock into me.

I moaned as one of his hands slipped in the front of my panties and found my clit. He slowly rubbed his fingers against the sensitive bundle of nerves and nipped at my neck. "I love how wet I make you, baby."

Ryker moved us forward until my knees hit the edge of bed. He continued to expertly massage my clit as his other hand came up and gripped my ponytail.

He tugged my head back before his mouth claimed mine. His tongue parted my lips as his fingertips added fuel to the flames he was stoking inside my core. My body involuntarily quivered from his sinful touch, escalating closer to release with each stroke of his fingers.

Our lips broke apart as Ryker let go of my hair and bent me over the mattress. Climbing on, I knelt at the edge of the bed, eager for him to sink into me and ease the blissful ache he was building inside me.

I groaned in protest as his hand left my clit to pull off my panties. I heard him unzip his pants, then he grasped my hips and pressed his hard cock against my bare ass.

Oh, God, yes.

I felt the tip of his length nudge my opening, but he didn't enter me. Instead, he began to rub his thick shaft between my wet folds, continuing to blissfully torture me.

I shifted back against him, wanting, no, needing him to relieve the ache between my thighs. Gripping the sheets, my voice came out a strangled plea, "Ryker, please."

A shudder ran through me from the strokes of his cock against my sensitive flesh. "Please, what, baby? Fill your sweet pussy with my cock?"

I gasped as his length roughly pressed against my clit. I was too overwhelmed by the sensations taking hold of my body to respond intelligibly. A throaty moan escaped me, expressing my need loud and clear without words.

Ryker continued to torment me for what felt like an endless eternity before he slowly filled me. Pushing back, I sank myself on him, unable to wait any longer to feel him completely inside me.

He grasped my hips before pulling out and slamming back into me over and over again. I cried out in pleasure as Ryker grabbed my ponytail and tugged lightly, forcing my head to tip back. "I want you to come all over my cock, baby."

Fuck me.

That definitely wouldn't be a problem. I was already so close to coming, and Ryker knew exactly what to do to send me into that heavenly oblivion. Every. Single. Time.

He roughly thrust himself deep inside me before pumping his cock in and out of my pussy, stroking my walls and building up the orgasm that was on the cusp of overtaking me.

Ryker's hand trailed around my hip before I felt his fingers dancing along my clit again, causing me to cry out as my body trembled in anticipation of climax. I bit down on my lip as I fought against the sensations rushing through me, wanting to prolong the pleasure I was experiencing for as long as possible.

Ryker's ministrations intensified as he grunted huskily. "Come for me, baby. Come all over my cock."

I whimpered and slumped against the bed. My ass was up in the air as I buried my face in the mattress while Ryker relentlessly pounded into me. My whimpers morphed into moans as he hammered deeper into my sex and played with my clit. I writhed under him, struggling to maintain control over my body even though I knew I was fighting a losing battle—my body was Ryker's; always had been, always would be.

I cried out as my body shuddered and finally succumbed to the release I'd been resisting. I knotted my hands in the sheets as my orgasm ran through me while Ryker continued to thrust into my throbbing core. His grip tightened in my hair as he groaned and stilled behind me, coming inside my tight warmth.

He fell on the bed beside me a few seconds later. I relaxed against the mattress as Ryker draped his arm over me and pulled me closer to him. He kissed my sweaty forehead. "Better finish getting ready."

Smiling contently, I closed my eyes, still enjoying the waves of bliss streaming through me. I felt the mattress dip as Ryker got up, and then I heard the shower running a few seconds later.

I stretched lazily before getting out of bed and walking to the bathroom. I scrunched my face as I took in my disheveled appearance. Pulling out my ponytail holder, I ran my fingers through my hair to fix the flyaways and tangles from our tryst in the sheets.

"Wanna join me?" Ryker asked from behind me.

I met his eyes in the mirror as one side of his sexy mouth curved up in a lopsided grin.

"I think that would make us later than we already are." I smiled flirtatiously back at him. "Wouldn't want to keep your brother waiting."

Ryker chuckled. "He won't mind. Ethan is a very patient person."

Turning around, I leaned back against the counter as our gazes locked again. Steam from the hot water fogged up most of the shower, but I could still see those captivating eyes. Heat manifested between my thighs as Ryker's sinful stare penetrated me, rekindling my desire even though he had just sated it. "Get in here now, Warrior," he growled.

The dominating tone of his voice intensified my want. I quirked an eyebrow in challenge. "And if I don't?"

His eyes narrowed mischievously as his lips curved up in a sexy smirk. "I'll have to punish you."

Yes, please.

I couldn't fight the primal lust coursing through my body, drawing me to him as if he had some kind of gravitational pull. I stopped when I reached the glass door and looked up at him. "Now or later?"

I stepped back as he slowly pushed the shower open, revealing all of his naked perfection without the mask of fog clouding it. My eyes couldn't help but travel over every inch of his golden skin as he huskily replied, "Now."

Unable to resist his sexual magnetism, I entered the shower. Ryker closed the door and caged me between his muscular form and the glass. His mouth found my neck as he nipped the tender skin along the jawline.

Seconds later, his rough, inked hands were gripping my ass as he lifted me up and whirled me around. My back met the tile as he pressed me against the wall and roughly thrust into me. The water rained down on our entangled bodies until we both reached ecstasy again.

Needless to say, we were late because of our shower escapade. Ryker and I had planned to meet Ethan for brunch, but it was more like lunch by the time we got there.

I was already nervous about meeting Ryker's brother, and to top it off, I was now flustered about the reason we were so late. It was definitely not the first impression I wanted to make.

Hi, I'm Kaiya. Sorry we're late, but your brother and I got caught up having sex and lost track of time. Nice to meet you.

That would go over well.

I snorted at my inner ramblings, causing Ryker to glance over at me from the driver's seat of his truck. "Something funny?"

He turned his attention back to the road as I replied. "Just thinking about what reason we're going to give Ethan for being so late." I looked at my phone and shook my head. "We're almost thirty minutes late, Ryker."

He chuckled and turned right onto the street where the restaurant we were meeting Ethan at was located. "Don't worry, babe. I already texted him that we were running late when we left. He was fine with it."

"I'm so nervous," I said as I wiped my sweaty palms on my skirt. "And I'm making a terrible first impression by being so late."

Ryker placed his hand over mine on my lap. "No, you're not, Ky. Ethan's going to love you, just like I do." He rubbed his thumb over the back of my hand reassuringly and gave me a sweet smile.

Turning my hand over, I linked our fingers together and squeezed tightly. I darted my gaze out the window. "I hope so." Even though I had some animosity toward Ethan because of what he did to Ryker, he was the only family Ryker had left. I wanted to support Ryker's decision to make amends, and I didn't want to cause any more problems between them.

Once we parked and started walking to the restaurant, Ryker called Ethan. He talked to him on the phone as he navigated us to where Ethan was seated in a booth near the back.

Ethan stood once we reached him. "Finally. I'm starved," he greeted jokingly. Our eyes met and a huge smile curved over his lips. "You must be Kaiya."

Ethan looked a lot like Ryker, with a defined jaw, golden skin, and dark hair, but Ethan had green eyes instead of brown, and he wasn't built like Ryker was. Ryker was pure muscle, and while Ethan had a nice physique, he had nothing on his brother's immaculate body. Ethan also dressed totally different than Ryker and looked like he was ready to go to the country club with his pressed button-down, sweater vest, and khakis. Ryker was definitely more casual in his faded jeans and fitted Henley.

"I am." I nervously flung out my hand to shake his, but Ethan wrapped me in a hug instead, taking me by surprise. My widened eyes met Ryker's over Ethan's shoulders, and he grinned before patting his brother's back. "Don't scare her away now. You just met."

Ethan pulled back and turned his attention to Ryker. "If you haven't done that by now, I don't think there's anything I could do that would scare her off."

I smiled at their exchange. "Now, now, boys. It takes a lot more than that to scare me." I glanced down at my stomach before meeting Ryker's eyes. "I think you're stuck with me."

Ethan laughed, gesturing to the seat in the booth. "Please sit." He waited for me to scoot in before sitting on the opposite side and picking up a menu. "I think it's too late for brunch." His eyes darted back and forth between us knowingly, as if he knew the reason why we were late, before they settled on the menu in his hand. "But the lunch here is just as good, so no big deal."

My cheeks heated in embarrassment as I looked accusingly at Ryker, who shrugged his shoulders and picked up his own menu.

Ugh, men. Ryker probably text him all of the intimate details.

I rolled my eyes and picked up another menu, browsing over the lunch specials for that day for a few minutes. When I set my menu down, the brothers were already in a discussion about sports.

Kill me now.

Thankfully, the waitress saved me for a few seconds as she took our drink order, and I swiftly changed the topic of conversation once she left. "So, Ethan, Ryker told me that you're in commercial real estate."

Not exactly the most stimulating conversation topic, but it's better than sports.

"That I am. The market has been very good, but I don't want to bore you with the details. Tell me more about you—I want to learn more about the woman that changed my brother's life."

I stole a quick glance at Ryker, who smiled sheepishly and avoided my eyes. My mouth quirked up to one side as I thought about how rare it was to see Ryker embarrassed.

How sweet. I wonder what he told him about me.

Turning my attention back to Ethan, I stumbled for words as I tried to tell him more about me without divulging the crazy.

Yeah, good luck with that.

"Um, well, there's not that much to tell. I'm pretty boring. I'm a project coordinator for a marketing and public relations firm here in Boston. I live with my older brother Kamden in Cambridge, and I enjoy long walks on the beach."

Both Ryker and Ethan chuckled at my corniness as the waitress dropped off our drinks. I couldn't help but notice how she basically devoured Ryker with her eyes before walking away again.

You better think twice, bitch.

Ryker's eyes caught mine when I released my death stare from the waitress' back. His lips twitched as he stifled a laugh, but it broke through after a few seconds.

I smacked his arm. "It's not funny, Ryker."

"Am I missing something?" Ethan questioned as he cocked an eyebrow in confusion.

"It's nothing," I answered.

At the same time as Ryker said, "Kaiya's jealous that the waitress was checking me out,"

I narrowed my eyes and frowned. "I am not."

Ethan cleared his throat. "So, Kaiya, how did my brother manage to land someone as beautiful and sweet as you?"

My expression eased as I looked away from Ryker to Ethan. "Well, I started working out at his gym and ended up taking his self-defense class." Both corners of my mouth started to tip up as I remembered our first meeting. "He saved me from a painful treadmill death."

Ethan's eyebrows raised in intrigue. "Really? Oh, I've got to hear this."

I proceeded to tell the story of my graceful first encounter with Ryker, and Ethan was howling with laughter by the end of my mortifying tale.

"See, Ethan, I'm a regular knight in shining armor," Ryker joked.

Ethan was too busy laughing to respond to Ryker, and our whore of a waitress finally decided to come back and take our order. She continued to ogle Ryker, pissing me off more with every passing second.

Calm down, Kaiya, You don't want to make a scene.

Taking a deep breath, I stared her down, then placed my order as calmly as I could before placing my hand on Ryker's leg.

"And for you, handsome?" she flirtatiously asked Ryker as she batted her eyelashes.

The anger I was trying to temper threatened to boil over. Didn't she fucking see me sitting right next to him?

Ryker draped his arm over my shoulders and pulled me closer to him as he gave her his order. I watched her face fall in disappointment, causing a smug smile of satisfaction to replace my jealous scowl.

Yeah, that's right, he's mine.

I linked my fingers with Ryker's. "Thank you," I said dismissively after we'd all placed our orders. Her lip practically curled up in fury before she huffed under her breath and walked away.

"You know you have nothing to worry about, right, Warrior?" Ryker asked as he stroked the back of my hand with his thumb.

I felt a slight pang of embarrassment as I leaned my head against his shoulder. "I know." I squeezed his hand. "These pregnancy hormones are something else," I joked, even though I knew I would've felt the same way even if I wasn't pregnant. My insecurities and low self-esteem were hateful bitches that caused unwanted emotions and drama that I didn't need. I'd dealt with them my whole life, and I wished they'd just go away so I could live without the heavy weight of them bearing down on me constantly.

Yeah, wishful thinking.

Ryker pressed a kiss to my temple, then directed his attention back to his brother.

The remainder of our lunch was filled with conversations about Ethan and Ryker's childhood, my pregnancy, and sports. Thankfully, my past was never brought up. I discussed my demons enough in therapy with Kamden and I didn't want to think about Kaleb any more than necessary. Ethan knew about the shooting, so I assumed that Ryker had asked him not to bring up anything involving Kaleb, which I appreciated more than he would ever understand.

Once we finished our meals and paid the bill, Ethan gave me another tight hug and spoke low into my ear. "Thank you for whatever you did to bring my brother back."

My mouth slightly gaped open out of shock from his words. "I didn't do anything," I quietly replied back.

Ethan pulled away, keeping his hands on my shoulders as he smiled broadly at me. "Yes, you did." He rubbed my shoulders affectionately. "It was a pleasure meeting you, Kaiya."

I smiled back. "You, too."

He turned his attention to Ryker. "Sox game next Saturday, bro?"

They joined hands, then hugged. "For sure," Ryker answered as he threaded our fingers together. "Text me later."

I was exhausted by the time we got home, so I told Ryker that I was going to take a nap. He had some fitness plans to finish, so he headed to our home office to work on them.

I'd just laid down in Ryker's bed and turned on my side when I felt a jolt in my stomach.

Oh my God, is that?

Rolling onto my back, I placed my hand over the spot where I felt the movement. A few seconds later, I felt the twitching in my stomach again.

"Ryker!" I yelled out excitedly. "Come here! Hurry!"

I heard his footsteps pounding before he rushed into the room. "What is it? Is everything okay?"

I giggled. "Everything's fine. Come here." I patted the bed next to me.

He gave me a confused look as he sat down next me. I grabbed his hand and placed it on my belly where I'd felt the baby kick.

Ryker started to speak, "Wha—"

"Shh. Just wait," I whispered as I held his hand to my abdomen.

He looked down at my stomach. About a minute passed and I was about to give up and take his hand off when the baby finally moved again.

"Did you feel that?" I asked excitedly, unable to stop my lips from spreading into a huge grin.

Raising his eyes to mine, he gave me that beautiful smile of his and nodded.

I placed my hands outside his so that I could feel the baby kick again. "Isn't it amazing?"

We both stared down at my stomach in wonder for several seconds before Ryker answered, "You're amazing."

I looked up to see Ryker gazing at me. He kept his hand on my stomach and cupped my cheek with his other as he leaned in and kissed me.

He continued pressing kisses down my chest to my stomach. Lifting my shirt, he placed one last kiss in the center of my pregnant belly.

The baby kicked again. "I think he or she likes that," I said.

"Oh, yeah?" He raised an eyebrow as the side of his mouth lifted in a lopsided grin.

I smiled down at him and ran my fingers through his hair. "Yeah."

Keeping his eyes fixated on mine, Ryker kissed the middle of my stomach again, then all around my abdomen. The baby kicked a couple of times throughout, and each time made the smile on my face spread wider. "I was wondering when the baby would start moving. I was going to ask Dr. Wallace about it at my appointment next week."

Ryker sat up next to me. "It's next week already? We find out the sex of the baby at this one, right?"

I nodded. "I can't wait. I'm dying to know what we're having."

"Me neither." He placed a hand on my stomach. "I think it's a boy."

I looked down at his hand. "I don't care either way. I just want to start buying cute baby outfits already."

Ryker chuckled. "We can go right after the appointment. Start looking at cribs, get some clothes and other baby shit."

"Baby shit, huh?" I laughed.

"I don't know what things babies need, okay? Give me a break here."

"I have a general idea, but maybe you should ask Ethan," I suggested. "I'm sure he remembers what they had to buy for Tristan. Plus, Molly is pregnant again so it's probably on his mind anyway."

His brows furrowed. He didn't seem to like that idea. "Maybe." He took his hand from my stomach and rose off the bed. "Get some rest, Warrior."

Being reminded about my nap made my eyelids feel heavy. "Okay," I yawned.

Ryker gave me a loving smile before walking out and shutting the door behind him. I placed both hands on my stomach as I closed my eyes and smiled contently. It didn't take long for me to drift off to sleep.

Chapter Sixteen

Ryker

Time seemed to be moving backward as we sat waiting in the doctors' office. I had been dying for this appointment because we were going to find out whether we were having a boy or a girl. Since finding out about the pregnancy, I'd wanted a son, but now I didn't care either way as long as they were healthy.

Kaiya was flipping through a baby magazine as my leg bounced anxiously. She glanced at me out of the corner of her eye and suppressed a smile. "Nervous?"

I drummed my hands on my knees. "Nah, just excited. I wanna find out already."

Kaiya laughed softly. "Me too. The doctor shouldn't be too much longer."

About fifteen agonizing minutes later, the receptionist called us back. Then, we had to wait another twenty until the doctor and ultrasound tech finally came in.

Dr. Wallace gave us a warm smile. "How are you feeling, Kaiya?"

"Excited. I can't wait to find out what we're having," Kaiya replied enthusiastically.

The doctor's smile spread. "Any stomach pain? Nausea? Cramping?"

"No, everything's been good," Kaiya smiled as she rubbed the small bump of her belly.

"Great. Now, let's get to what you've been waiting for."

The ultrasound tech wheeled the cart next to Kaiya and got her prepped. The computer lit up with the image of our baby as soon as the sensor pressed against Kaiya's belly.

"There's the head. Let's move down a little to see if we can get a glimpse between the legs." The tech said as she moved the wand down. "There."

We stared at the screen where the mouse cursor was pointing at something. "Is that?" I started to ask.

The tech grinned. "Yep. Congratulations, you're having a boy!"

A boy… I'm going to have a son.

My chest swelled with pride and a huge smile spread across my mouth. I leaned down and kissed Kaiya's forehead. Her face beamed with joy as she gazed up at me when I pulled away. "I wanted a little Ryker."

The doctor handed Kaiya the sonogram picture after it printed out. Her smile was from ear to ear as she looked at the image. "Hayden."

"Hayden?" I repeated.

"That's the name that comes to mind when I look at him." She brought her eyes to mine. "What do you think?"

I rubbed the stubble on my chin. "I like it. Sounds strong."

"And it's not that common. I don't want him having a name that everyone else has, like John or Mike."

I smiled. "Hayden it is then."

We thanked Kaiya's doctor and the ultrasound tech before leaving. Kaiya linked our hands together and squealed excitedly. "I can't wait to go shopping!"

At class the next day, I planned to demonstrate another small circle hapkido technique. I'd been researching various maneuvers over the past couple of weeks, but had only been teaching the basics and integrating them into defenses that we'd already learned since many of the moves were very intricate. They weren't necessarily hard. They just required that everyone pay attention to detail.

After working on the bags, I gathered the class on the mats. "As you know, we've been going over the basics of small circle hapkido—all of the various locks and grabs. The reason for this is that I wanted to have a solid foundation to build on for the more intricate defenses. The first one I taught was a simple, introductory move to get your feet wet."

I motioned Mark to come to me. "Today, we're going to work on small circle defense against a lapel grab. This would even work against a frontal choke."

I walked the class through the steps of the maneuver before instructing them to get with their partners. Kaiya smiled as I approached her. "This one looks like it's going to hurt."

"All of them hurt, babe. That's why they're so effective."

She playfully rolled her eyes. "Okay, sensei, let's get started."

I patted the left side of my chest, over my heart. "Grab my shirt here." I waited for her to grip my tee before continuing. "Since you're holding me with your right hand, I'm going to bring up my left hand and grab your wrist with it. I can use my right hand to block if my attacker tries to punch me, or even to get some hits in to slow them down before I continue the technique."

I wrapped my hand around her wrist and brought my right arm up in blocking position. "I can do some jabs to the face, maybe even some sudos to the throat from this angle if I want. Then, I'm going to bring my hand over to the one you're holding me with, and grab your thumb." I gripped her thumb, using my fingers to push into the pad of her palm at the base of her thumb. "Now I slide my thumb onto the web between your index finger and thumb. Then, I secure it there before pressing down and away, prying your hand off of me while making a circular motion and bending the wrist at a forty-five degree angle."

Kaiya's face contorted and she hissed in pain as I executed the maneuver, but she didn't tap out; she rarely did. I still let go, not wanting to hurt her because of her stubbornness. "Once you get them to release you and into that position, you can throw in whatever you like since they will basically be at your mercy. A roundhouse to the ribs, maybe a side kick to the knee. You could even let go and finish with a back fist, followed by a ridge hand right to the face."

Kaiya rotated her wrist and rubbed it. "That hurt—even for me." That pretty mouth of hers curved up in a smirk. She tried to fight a laugh, but she couldn't hold it back. "You're going to tap out so fast."

I cocked an eyebrow and crossed my arms over my chest. "You think so, huh?"

She continued to giggle as she nodded. "Oh, yeah."

I narrowed my eyes in challenge. "We'll see about that."

She was probably right, but since she was talking shit, I had to prove her wrong. I grabbed the strap of her tank top with my left hand, knowing full well that I would definitely tap out if I used my right due to my injury from the shooting.

Kaiya initiated the move without my guidance. She had some trouble slipping her hand in the right place and securing mine, but with practice, I had no doubt she would be able to execute it efficiently.

"Need some help?" I teased as she continued to try and get her hand placed correctly.

She frowned and glared up at me, giving me her answer without words. I knew I was going to pay for that comment in a minute or so.

Kaiya's narrowed eyes spread wide in excitement when she finally gripped my hand right. She twisted it away from her in a circular motion, and I immediately wanted to tap out from the pain. I didn't understand how women were so damn flexible. I ground my teeth together to keep from tapping, my stubborn pride outweighing the worry of injury.

Our eyes met and the corner of Kaiya's mouth lifted before she let go. "I don't want to hurt you because of your stubborn pride."

I shook my wrist out and smirked. "It's called determination. You know I never back down from a challenge."

Her lips spread wider into a full, seductive grin. "I know."

We practiced a few more times before I ended class. Some students complained about the difficulty of the maneuver, but most enjoyed the technique and its simple effectiveness. Others preferred the larger body attacks and felt like they had more control and power with punches and kicks. I had to agree, but I still wanted Kaiya to participate in class, so compromises needed to be made.

After closing up the gym, I mentioned some thoughts I'd been having to Kaiya as we walked out. "So I'm thinking about doing small circle hapkido for one class per week, and then normal self-defense for the other two."

She nodded. "That sounds good. From what I've heard, most of the girls like the small circle hapkido, but prefer the regular self-defense techniques better."

"Yeah," I agreed, grabbing her hand as I led her to her car. "Some of the hapkido techniques can be very intricate and some people don't have the patience for that."

"I'm surprised you do," she joked as we reached her car. Turning around, she leaned back against the driver's side door and smiled knowingly. "You're one of the most impatient people that I know."

I placed my hands on the outside of her shoulders against the window, caging her in between my arms. "Depends on the situation." I leaned forward and barely grazed my lips over hers. "With you, I was definitely impatient. When I want something, I have to have it. But with self-defense," I said as I pulled back, putting some space between our faces, "you have to be calculated and precise. Any wrong move could mean injury or death during an attack, so patience is a must."

"Wise words, Master Campbell," she replied with a playful grin. Her stomach growled loudly, causing us both to look down at her baby bump and laugh. "I think Hayden is hungry," Kaiya giggled.

I took one of my hands off the car and placed it on her belly. "Well, he's a growing boy. Let's go get him something to eat."

Kaiya stood up on her tiptoes to kiss me. "I think we have some leftover Italian chicken and risotto from earlier this week." She looked down again at her stomach and smiled. "We both really liked that."

I gave her a kiss before grabbing the door handle and opening the door for her. "I'll meet you at home."

"Okay. Be careful," she replied as she got in.

"You, too, baby," I said, shutting the door.

Kaiya smiled at me through her window and started her car. She waved as I backed away toward my truck.

I followed Kaiya back to her apartment. We parked next to each other in front of her building before heading up the stairs to her place.

"Kam, we're home," Kaiya announced as we walked inside. All the lights were off, leaving the room completely dark.

Kaiya flipped on the light to living room and called out to her brother again. "Kamden?"

Still no answer. A month or two ago, this would have been typical, but since Kamden stopped drinking, he was usually home, either watching TV or working on his computer.

Kaiya dropped her purse and gym bag on the coffee table, then went into the dining room and kitchen, turning the lights on in each room. When she came back into the living room, there was no denying the look of worry on her face.

"What's wrong, baby?" I questioned as I scanned over her wide eyes and the tight line that had replaced her normal smile.

"There's an empty bottle of Jack on the counter, plus a bunch of empty beer cans."

Shit.

Kaiya whipped around and sped to Kamden's room. Seconds later, her shriek pierced my ears. "Oh my God, Kamden!"

Chapter Seventeen

Kaiya

Rushing to Kamden's side, I knelt beside his limp body on the floor. An almost empty bottle of Jack was next to him, along with a folded letter, envelope, and a handful of pictures scattered around the hardwood.

One photo caught my eye—Kamden and Kaleb back in high school with their arms draped over each other's shoulders and wide smiles on their faces.

"What is it, Ky?" Ryker asked from behind me.

I jerked slightly, startled by his voice, but I didn't respond. My fingers hovered over the letter and my eyes scanned the pictures. All of them were of Kaleb and Kamden, ranging from when they were toddlers to teenagers.

Where did he get these?

Snatching the letter off the ground, I unfolded it and started reading:

> **"Let these pictures be reminders of the horrible sin you committed. You're a murderer and deserve to suffer for what you did."**

I stared at the paper in shock for several seconds before crumbling it into a ball with my fist. I threw it angrily across the room as tears streamed down my cheeks.

I grabbed the envelope and looked at the return address, even though I knew who the letter was from. My fucking mother.

There was no name, just a P.O. Box, but I knew it was her. No one else would be so heartless and have those pictures. Only her.

I dropped the envelope and focused back on my brother. A choked sob shuddered through my chest as I looked down at his face. "Please, God, no," I whispered as I reached out my hand toward him. Shaking his shoulder, I pleaded, "Kam, wake up." After several seconds, I shook more forcefully. "Wake up, Kamden!" I cried out desperately.

He was on his stomach, face down, and I couldn't tell whether he was breathing or not. I tried to turn him over, but he was almost as big and bulky as Ryker, so it was like a chihuahua trying to flip over a pitbull.

Ryker was next to me in an instant, helping me turn Kamden over onto his back. His skin was pale and cold, and I feared for the worst.

Please be alive, please be alive, please be alive.

As I pressed my ear against his chest, a chill ran up my spine. An overwhelming case of déjà vu came over me—I was doing the same thing less than a year ago when Kaleb had come for me.

Tears blurred my vision as I waited to hear my brother's heartbeat. I could vaguely hear Ryker talking on the phone, giving my address and describing the situation to whoever was on the line. "An ambulance is on its way."

I didn't reply, too focused on listening for Kam's heart to say anything. It felt like hours had passed when I finally heard the weak thump. I closed my eyes and sighed in relief. "He's alive."

I stayed by Kamden's side, holding his hand until the paramedics came. Ryker followed me in the ambulance to the hospital, and I had to be pried off of Kam when they took him back to work on him.

My eyes burned from the non-stop flow of tears as I sat in the emergency room waiting room. Ryker sat next to me and draped his arm around my shoulders, hugging me tightly to him and giving me the comfort I needed.

About an hour passed when a doctor walked into the waiting area. "Kaiya Marlow?"

I popped out of my seat. "That's me. Is my brother okay?" I urgently asked.

The doctor scanned my face. "We had to pump his stomach because of the amount of alcohol he consumed. We're replenishing his fluids, and he's in recovery now. We want to keep him for observation for twenty-four hours, but you can see him now for a few minutes if you'd like."

Some of the heavy weight bearing down on me receded. "Please," I croaked, my voice tangled up with emotion.

The doctor led us to Kamden's room, where he had a tube in his nose and an IV stuck in the top of his hand. He slowly turned his head to look at me through half-lidded eyes. "Hey," he rasped.

My bottom lip trembled, and my eyes become watery again. "Hey." I sobbed, making my way to his bedside.

I grabbed his hand in a death grip, fearing he would slip away if I let go. "You scared the shit out of me."

His face fell in shame as he looked away. "I'm sorry."

My fear and worry transformed into outrage as I raised my voice in anger. "How could you do that, Kam? You almost killed yourself!"

Fuck, I shouldn't have said that. He's vulnerable and needs my support, not my reprimanding.

He met my gaze with narrowed, bloodshot eyes, but didn't reply. The hurt in his clouded stare was apparent, and I wanted to do whatever I could to take his pain away.

"I'm sorry." I sighed, stroking the back of his hand with my thumb. "I'm just upset. I thought I lost you."

He squeezed my hand, and his face softened as he looked at me apologetically. "I know. I'm sorry. The letter hurt so much, and the pictures were the icing on the cake."

Thinking about what my mother had sent him made rage burn through my veins. "Fuck her," I gritted out angrily.

Tears welled in his eyes. "She's right."

I clenched his hand tighter. "Don't start this again, Kam. She's bat-shit crazy and has no fucking idea what she's talking about."

He glared at me stubbornly. "Facts are facts. I killed my brother, my own flesh and blood. That's a fucking fact."

I scoffed in exasperation before arguing back. "Protecting me! You did what you had to do to defend yourself. If you hadn't, Kaleb would've killed you, Ryker, and me. If anything, this is all my fault."

Some tears trailed down his cheeks. "I just want the pain to go away."

The anguish and sorrow present in his voice washed away my anger and replaced it with sadness. I didn't think I could loathe my mother more than I already did, but my hate for that bitch increased tenfold for the pain she was causing my brother.

I released his hand and leaned over, wrapping my arms around his neck and hugging him. He copied my actions, holding me tightly to him as he buried his face in my chest and sobbed.

My own tears poured from my eyes as everything overwhelmed me. Helplessness for not being strong enough for my brother, fury at my mother for her actions, guilt for causing this whole fucked-up mess, all combined with my hormones to create an avalanche of emotion.

Kamden was still crying after I finally stopped. I continued to hold him, hoping to guide him back from the limb of hopelessness he was balancing on. He needed me now more than ever, and I was going to be there for him.

"Tell me about your week," Dr. Lowell prompted at our next session following Kamden's incident. It had been almost a week since that night, and I'd made sure that he hadn't had anything else to drink. I felt like an overprotective mother. I knew I was annoying the hell out of him, but it had to be done.

Kamden let out a deep breath. "I relapsed. Ended up in the hospital with alcohol poisoning."

Dr. Lowell adjusted her glasses and sat up straighter, the concern obvious in her voice as she spoke. "What brought this on? You were doing so well."

Kamden ran his hands over his face, then his buzzed head. "I got a letter. Pretty sure it was from my mom, even though it didn't say it was."

Dr. Lowell wrote on her notepad. "Tell me more about this letter. What did it say? How do you know it was from your mother?"

"Are you sure that he should be talking about this so soon after? It was a traumatic experience for both of us. I thought... I thought he was dead when I found him. I was terrified."

Kamden placed a hand on my knee. "Ky, it's okay. We need to talk about it if we're going to move past it."

I searched his eyes. He still looked wounded, but strong at the same time, like he was ready to move on, but needed support to do so. And I would be that support.

I smiled proudly at him. "Okay."

Kamden gave me a soft smile back, then directed his attention to Dr. Lowell. "Along with the letter, the envelope contained pictures— pictures of me and Kaleb when we were younger. No one would have those except her."

The psychiatrist nodded. "And what did the letter say?"

Hearing Kamden repeat the words from the letter caused my anger to resurface.

How dare she? She just wants everyone to be miserable like her. Stupid bitch. Kamden was doing so well.

"What made you turn to the alcohol after so long?" Dr. Lowell asked.

The answer was obvious, and even though I hated the stupid questions that Kamden's therapist asked, I knew they were necessary to get him to open up and address his issues.

"I couldn't take it. The guilt was so overwhelming, and those pictures." He paused and exhaled a shaky breath. "Those pictures were branded into my mind. I couldn't stop seeing them even when I wasn't looking. I just wanted the pain to go away."

Tears rolled down his flushed cheeks, and I rubbed his back in an attempt to soothe him. "It was a stupid moment of weakness." He looked over at me and apologized. "I'm sorry, Ky."

His voice was meek and sorrow-filled. I gave him a comforting smile. "Don't apologize—it's not your fault. It's our bitch of a mom's fault."

His face hardened as his lips formed into a tight-lipped frown. "I should be stronger by now. I need to be stronger."

"It takes time to heal. There will be bumps along your road to recovery, but you will get there," Dr. Lowell said with an assuring smile.

Kamden nodded. "I hope so."

"You will. I have total faith in you," I interjected. "You've helped me through so many hard times, and I know you're gonna pull through this one."

My brother gave me a weak, but genuine smile. "Thank you, *sorella*. You don't know how much that means coming from you."

Giving him a perplexed look, I scrunched my eyebrows together and slightly pursed my mouth. I didn't understand why my statement was more meaningful than anything Dr. Lowell had said; she was the expert. "Why?"

Kamden's shoulders bobbed as he chuckled softly. "Ky, you've been through so much—things that would make some people go insane." He softly took my hand in his and looked into my eyes. "Hearing that you believe in me after what you've endured in your life is empowering. If you can overcome your demons and live with their scars, then I can do the same with mine."

I was so wrapped up in his words that I didn't notice I was crying until a tear rolled down each cheek. My throat was clogged with my emotion, preventing me from speaking, so I just threw my arms around my brother and hugged him tightly. Neither of us needed to say anything as an unspoken understanding passed between us. We were each other's support, beacons that guided each other through the dark, stormy times. Kamden had been mine for so long, and now it was my turn to be his.

It was Saturday, and I was absolutely ecstatic to finally go shopping for some stuff for Hayden. We hadn't been able to go the last weekend because of what had happened with Kamden. I'd been too scared to let him out of my sight once we had brought him home from the hospital, so I stayed in the apartment the whole time.

Ryker and I walked into the baby store, which heightened my excitement. I'd been a couple of times before to buy gifts for coworkers' baby showers, but this time was completely different, a whole new experience now that I was a first-time mom-to-be.

Many of the mothers at my work had told me not to buy things like bottles, diapers, bathing items, or baby toys yet because I would be getting a lot of that at my baby shower. I just had to pick the ones that I wanted and scan them onto my baby registry.

My heart warmed as I took in the rows and rows of baby clothes, strollers, car seats, and nursery furniture. Ryker looked overwhelmed, his eyes wide as he gazed around the huge store. "Wow." He whistled.

I laughed. "Lots of baby shit, huh?"

"No kidding. This is nuts." He chuckled.

I stopped near the baby registry kiosk and looked at Ryker. "We should probably do our baby registry while we're here. Nori told me she wanted to include it in our shower invitation, and she's going to be sending them out in the next few weeks."

"All right. You do the honors, Momma." He gestured to the kiosk area.

A smile crept over my lips, and my heart fluttered. He just called me Momma.

Oh my God, that's the sweetest thing ever.

I walked to the kiosk and started pressing buttons on the screen. After completing the registration and getting the price scanner, Ryker and I headed to the first section of the store and began scanning items.

Once we had made our way to the clothes section, we'd already picked out a bottle set, a baby bath tub and towel set, a mobile to hang above the crib, packs of diapers and wipes, and nursery items to match the adorable crib set we picked out.

I wanted to find the perfect outfit for Hayden to wear home from the hospital since it was going to be the very first outfit he ever wore, and I was definitely planning on keeping it.

We found some cute outfits that we put in our cart, but none that stood out to me as "the one." I was about to give up and leave when I caught sight of the perfect outfit.

"Oh, Ryker, look!" I cooed. Tugging his arm, I walked in the direction of the adorable clothes set.

The outfit consisted of a dark brown onesie with turquoise trim. A puppy playing with a red ball was centered in the middle and teal and brown plaid shorts with the same puppy on them complimented the shirt.

"It's so cute." I ran my fingers over the shorts. "Oh, look at the shoes!"

A matching pair of slip-on shoes, socks, and a beanie that looked like the top of a puppy head accompanied the set of clothes.

"This is it." I grabbed the hanger. "Can you get the shoes and socks?"

We headed back to the customer service desk to turn in our registry before purchasing the items we had chosen. Ryker carried our bags to the truck before helping me in—it was beginning to get awkward to step up into his lifted Chevy due to my size.

"Happy, Warrior?" Ryker asked as he started the truck.

The smile that had been on my face since we entered the store curved higher. "I've never been happier."

Chapter Eighteen

Ryker

Kaiya's birthday was in a few days, and I had finally decided what I was going to get her. Now I was standing in a pet store full of yapping puppies, meowing kittens, and screeching birds. Great fucking idea.

"Is there something I can help you with today, sir?" A blonde, teenage girl with braces asked. She smiled politely as she waited for me to answer.

I looked around the store before meeting her eyes. "Um, yeah, I'm trying to find my girlfriend a pet for her birthday."

The girl's smile shifted from professional to genuine. "Aw, that's so sweet. My name is Becca, and I can help you find the perfect pet for your girlfriend," she said before pursing her lips to the side in thought. "I, for one, love kittens. Most girls do."

I thought about having to deal with cat litter and claws scratching me, then furrowed my brows. I didn't think Kaiya would like that shit either. "I was thinking a puppy. My girlfriend is pregnant, and I think a litter box would be too much maintenance."

"Well, cats are very independent, but pregnant women aren't supposed to be around cat urine, so I think a puppy is a great idea." She walked and talked over her shoulder. "Let me show you the puppies we have available."

I followed her to the center of the huge store, which had a big sign in the shape of a dog over it. The barking got louder the further we walked into that section. Dog food, leashes, collars, chew toys, and every other kind of dog essential lined the shelves in that, and a glass wall with puppies was in the very back.

"Are you looking for a small or large dog?" Becca asked as I scanned over my options. I loved big dogs, but I knew Kaiya would think a little dog was cute and would probably dress them up and all that prissy shit. "Small," I answered.

The girl nodded with a smile. "Our smaller dogs are on this side." She guided me to the far left side of the transparent wall of puppies. Some were sleeping, others were playing around, and a few wagged their tails and barked at us.

"Ryker?"

I froze in my tracks. That voice was like nails on a chalkboard for me.

"Ryker, is that you?"

Fuck me sideways.

I turned to face someone I hadn't seen in years; someone I could have gone the rest of my life without seeing.

Molly.

"It is you! Fancy meeting you here," she commented as she approached me. "How have you been?"

Great until now.

I forced myself to respond. "Fine. How about you?"

"Good, thanks." She placed a hand on her small baby bump as her eyes ran up and down my body. "You look amazing."

Pushing the thought of her being pregnant and all the bad memories it caused to resurface, I crossed my arms over my chest. "What do you want, Molly?"

She shifted uncomfortably and a look of hurt flashed across her face. "I can't ask an old friend about how they've been?"

I scoffed. "Old friend? If you treat your friends like you treated

164

me, I'd hate to be your enemy."

She stretched out a hand out to touch my shoulder. "Ryker, don't be that way."

Stepping back, I moved out of her reach. "What way, Molly? You want me to be happy to see you after what you did?"

She narrowed her eyes at me. "That was over five years ago, Ryker! Are you ever going to let it go? Ethan said you had, but that doesn't seem to be the case."

Let it go? Is she serious?

I turned and walked away. "Nice seeing you, Molly."

"Ryker, wait," she called after me. I could hear her heels clacking on the floor behind me. "Please. For Ethan."

Damn it.

I stopped as I thought about my brother and our mending relationship. I wanted to get back to how we used to be, and unfortunately, Molly was a part of that.

Fuck, fuck, fuck.

"Fine." Clenching my fists, I turned back around. "What do you want?" I ground out, pissed off about the situation.

She paused, giving me a hesitant look before finally speaking. "Well, I, uh, want us to be friends."

I cocked my eyebrow at her in disbelief. "Friends?" I repeated sarcastically.

Molly rolled her eyes. "Okay, maybe not friends, but I want us to be civil. Ethan is so happy that you're talking again and fixing your relationship, and I don't want your grudge against me to hinder that."

Damn it, she's right.

No matter how much I hated Molly, I loved my brother more, and I didn't want my stubbornness to fuck up the progress we'd made.

I dropped my arms by my sides and sighed, feeling somewhat defeated for having to give in to what Molly wanted. "You're right." I forced myself to say. The words left a bad taste in my mouth. "I'll try. For Ethan."

Molly's eyebrows rose. She must have been surprised that I agreed with her. "Great," she stammered, then smiled. "I'm glad you're going to at least try."

"I'm not making any promises."

She nodded. "I know, but I have faith in you." Turning around, she called over her shoulder. "I'll see you around."

I stood there, dumbfounded by what had just happened.

Did I just agree to be civil with Molly? Damn, I'm going soft.

"Sir? Are you ready to see the puppies?"

I'd forgotten all about Becca and where I was. Molly had a way of flipping shit upside down like that, and not in a good way. I turned to face the employee helping me. "Yes, sorry."

"No problem." Becca pointed at one of the sleeping pups. "This little guy here is a Maltese. Like all of our puppies, he has all of his shots and is free of any parasites and diseases."

The dog she showed me was completely white with long hair. I thought about the white strands being all over the place and the maintenance he would need to stay that clean and white. "Maybe something not so white and fluffy," I chuckled.

The teen smiled in understanding. "How about this one? She's such a sweetheart—very playful and loving."

Becca pointed out a tiny Chihuahua. Normally, I didn't think that the mascot of Taco Bell was cute, especially considering most Chihuahuas had bug eyes and yapped all the time, but this one was different. She didn't look like most Chihuahuas—she had chocolate brown fur and green eyes.

I moved closer to the wall of dogs and the small puppy started wagging its tail and scratching at the glass barrier between us. "She's cute." I grinned.

"Would you like to hold her?" Becca asked.

I hated handling small things—I always felt like I was going to break them somehow with my bulky, clumsy hands. But I definitely needed practice for when Hayden was born, and the little ball of fur in front of me might be perfect for the job.

"Sure," I replied, then hesitated. "Wait, she's not going to piss on me or anything, right?"

The young worker giggled as she took out a set of keys. "She shouldn't. We take the puppies out to relieve themselves every hour since they are still potty-training, and I took them out right before you got here."

I nodded. "All right, but if she pees on me, I'm sending you the dry cleaning bill," I joked.

Becca stuck one of the keys in a lock on the right side of the glass box that held the Chihuahua. "Come here, cutie." She baby-talked as the puppy bounded to her excitedly.

She turned around, puppy in hand, and extended her arms out toward me. "Here you go."

I awkwardly grabbed the pup and held her in my hands. She was wagging her tail so hard that her whole body shook with her excitement. She wiggled and stretched in my grasp, trying to get closer to me, so I pulled her against my chest so I wouldn't drop her.

"She likes you," Becca cooed as the tiny dog licked my chin and whined in excitement.

"Okay, okay, stop." I laughed, pulling my face out of reach of the pup's searching tongue.

"So, what do you think?" Becca inquired expectantly.

I looked at the squirming animal in my hands, whose tongue was now hanging out as she panted at me. I chuckled. "I'll take her."

I calculated that I would have maybe ten minutes to spare getting everything ready for Kaiya's birthday. I planned to surprise her with the puppy, then take her to meet Kamden and Nori at her favorite restaurant for dinner.

Becca, being the expert salesperson she was, talked me into buying almost one of everything in the dog section for Kaiya's new puppy: leash, collar, crate, food and water bowls, puppy food, shampoo, bed; you name it, I bought it.

I wasn't good at the romantic boyfriend thing, but I was trying my best to make Kaiya's birthday special. I wanted the puppy to be a complete surprise, so I got a cardboard gift box, poked some holes in the top, put the dog inside, closed it, and slipped a pink bow around it.

Becca had given me a puppy starter kit that had more essentials that we would apparently need for our new addition. I put everything I had bought and arranged it in the puppy's bed before hiding it in my closet.

About fifteen minutes before Kaiya usually got home, the puppy started whining and scratching inside the box. I decided to hold the box in my lap on the couch, hoping that would silence the puppy's cries.

The pup still whimpered, so I tried talking to her to calm her down. "Shhh, little one. It's okay. Just a few more minutes."

Thankfully, my plan worked, and Kaiya's present cooperated with me. "Good girl. Mommy will be home soon."

When I heard Kaiya twisting her key in the door, I stood with her present in hand. Her eyes immediately found me as she walked in. "Hey, baby."

I walked toward her. "Happy birthday, Warrior." I presented the gift to her. "I got something for you."

Kaiya smiled sweetly as she took the box. "Ryker, you shouldn't have. The flowers at work were enough, and I know you planned something with Nori."

I smirked. "Just open it, babe."

She rolled her eyes playfully and took the box over to the dining room table. She slipped the bow off and neatly laid it down before removing the top. I heard her gasp right before she squealed, "Oh my God, Ryker!"

I could see the puppy's head bobbing as it tried to jump out of the box. Kaiya scooped her up and hugged her to her chest as she twirled around and faced me. "She's precious!" The smile she had lit up her whole face, and caused a matching one to form on mine.

"You like her?" I asked.

Kaiya gave me a look of disbelief. "Like her? I love her!" She walked over to me and wrapped her free arm around my neck, squeezing me tightly to her. "She's adorable. By far, the best birthday present ever!"

That's what I was hoping for.

"What are you going to name her?" I asked as Kaiya pulled away.

Kaiya held the puppy out in front of her and looked her over for several seconds. "Brownie."

I snorted. "Brownie?"

Kaiya hadn't taken her eyes off the puppy. "Yes, Brownie. Look at her—her fur is the same color as a brownie."

My chest rumbled with soft laughter. "Maybe we should call her Princess Brownie."

Kaiya leveled me with an annoyed glare before turning her attention back to Brownie. "Aren't you just the cutest thing ever? Yes, you are. Yes, you are."

I chuckled before leaving the two divas to go to my closet. I grabbed everything I'd bought for Brownie and took it out to the living room. "I think I got everything we need for her, but we can always go back to the pet store and get more."

Kaiya scanned over the pile of items with wide, shocked eyes. "Wow, I can't believe you thought to get all of this."

I grinned. "I had help."

"That explains it," Kaiya teasingly replied as she sat down on the couch with Brownie. "Especially since everything matches."

All of the items that Becca had picked out had a pink leopard print design. "The girl that helped me said you would like it."

Kaiya rubbed Brownie's belly. "She was right. Now, all we need is to get some cute dresses. Isn't that right, princess?"

I smiled as I took Brownie's bowls and food out of the bed, then headed to the kitchen. I knew she would want to dress the dog up. "We need to leave in about forty-five minutes."

Setting the bowls on the counter, I turned on the sink and filled one of the dishes with water.

"Why?" Kaiya asked.

I ripped open the bag of food and scooped some of the contents into the other bowl. "It's a surprise."

"Ryker, wh—"

I interrupted her. "No questions. Now go get ready."

Her lips fought a smile as she bent over to put Brownie down on the floor. "Fine," she huffed playfully before standing.

Once I set Brownie's bowls on the tile in the kitchen, she scampered over to them and started eating.

"Babe, what should I wear?" Kaiya called from down the hall.

I left Brownie to finish her dinner and headed to my room. Kaiya was in the closet in only her bra and lace boy shorts with her back to me when I entered, causing my dick to twitch.

You don't have time right now.

I cleared my throat and focused on her question. "Whatever you want. You look great in everything."

That's the right answer, right?

Kaiya turned to face me and the right corner of her mouth lifted. "I mean, how should I dress? Fancy? Casual? Something in between?"

Duh, dumb ass.

Her sexy smirk made my cock harden. I crossed my arms over my chest to keep from walking over there and taking her against the door frame.

Focus on the question.

"Something in between."

Kaiya disappeared into the closet after I answered. I started to make my way back to the living room when a brown blur flew past my feet and into the bedroom.

I turned around to hear Kaiya giggling before speaking in a high pitched voice. "Hi, cutie. Is your belly full? Did you like your dinner?"

I entered the closet to see Kaiya squatting down and rubbing Brownie's exposed stomach. She continued to baby talk the puppy. "Who's the prettiest girl? Who's the prettiest girl? You. Yes, you are. Yes, you are."

I checked the time on my watch. "Babe, we have reservations."

Kaiya glanced up at me, then back down at Brownie. "Daddy's a party pooper, Brownie. He won't let us play."

A warm smile spread over my face as my stomach tightened from hearing Kaiya call me "daddy."

God, I love her.

Brownie rolled off her back and stood. Her butt shook back and forth from how hard she was wagging her tail. Kaiya patted her on the head and smiled. "Go play with Daddy. Mommy has to get ready now."

Kaiya rose back up. "Maybe you should take her outside before we leave," she suggested as she resumed her search through her clothes on the rack.

"Okay." I picked Brownie up and carried her to the bedroom door. "You better be ready by the time I get back," I joked.

"Yeah, yeah, whatever," Kaiya shouted as I walked down the hall. I knew she wasn't going to be anywhere near ready when I came back inside.

"Your momma is a smart ass," I said as I scratched our new puppy's neck. "But I wouldn't want her any other way."

Chapter Nineteen

Kaiya

I could hardly wait to see where Ryker planned to take me for my birthday. My family had never been big on parties growing up. As adults, Kam and I wouldn't do anything extravagant when our birthdays came around, much to Nori's displeasure. She'd always wanted to throw both of us a huge party, but we usually ended up just doing dinner and dancing for my birthday and barhopping for Kam's.

"Just tell me where you're taking me," I pleaded for the fifth time since we started driving. The anticipation was killing me.

Ryker chuckled. "Nope. It's called a surprise for a reason."

"Damn it," I mumbled under my breath before huffing like a bratty child.

Ryker placed his hand on my thigh, which was slightly exposed by my new dress. I couldn't figure out what to wear so I ended up going to buy one for the special occasion. "You'll like it, Warrior. Trust me." He grinned with a wink.

My lips curved up at his sexy smile. "Yeah, you do know what I like."

That was a big understatement—Ryker always knew how to please me. His smile morphed to a cocky smirk from my words as his fingers danced higher up my thigh. The tender skin tingled with pleasure until he reached the juncture between my legs and stilled.

His eyes were filled with lust as they locked on mine. My lips parted to release a small gasp as he started to rub his fingertips against my panties.

He moved to the edge of my lace boy shorts and snaked his hand underneath the fabric. His gaze left mine as he looked back at the road, but his fingers didn't stop their course. They slowly continued, tracing their way along my skin until they found my heated core.

Ryker played within the sensitive folds, massaging my clit using his expert touch. "Guess I do know what you like—that sweet pussy is soaking wet for me," he growled, his voice thick with lust.

Leaning my head back, I closed my eyes and bit down on my lower lip as Ryker slipped the tips of two of his fingers inside me and quickly dragged them out.

I squirmed as he toyed with my clit again, aching for him to sink his fingers deep in me again. A moan left me as he teased my entrance, knowing he was going to make me come completely undone before giving me release.

After several blissfully tortuous seconds, Ryker slowly pushed his fingers inside my pussy, causing me to cry out. I gripped the edge of my seat as he pulled them out again and groaned in protest, "Ryker, please."

"Not yet, baby. I'm not ready for you to come yet."

Damn it.

I hated and loved every second of Ryker's pleasurable torment. I wanted him to end it, yet didn't want him to stop. I didn't know how long he continued his heavenly ministrations, but after some time, he took his hand away and huskily spoke. "We're here."

My eyes snapped open and met his. "Don't stop," I whimpered as I writhed against the seat, wanting, no, needing release.

Ryker chuckled before sticking the fingers that had just been inside me into his mouth and sucking them.

Holy fuck. That's one of the hottest things I've ever seen.

I licked my lips, then closed my mouth, which had parted as I watched Ryker savor my arousal.

His eyes darted to my lips and back as the right side of his mouth curved up into a sinful smirk. "We'll be late if I don't stop," he said in a sensual rasp.

Sparks of lust flared in the silence that followed his statement, then our lips crashed together. Ryker gripped my hips as he lifted me over the center console of his truck and onto his lap. His hands roamed under my dress and grabbed my ass as I fumbled with his zipper.

A smack on the window broke us apart. "Hey! Quit that shit! You bitches have a party to attend!"

I turned my head to see Nori outside Ryker's door. A mischievous grin lined her lips as she took a drag from her cigarette and blew out the smoke from the corner of her mouth.

I buried my face in Ryker's chest, which moved up and down with his laughter. "Perfect timing," I mumbled against his shirt.

Ryker rubbed his hands up and down my back. "Guess we better go. Don't want to keep her waiting."

I groaned in protest, still craving release, but raised my head and opened the door to the truck. Nori snickered as I climbed down. "Sorry, I hope I didn't interrupt anything important," she teased before taking another puff of her cigarette.

Narrowing my eyes, I glared at her. "Cock block."

Nori laughed and flicked her cigarette to the asphalt. "Sorry, girl. You know how impatient I am, and I've already been waiting fifteen minutes for you."

I heard the truck door close behind me, followed by the beep of the alarm locking. "Hey, Nori," Ryker greeted once he reached us.

Nori smiled with amusement. "Hey. You were supposed to get her here on time, not be the reason she was late."

Ryker shrugged. "Sometimes I just can't help myself." His eyes ran over my body and a smirk tipped his lips. "Look at her."

I looked down at myself and scoffed. "I look like a fat cow."

Nori snorted as Ryker draped an arm over my shoulder and pulled me into him. "No you don't, Warrior. You're the most beautiful woman I've ever seen."

A small smile curved my lips. "You have to say that."

Ryker was about to reply when Nori interjected, "All right, lovebirds, let's go." She walked toward the restaurant, which I finally noticed was Luciano's now that I wasn't caught up in Ryker. I looked up at him and grinned widely. "Luciano's?"

Ryker led me behind Nori, keeping his arm around me as we walked. "Your favorite for such a special occasion."

I knew it wasn't anything major, but all the little things that Ryker did to make me feel special meant the world to me. No one had ever done so much to make me happy. I squeezed him around his middle. "Thank you."

Ryker kissed the top of my head. "Anything for you, Warrior."

My phone chimed as we neared the entrance. I pulled away from Ryker and stopped to fish my cell out of my purse. "Let me grab my phone real quick."

A text message popped up when I swiped my screen:

Unknown: Happy birthday hope you get everything your heart desires

My stomach clenched as fear rooted deep throughout my insides. My head darted frantically around the parking lot, searching for anyone suspicious.

Who the fuck is this?

Ryker placed his hand on the small of my back, causing me to startle and jerk away.

"Whoa, babe, it's just me." Ryker calmly spoke as if talking to a spooked animal. "What's wrong?"

I gulped, then exhaled a shaky breath. "Nothing. I'm fine."

Ryker gave me a knowing look. He wasn't buying it. "Kaiya." His tone was like that of a disapproving parent who caught their teenager in a lie.

"Hey, I'm starving here. Hurry the fuck up," Nori interrupted.

Thank God.

I forced a smile. "I'm fine, really. Let's get inside."

He narrowed his eyes and reached out his hand. "Let me see your phone."

No. He can't find out. He'll be upset and even more worried.

"Can we not do this right now?" I deflected and crossed my arms over my chest. "It's my birthday."

His features softened as he sighed in defeat, then quickly hardened again. "We *will* be talking about this later." His tone left no room for argument.

Fuck. Shit. Damn.

"Okay," I replied in resignation, then walked toward the door, hoping that he'd forget by the time the night was over.

Wishful thinking.

When we got inside, we followed Nori to a table in the back of the restaurant where Kamden sat with a bunch of pink balloons and cupcakes.

"Happy birthday!" Nori and Kam shouted in unison.

My mood shifted, even though a tiny sliver of dread lingered in my gut. I buried it down, determined not to let some psycho asshole ruin my birthday. I'd dealt with that enough in my life.

Tears welled in my eyes from the thoughtfulness that had been put into this surprise. I knew I'd be crying more than once before the night was over. "You guys." My voice cracked as emotion clogged my throat.

"Geez, you're like a faucet lately," Nori joked as she hugged me. She pulled back and smiled. "It's your party, and you can cry if you want to?"

I snorted with laughter and swiped the moisture from my lashes. "Yeah. Thank you for all this." My eyes drifted from face to face of each of my loved ones. "All of you."

The night was filled with laughs and joyful banter. No talk of Kaleb, no talk about Kamden's drinking or rehab—just happiness. I prayed that we would have more times like this in the future, especially once Hayden was born.

Once we were almost finished eating, Kamden pulled out a small, wrapped box from under the table and presented it to me. "Happy Birthday, Ky."

I took the gift from him. "Kam, you didn't have to get me anything." Everything he'd done for me was enough to last me a lifetime.

"I wanted to." Motioning with his hands, he urged me to open the present. "Go on, open it."

Ripping the paper off, I revealed a small cardboard box. Inside that was a black jewelry case. I opened the lid and stared down at a necklace with two hearts; a large heart that had the word "*sorella*" engraved on it dangled from a smaller, open heart.

My vision was clouded as I looked up at Kam. His lips curved up slightly as he grabbed my hand. "The little heart is you—holding me up when I need it most. Thank you for being there to support me through everything."

I squeezed his hand back, unable to speak as tears trickled down my cheeks. After I wiped my face with my free hand and took a deep breath to compose myself, my words came out soft as cotton when I replied, "Thank you."

Kamden smiled warmly. "You're welcome. Let's see how it looks."

I took the thin, delicate chain out of the box and clasped it around my neck. I made sure it lay correctly against my skin before looking back up at my brother. "I love it, Kam."

"Good, I'm glad. Shopping for you was hard." He chuckled.

"It's perfect. You made a great choice," I replied genuinely.

"My turn!" Nori squealed as she handed me a card and a gift bag.

"Not you, too. You guys didn't have to do all this for me."

"Just shut up and open the damn gift," Nori playfully demanded.

I smashed my lips together, fighting the smile trying to break through. "Fine." I huffed as I tore the envelope open and slipped out the card that was inside. A gift certificate to my favorite spa fell out as I opened the card and read what Nori had wrote inside:

"We may not be sisters by blood, but you're the only sister I'll ever need. I love you and can't wait to be a part of this next chapter in your life. Happy birthday!"

My eyes watered again as they drifted up to Nori. She shook her head, fighting tears as well. "Cut it out, damn it. You're going to make me cry."

I chuckled and wiped my eyes before opening my arms to her. She leaned over and hugged me. "Happy Birthday, Ky."

I pulled back and smiled. "Thank you."

"Don't forget the gift," Nori reminded.

I took out the pink tissue paper and looked in the bag. I pulled the little baby outfit out and held it up. It had a bib, onesie, and pants; both the bib and onesie read "My aunt is cooler than your aunt."

I laughed as I showed Ryker, who snorted. "I love it," I said, hugging Nori again. "You're more family to me than my real family ever was. Well, besides Kam, of course."

She squeezed me tight. "I know, girl. Same here. I'll always be there for you."

When I pulled back, I looked around the table at the amazing people with me. My family. A smile spread over my face as I placed a hand on my bulging belly and gazed down.

I had everything I ever needed right there with me.

As soon as we set foot in Ryker's apartment, he questioned me. "What happened earlier?"

I played dumb, even though I knew he wasn't going to buy it. "When?"

He lowered his head to make eye contact with me, making me uneasy. My eyes flitted away, then back to his. "Don't act stupid, Kaiya," Ryker responded abrasively.

Shifting uncomfortably, I rubbed my hands up and down my bare arms. "It was nothing."

"Bullshit," he growled. His face was lined with anger. His jaw set, and his eyes burned with fury. "Don't fucking lie to me."

Damn it, how does he read me so well?

My brain raced as I held his gaze, trying to think of a believable lie.

I'd lied to everyone about Kaleb for most of my life, so lying was a natural defense mechanism for me. I swallowed the lump in my throat as the perfect thing came to mind. "I just…" I started, then paused and sighed. "My mom text me."

His face fell as guilt washed over, making me feel like a piece of shit for lying. He opened his arms and moved toward me. "Baby, I'm sorry. I shouldn't have pushed you to tell me." His arms wrapped around me and pulled me against his strong frame.

Resting my head against his chest, I sighed, still feeling disgusted with myself. "Can we just forget about it? Please?"

Ryker rubbed his hands up and down my back. "Yeah, Warrior. We can."

Chapter Twenty

Ryker

Cheering sounded throughout the bar as Ortiz hit a home run with two players on the bases. I took a swig of my beer as my brother clapped wildly. "Go Sox!" he shouted before turning from the T.V. to face me. "Can you believe that hit? Two strikes in the bottom of the ninth and then he blows it out of the park to tie it up. Unbelievable."

"Yeah, it was a pretty good hit," I replied unenthusiastically.

Ethan's brows furrowed. "What's wrong with you, bro?"

My argument with Kaiya and encounter with Molly were still weighing on me a week later. "Just have a lot on my mind."

"Molly told me she ran into you last week."

I nodded. "Yep. It was awkward at best."

He chuckled. "Well, at least you're trying."

I took a long pull from my bottle. "Doing my best. I'm not gonna lie, it was hard to take that step."

He patted me on the shoulder. "It'll get better. Time heals all wounds."

I snorted. "We'll see."

"Have faith, bro." Ethan smiled warmly. "I do. You both love me too much to let what happened come between us again."

"The past is the past, right?" I asked rhetorically.

He raised his beer toward me. "Cheers to that."

I tapped our bottles together. "To moving on."

Ethan's smile broadened. "To moving on."

We both took a drink, then Ethan asked, "So does that mean we can all go out to dinner or something soon?"

I thought for a second before replying, "I'm not so sure about that yet."

"Come on, Ry. Kaiya's going to have the baby in a couple of months, and you've already gone through the worst part."

He had a point. I hadn't wanted to see Molly, but I'd gotten that confrontation over with, even though it was tense and awkward.

"I'll talk to Kaiya about it and let you know. Her baby shower is in a few weeks—maybe you can bring Molly and Tristan to that."

Ethan grinned broadly. "I'd really like that."

I left the bar feeling better, but I couldn't get the argument with Kaiya out of my mind. Even though she'd said her mom had texted her, which would have caused her to react the way she had, I had a sick feeling she was keeping something from me. My gut was usually right, just like with Molly.

Kaiya isn't Molly. She wouldn't do that.

The problem was that I wasn't sure. Doubt lingered in the back of my mind.

Old habits die hard.

My past had made me distrusting of everyone, especially women. Kaiya had broken through most of my walls, but the way she'd been acting over the past few months was making me want to build them back up again.

By the time I got home, I had enough time to think and had made myself even more conflicted than I already was. But as soon as I saw Kaiya napping on the couch with her hand on her huge belly, the love I felt for her quickly eradicated the negative emotions I was feeling.

Brownie was cuddled up in between her legs, but started moving when I shut the door. Her tail wagged as she stood up and paced back and forth on the couch, looking for a way to get down. Then, she started whimpering and scratching at the cushions.

"Shh, mommy's sleeping," I whispered, picking her up.

After putting Brownie down on the floor, I grabbed the blanket from the top of the couch and draped it over Kaiya, who stirred but didn't wake up.

As I turned around, I glimpsed Kaiya's phone on the coffee table. My eyes darted back and forth between her and the device several times before I finally picked it up.

I swiped the screen, but it asked for a password.

Since when does Kaiya have a lock on her phone?

I stared at the locked screen, which had a picture of us from her birthday party as the background.

What is she hiding?

I put her phone back down on the table before directing my attention to Brownie, who was pawing at the bottom of my jeans. "You need to go outside?" Her ears perked up. "Let's go outside."

I needed to get out and clear my head. I thought I was over the whole Molly thing, but Kaiya's mysterious calls and seeing Molly again triggered my doubt and caused a sick feeling of dread to settle in my gut. I'd been down this road before and Kaiya was acting the exact same way Molly had when we'd been together.

Brownie bounded to the door and circled in front of it happily. I took her leash off one of the key hooks on the wall and tried to get her to sit still long enough for me to attach it to her collar.

Once I did, I walked Brownie to the pet area. The thoughts swirled around in my head, creating a lethal mixture of paranoia and suspicion. The more I tried to block, defuse, and deny them, the more they screamed not to ignore them.

.When I went back to my apartment, Kaiya hadn't moved from when I covered her. After I removed Brownie's leash, she ran back over to the couch and attempted to get back on.

She hopped repeatedly, reminding me of a bouncing bunny as she kept trying to jump on the sofa. "Need help?" I chuckled.

I helped her get on, then she proceeded to slip beneath the blanket and curl up with Kaiya again. A smile curved up the right side of my mouth as I watched them.

My smile faded as the question I had from earlier resurfaced.

What is she hiding?

The following Saturday, Drew texted me, asking to meet up for a couple of drinks at our old bar. I hadn't been out with him since we found out that Kaiya was pregnant, so I decided to go, needing some guy time.

Maybe it'll help clear my head.

A knock sounded on the door, breaking through my thoughts. I heard Kaiya greeting Nori, who had come over to have a girl's movie night with Kaiya while I went out.

I checked myself one last time in the mirror before walking out to the living room, where Kaiya was scanning over the DVDs in Nori's hand.

"I brought *Steel Magnolias, Dirty Dancing,* and *The Sweetest Thing.* Which do you want to watch first?"

Kaiya gave her an 'are you serious' look. "Nobody puts Baby in a corner."

Both women burst out in laughter. A smile spread across my lips as I walked over to Kaiya and kissed her on the cheek. "You girls have fun."

Kaiya linked her fingers with mine. "You too. Be careful."

I squeezed her hand. "Always."

Letting go, I traveled the rest of the way to the door and left. I took out my phone and called Drew as I trotted down the stairs. "Hey bro, I'm on my way."

"You're always late." He chuckled. I could practically see him shaking his head at me through the phone.

"I know, I know. You there already?"

"Not yet. I knew you'd be late, so I took my time. I'm on the way, though," he answered.

I unlocked my truck and hopped in. "I'll be there in ten."

"All right, see you then."

Drew was already seated at the bar when I walked in. What I assumed was a Jack and Coke sat next to him on the bar top as he drank his beer. He tipped his chin up at me as I approached. "'Sup?"

I patted him on the back before taking the seat next to him. "Not much. How's everything with you?"

"Good." He paused and took a swig from his bottle. "Things with Nori are getting kinda serious."

I cocked an eyebrow. "No shit?"

His goofy, love-struck smile told me he was head over heels for her before his words did. "I think I love her."

Nori and Drew had been dating since right before the shooting. They'd been pretty casual the whole time, and it had been awhile since Drew and I had really talked, so I had no idea they had gotten serious. "Have you told her?"

He shook his head. "Nah. Everything has been going so well, and I don't want to jinx it."

I nodded. "I feel you. If it ain't broke, don't fix it."

He tipped his bottle to me. "And you? How are things with Kaiya?"

"Awesome." That was partially a lie; a lie based on me making assumptions, but still. "Only a couple more months till Hayden is born."

"Damn. I still can't believe it sometimes. After Molly, I never thought you would settle down." He made an 'oh shit' face, then rushed his next statement. "But things with Kaiya are totally different. She'd never do what Molly did."

I wasn't totally sure, but I agreed anyway. "Yeah. She wouldn't."

"When's his exact due date again?"

"August 2," I answered before taking the first swig of my drink.

"Damn, so two and a half months, huh? Bet you're excited."

"I am. Nervous, too."

"I'd be shitting bricks if I were you. I know nothing about babies."

"Thanks," I replied sarcastically. "That makes me feel so much more confident."

He slapped me on the shoulder. "I'm sure you'll be a great dad. That kind of shit comes naturally once the baby is born."

"I hope so. I'm in the same boat as you."

"Maybe you should buy some parenting books."

I gave him a look of disbelief. "You're kidding, right?"

A teasing grin lifted his lips. "Not if you're that worried."

I scoffed. "I'm not going to read a parenting book. I'm sure I'll be fine."

He shrugged. "Suit yourself."

I noticed a woman at the end of the bar eyeing me seductively. In the past, I would've have been all over her in a second, buying us a few rounds of drinks before taking her home later that night. But I wasn't that guy anymore. Instead, I ignored her signals and directed my attention back to Drew, who was back to analyzing his feelings for Nori again.

An amused smirk curved the corner of my mouth.

How things have changed.

After a few more drinks, I looked at my phone to see if Kaiya had text me. Nothing.

I wonder what she's doing.

My mind conjured up images of Kaiya in bed with another man, her girls' night with Nori just a ploy to get away from me without suspicion.

I pushed the thoughts back as I turned to Drew. "Hey, has Nori texted you?"

He took his phone out of his pocket, then looked at the screen. "No. Why?"

I laughed inwardly at my crazy imagination. Kaiya fucking another man with her huge, pregnant belly.

I slipped my phone into my back pocket. "No reason."

By the time we left, I had a nice buzz. "We have to do this again soon. It's been too long, bro. You're all domesticated and shit," Drew teased as we walked to the parking lot.

I punched his arms. "Just wait until you have a kid on the way, dick. Things will be different." We clasped hands once we reached our cars. "I'll hit you up next weekend."

No matter how much I tried, I couldn't completely push out the thoughts of Kaiya with another man as I drove home. The way she'd been acting lately, along with the lengths she was taking to keep her phone from me made me suspicious of her.

And the same question kept plaguing me.

What is she hiding?

When I got home, my muscles tensed in anticipation as the images of me walking in on Kaiya having sex with someone played in my head.

I exhaled and unlocked my front door before entering. I hoped that my fears were unrealistic, and that I wouldn't be made a fool twice.

When I walked in, I found Nori and Kaiya both sleeping on the couch. Brownie was balled up in between them on top of the blanket that covered their legs. Their feet were propped up on the coffee table and Kaiya's head rested on Nori's shoulder.

I laughed lightly at my ridiculous thoughts from moments before.

What was I thinking?

I turned the TV off, then carefully went to scoop Kaiya off the couch so I wouldn't wake up Nori. Neither woman stirred as I picked Kaiya up and carried her to our bedroom.

As I tucked Kaiya in bed, a new question surfaced as I stared down at her.

Am I really just imagining things, or am I too blinded by my love for her to see the truth?

I swallowed deeply and my stomach knotted uncomfortably. I didn't know the answer.

Chapter Twenty-One

Kaiya

Ryker's apartment was madness as I watched Nori and some of the girls from my office run around trying to get everything ready for my baby shower while I sat on the couch.

There was blue everywhere. And I mean *everywhere*. Streamers, balloons, banners, and other decorations were spread out over the living room, dining room, and kitchen. It was kind of overwhelming.

Finger foods were arranged on decorative plates on the counters in the kitchen, and presents sat on the coffee table in the living room. I snacked on some chips and dip as Nori set out the cake. "How you doing, girl? You need anything?"

I finished chewing my chip. "I'm good, just going to grab some fruit." I started walking to the fruit tray.

"I'll get it. You go sit down and relax," Nori ordered as she softly grabbed me by the shoulders and stopped me.

I rolled my eyes. "You sound just like Ryker and Kamden."

She gave me her take no shit look. "Go."

"Fine," I huffed before turning around and walking into the living room. My feet were already hurting anyway, so I didn't mind following Nori's demand. I needed to relax some before Ethan and Molly showed up.

I was so anxious about them coming over. I'd asked Nori a dozen times if my outfit looked okay, even though I felt like a walrus. I'd straightened my hair repeatedly, wanting my hair to look perfect for the occasion. Not to mention I couldn't stop stuffing my face with food

I'd met Ethan a couple of times before, but not Molly or their son. To be completely honest, I really wasn't looking forward to meeting Molly for obvious reasons. I already disliked her because of how much she hurt Ryker, but I was going to try to be as nice as possible for his sake. I wanted to give him all the support that I could.

Ryker wasn't too thrilled about having to deal with Molly either, but he was making the best of it to mend his relationship with Ethan. Both he and Molly were at fault, but Ryker had found that it was easier to forgive Ethan since they were brothers and put most of the blame on Molly.

I waddled over to the couch to sit down before they arrived. I felt like a bloated cow ready to be milked, and everything was swollen—my feet, my legs, my stomach, everything. I was more than ready for this pregnancy to be over with so I could finally hold Hayden in my arms.

Only nine more weeks.

Ryker brought me a bottle of water and sat next to me. "How you feeling, Warrior?" He gently rubbed my stomach.

"Fat," I answered with a sarcastic laugh. "I don't know how you can stand to look at me."

He tucked a strand of hair behind my ear. "I think you look beautiful carrying my son." His fingertips trailed along my cheek as he looked down. "How's my little man doing?"

I followed his gaze and smiled. "I think he knows we're having a party for him—he's been moving around a lot."

Ryker focused on my bulging belly. "Oh yeah? Where is he now?"

I grabbed his hand and moved it to the opposite side, right under my ribs. "He's been kicking me here for a while. It's so uncomfortable."

Ryker narrowed his eyes at my stomach. "Quit kicking Mommy, Hayden."

I couldn't help but giggle at how adorable he was. I caressed his scruffy jaw with my fingers.

God, I love him.

Ryker looked up at me and smiled. His rugged beauty still caused my heart to stutter when I looked at him.

How did I get so lucky?

Just then, the doorbell rang. Ryker glanced over his shoulder as he said, "That's probably Ethan." He stood and reached his hand out to help me up.

I stopped him. "Wait, do I look okay?" I asked as I ran my fingers through my hair and straightened my dress.

Ryker pulled me closer to him and kissed my cheek. "You look great. Don't worry." He led me to the entryway and opened the door. "Hey, come on in," he greeted.

Ryker closed the door behind the family that walked in. He came by my side and rested his hand on my back. "Ethan, you remember Kaiya, right?"

Ethan grinned and stretched his arms out towards me. "How could I forget? Nice to see you again, Kaiya."

I smiled and accepted his hug. "You too. Thanks for coming."

When he pulled away, he gestured to his family. "This is my wife, Molly, and our son, Tristan."

Molly had blonde hair and hazel eyes, and her pregnant stomach protruded from her tiny frame. She was about ten weeks behind me, but I looked a hell of a lot bigger than she did, even when I was at that stage in my pregnancy. That made me hate her even more. I knew I was being juvenile but I didn't care.

Tristan looked identical to Ethan, just like Ryker had said. I smiled as I pictured Hayden looking like Ryker. I definitely didn't want him looking anything like me or *him*. I wasn't sure how I'd cope with seeing a replica of Kaleb everyday.

I quickly swiped the thoughts of Kaleb away before they spun out of control, not wanting to ruin my special day because of him. He'd ruined too many days of my life, and now that he was gone, there was no reason to let him continue to do so.

Molly stuck her hand out toward me. "Hi, nice to meet you."

"Kaiya," I greeted as nicely as I could, with one of the most fake smiles I'd ever forced before. Inside, I wanted to rip her a new asshole and give her a piece of my mind for everything she had done to Ryker. But on the surface, I tried to stay calm and courteous.

"Ethan has told me so much about you." She sounded phony, like she was trying too hard to be enthusiastic about meeting me.

She turned her attention to Ryker. "Hey, Ry. Good to see you again."

Sure bitch.

Ryker gave her a strained smile before looking at Ethan. "Thanks for coming. We have plenty of food and drinks in the kitchen. Make yourself at home."

"Thanks, bro." Ethan replied before leading Molly and Tristan into the kitchen.

Ryker pulled me into his side and kissed the top of my head. I glanced up at him as he asked, "You okay?"

I breathed a sigh of relief, more comfortable now that Molly wasn't right in front of me. "Yeah. That wasn't as bad as I thought it was gonna be."

"Good. It'll take some time before things aren't so awkward, but we just took a big step."

I nodded. "You're right."

Leaning down, Ryker pressed his lips to mine and placed a hand on my belly. He couldn't seem to keep his hands off me, but I wasn't complaining; I loved it.

When he pulled away, he smiled down at me lovingly and caressed my stomach one last time, then led me back into the living room.

We mingled with some of my coworkers for a while before Nori dragged me away into the kitchen to get ready for one of the games she had planned.

Ryker was staring at me while Nori wrapped my torso with toilet paper. My stomach knotted as he gave me a seductive smirk.

"Hey." Molly drew my attention away from him.

What does she want?

Barely making eye contact, I forced a smile. "Hi."

Tristan was sleeping on her shoulder as she swayed back and forth. "He really loves you."

Nori glanced up at me as she continued to cocoon my abdomen. *What is she talking about?*

"Huh?" I questioned.

"Ryker. He really loves you. I can tell by the way he looks at you." *Because you're an expert? Pffft.*

I looked away from her to Ryker, who glanced away from Drew to me. He gave me another heartwarming smile as our eyes locked.

"He never looked at me that way," Molly added.

I didn't really care what she was saying because I was so caught up in Ryker. He patted Drew on the shoulder and told him something, then walked in my direction. My heart pounded faster with every step he took, and Hayden started kicking me again.

Molly was right about one thing—the way Ryker was looking at me displayed the love he had for me all over his face. He wrapped his arms around me when he reached me. "Hey, Warrior." He pressed a kiss to my forehead.

I smiled up at him. "Hi."

His hands came back around to my stomach. "Having a good time?"

"Much better now." I placed my hands on the outside of his forearms as I gazed up at him.

His eyes darted to my lips right before he leaned down and kissed me. The gentle press of his mouth on mine sent passion flaring through me. I shuddered a shaky breath when he pulled away.

Ryker smirked as he swept his thumb over my lips, then cupped my cheek. "I love you."

I nuzzled into his palm and closed my eyes. "I love you, too."

He looked down at my toilet paper-wrapped stomach. He grinned and raised an eyebrow in question. "Why do you have toilet paper wrapped around you?"

"For a game. People have to guess how many squares of toilet paper are wrapped around me."

He chuckled. "Weird."

I pulled him to one of the kitchen counter. "That's nothing. Check this out." I motioned down to the counter that had diapers with various melted chocolates on them. "People have to guess what chocolate it is by smelling it."

Ryker scrunched his nose in displeasure. "Gross."

I giggled. "It's just chocolate."

"Yeah, but it looks like shit."

"That's the point, genius," Nori teased as she interrupted.

Ryker scratched his forehead with his middle finger as he gave Nori a teasing grin.

Nori playfully returned his gesture, then looked at me. "Ready for the games?"

"Sure." I nodded and grabbed Ryker's hand. "Let's get started."

Nori made Ryker and me sit on the couch before starting the first game. Everyone was laughing and having a great time as we played the silly games Nori had planned for the shower.

By the time we had finished, my stomach was growling. I got up to go grab some snacks, then circulated around the apartment with Ryker to talk more to some of the guests.

"Time for presents!" Nori announced loudly as she came up to me. She grabbed my arm, then pulled me away from Ryker.

"Sorry, Ry," she giggled, leading me back to the couch, where she had arranged all the gifts on the coffee table.

Ryker sat down next to me as Nori handed me the first present. Kamden had a camera ready when I started unwrapping the gift.

Most of the presents were clothes and diapers, but we also got some bigger items from Nori, Kamden, and my boss. Nori had bought us a swing, Kamden had gotten the matching changing table to the crib set we had purchased already, and my boss had gifted us a set of bottles and the corresponding bottle warmer.

"There's one more gift," Ethan announced as he pulled an envelope from his shirt pocket. He handed it to Ryker, who gave him a quizzical look. Ethan chuckled, "Open it."

Ryker ripped open the envelope and took out a check. His eyes widened and his jaw dropped as he scanned over it, then looked at

Ethan in shock.

"That should cover what you needed for the house you wanted, right?"

I leaned over to look at the check in Ryker's hand.

Holy shit!

I blinked several times to make sure I wasn't imagining things.

Nope, still the same ridiculously large amount.

It was more than enough to pay for the remainder of the down payment that we weren't able to come up with for the house. And then some.

"Oh my God, Ryker," I gasped as I placed a hand on his leg. My eyes stung with tears when his eyes met mine.

"I… we… we can't accept this. It's too much, Ethan," Ryker said as he stood and handed the check to his brother.

Ethan put his hands up. "Nope. It's the least we can do after everything. Please take it."

Ryker looked at me, seeking my approval for what to do. That house was my dream house, so it didn't require much debate for me. Giving him a teary-eyed smile, I nodded enthusiastically.

He faced Ethan and stared at him for several seconds, then suddenly moved forward and threw his arms around him. Squeezing his brother tightly, Ryker's voice was drowned with emotion as he said, "Thank you. You don't even understand what this means to me."

A few tears spilled down my cheeks as Ethan hugged Ryker back. Even though what Ethan had done to Ryker was inexcusable, it made me happy to see them reconciling after so many years. Ryker would never admit it, but I knew he missed his brother greatly while they weren't speaking.

Ryker patted Ethan on the back before pulling away and looking at me. His eyes were glazed with unshed tears as he extended his hand to me.

Grabbing it, I linked our fingers together and stood by his side. He squeezed my hand and pressed a kiss atop my head.

My eyes found Ethan's. "Thank you so much. I don't think we can ever repay you."

Ethan smiled. "Just take care of my brother and nephew. God knows they need you."

My mouth curved up. Ethan had it backwards—I needed Ryker and Hayden more than he would ever understand. They were granting me a life that I never dreamed I could have, not to mention giving me a happiness I never knew existed.

I turned my head toward Ryker and my smile spread wider. Everything was falling into place for us, and for once, I couldn't wait to see what the future had in store for me.

The following Monday, I called our realtor as soon as her office opened to see if the house we wanted was still available. She'd sent us listings of a few more properties after, but none of them were what we wanted.

It had been months since Tanya had shown the property to us, but I was hoping that it was still available. We needed to find something soon—Hayden was due in a little over two months, and I didn't want to have to deal with finding a house and moving after he was born.

"Hello?"

"Hi, Tanya, this is Kaiya Marlow."

Her voice pepped up. "Hi, Kaiya. How are you? You're due soon, aren't you?"

I slipped off my shoes, hiding them under my desk. "I am—a little over two months now."

"Aww, I bet you're excited. I remember my first baby. I was so overwhelmed and excited all at once."

"Yep, I'm definitely getting more anxious each day. I can't wait to hold him." My heart warmed as I thought of holding Hayden in my arms. "I was just calling to see if that house we looked at back in March was still available. I know it's a long shot, but we we're able to get the money we needed for the counter offer."

"Let me check for you. I don't remember selling it, but that doesn't necessarily mean anything. I manage several properties at a time."

"I understand," I replied as a ball of anticipation tightened my chest.

Please, please, please.

I heard typing through the phone followed by the clicking of a mouse. "Do you remember the address or listing number?"

"9603 Briarwood Lane." I didn't think I'd ever forget that address.

More typing and clicking followed my response. "Here it is—looks like it's still on the market."

"Really?" There was no doubting the hope in my question.

"Yes. Just let me double-check something real quick..." After a few seconds of silence, her voice sounded back into the phone. "Yep, it's still available. Did you want to see it again?"

I couldn't stop the excitement that came over me. I sat up in my chair. "Can we just skip that and get to the paperwork?"

Tanya laughed. "I have to give your offer to the seller first. I'll do that as soon as we get off the phone."

"That would be great. Please keep me posted."

I could hear Tanya's smile in her voice. "I'll be in touch soon. You make sure that you stay well-rested for that baby."

"I will. Thanks again."

I text Ryker as soon as I hung up the phone to let him know the good news. Things were finally taking a turn for the better, and I wondered if they were too good to be true.

Chapter Twenty-Two

Ryker

"Where should I put this, babe?" I grunted as I hefted some chair that Kaiya had called a chaise through the doorway to our new house. It had taken about a month to get through the whole mortgage process, including extensive credit checks and employment verification, before we were finally able to move in.

Kaiya whipped around to face me, causing her ponytail to swing back and forth from the movement. "Um." She pursed her lips and walked toward me. "Right here should be fine."

I set the chair down where Kaiya indicated as she walked upstairs with a laundry basket full of baby clothes. I followed her with the box containing Hayden's crib, then put it down just inside his door.

I leaned against the door-frame and smiled as I watched Kaiya lay clothes on her enormous belly before folding them and setting them in the drawers of the dresser I had set up earlier.

I still had about two months left on my lease, so we were slowly moving stuff from both of our apartments into the house. We had also painted Hayden's room the week before, and Kaiya wanted to set everything up and have it ready before we moved in.

"Where do you want the crib?" I asked as I walked over to the cardboard. Gripping the edge, I started pulling at the top to open the box.

"Against that wall," Kaiya replied as she turned around and pointed across the room opposite of where she stood. "I want to put the rocking chair by the window."

I began to take the pieces out and arrange them on the floor so I could find them easily when I read the directions. After looking over the instructions a couple of times, I went downstairs to grab my toolbox out of my truck and get the tools I needed to assemble the crib.

Kaiya made several trips in and out of the room as I worked, bringing in the gifts we'd received at the baby shower and arranging them around the nursery. Everything was so surreal—moving into this house, becoming a father in just a month; basically settling down. If someone would have told me that this would be my life a year ago, I would've laughed in their faces.

Once I finished, I stepped back to survey my work. The crib looked just like the picture on the box. I gripped the edges of the crib and shook it a little to make sure it was sturdy.

"Finished?" Kaiya asked.

I looked over the crib again. "I think so." Bending down, I inspected the underside, then grabbed the legs and tested their stability. "Everything seems stable."

Kaiya came next to me as I stood and eyed the crib. "It looks good." She wrapped an arm around my waist and looked up at me with a loving smile. "Great job, Daddy."

I smiled from her words—I loved when she called me that. "Thanks, Momma."

Kaiya's mouth spread wider as she tiptoed up to kiss me. My hand automatically went to her stomach as our lips met; I loved feeling her belly and knowing that my son was inside her.

Or so you think.

My suspicious thoughts made me break the kiss and step back. "We have a lot to do. Stop distracting me," I deflected, hoping she wouldn't notice that something was bothering me.

She gave me a quick kiss on the cheek and smiled. "You're right. We don't have time to get carried away like usual."

Turning around, Kaiya grabbed the sheets we had bought for the crib and started putting them on the mattress. I went downstairs to get the rocking chair before bringing it up and putting it by the window where Kaiya wanted.

She walked toward me. "Thank you, baby." Sitting down in the chair, she looked out the window and sighed. "It's perfect."

I bent down and kissed her on the forehead. "I have some stuff to finish downstairs. Yell if you need me."

She smiled up at me. "Okay."

I ran my knuckles down Kaiya's cheek before walking out. Her phone rang as I walked out, so I stopped just outside the door to listen to the call.

The phone stopped ringing, but I didn't hear Kaiya answer it.

"Who was it, babe?" I asked as I stuck my head back in the room.

Kaiya jerked slightly before turning her phone over to hide the screen in her lap. The smile she gave me was forced, and I could tell she was trying to hide something. "Telemarketer."

Sure it was.

I nodded before leaving the room, trying to fight the sinking feeling that had crept in my gut.

Things between Kaiya and I had been getting tenser the closer she got to her due date. She was more irritable from the pregnancy hormones, and the suspicions I'd been having were growing the more I thought about them, making me trust her less and less.

I rented a couple of movies, hoping to relax and ease some of the tension between us. As we settled on the couch, my arm draped around Kaiya's shoulders as she curled up next to me, I could almost forget everything that had been bothering me.

That is until her phone vibrated and lit up during the first half of the movie.

Out of the corner of my eye, I tried to see the text message that had popped up, but as usual, she sneakily angled the screen away from me.

Anger lit my veins. We were a month away from having a kid together and she was hiding shit from me. Why would she be keeping things from me if she loved me and was about to give birth to my son. Unless...

He's not mine.

My mind ran a mile a minute, processing the revelation that dawned on me.

He's not mine.

The only reason she'd be so secretive was if she was cheating on me. If she really loved me, she wouldn't hide anything from me, especially weeks from having my kid. I knew the signs, and Kaiya had been flashing them brightly for months. I'd just been denying everything because I didn't want them to be true.

Then, another thing popped in my head. Whoever she was cheating with was the father. Not me.

He's not mine.

My heart felt like it was breaking into pieces, then being doused with battery acid. The pain that flooded me was unlike any other, and I knew there'd be no recovering from it. The wounds from Kaiya's betrayal would never scar, they'd be raw and open for the rest of my life.

Kaiya put her phone face down on the cushion next to her and focused back on the movie. Laying her hand on my chest, she snuggled closer to me, chasing away some of the harsh cold that had crept into my heart and replacing it with the warmth only she brought me.

No. Don't be weak. She doesn't love you. She's a cheating liar, just like Molly.

My teeth ground together as I thought about how stupid I'd been. Falling in love when I knew all women were the same. I needed answers; I needed to know why. "So, who is it?"

Kaiya kept her eyes on the TV. "Huh?"

Playing stupid, as always.

"Who are you cheating on me with?"

Kaiya sat up abruptly and looked at me with concern. "Ryker, what are you talking about?"

My heart pounded as my anger grew. "Don't lie to me anymore, Kaiya! Cut the bullshit and tell me!" I snarled.

Her eyes watered as she rested a hand against the middle of her chest. "Ryker, I would never-"

Unable to contain my rage anymore, I cut off her words, shouting over her. "Yeah, that's what she said! And look what happened!"

Tears poured down her cheeks. "I'm not Molly, Ryker! I'm not cheating on you!" she cried.

She's lying. Don't be fooled again.

I stood up and paced in front of the couch. "How do I know that, huh? You've been acting strange for the past few months. Secretly looking at your phone, angling the screen away from me so I can't see it, and getting calls from "wrong" numbers. Not to mention you added a password lock on your phone so I can't get in it."

Her face was blotchy as she looked up at me. "Here take it." She thrust her phone at me. "The password is Hayden's due date," she sobbed.

I stilled, starting to question my accusations.

Maybe she's not cheating. Maybe I'm just overreacting.

Don't be weak.

"It's too late for that now." I paused and took a deep breath before forcing myself to say the next sentence, even though it tore me up inside. "We're through."

The look of devastation that took over Kaiya's face constricted my heart, making me start to regret my words.

"Ryker, please. Let me explain," Kaiya pleaded desperately as she got up off the couch and grabbed my hands.

So she is hiding something. What else would there be to explain?

The coldness snaked back in as I steeled myself, preparing to do the hardest thing I'd ever done. I wasn't going to let her hurt me more than she already had. I was done letting my love for her blind me.

Forcing my steps, I made my way to the door. "Save it!" I yelled as

I grabbed my keys from the hook. "I don't want to hear your lies."

My chest tightened as I forcefully opened the door.

Don't go.

"Ryker, wait!" Kaiya started to beg. "Please don't g—"

I almost stopped, my love for her screaming for me to stay, to forget everything and take her in my arms, stop both of us from hurting. But I didn't. I walked out the door, slamming it behind me and cutting off Kaiya's sobs.

I had to get some air, and make sense of everything, make sure I was making the right decision.

You are.

As I got to my truck, I stopped. Every part of me, except my stubborn pride, told me to go back upstairs and quit being such a paranoid asshole.

Kaiya is eight months pregnant with your son. Don't leave her.

I almost went back, but what happened with Molly and me kept replaying in my mind. The way Kaiya had been acting over the past several months was similar to how Molly had acted before I'd found out about her and my brother.

I clenched my fists before punching the window of my driver's side door. Pain immediately shot up my arm, but I ignored it and got in my truck.

I should've never trusted her. I knew all women were the same.

I put the keys in the ignition, then stopped and gripped the steering wheel. Resting my head against it, I exhaled a heavy breath and closed my eyes.

Kaiya loves you. Go back up there and quit being a jackass.

Tightening my grip on the steering wheel, I started banging my forehead against it. "Fuck!"

You're letting your love for her blind you, just like you did with Molly. Don't be made a fool twice.

After starting my truck, I reversed and peeled out of the parking lot, ignoring pain in my chest and the knot forming in my gut.

Chapter Twenty-Three

Kaiya

Ryker's words held so much venom that I felt like my heart had been stung, injected with a lethal poison that was slowly corroding deep into my body and adding more irreparable scars to my broken soul.

How could he think that I cheated on him? I love him more than anything.

"Ryker, wait!" I cried out in despair. "Please don't g—"

I didn't get to finish my plea. The door slammed with his exit, and I felt like my heart had been smashed by it. All the pieces he had mended slowly fell apart again, shattering with every passing second that he was gone. Sinking to my knees on the floor, I sobbed into my hands as my world crumbled around me.

Why didn't I just tell him a long time ago? I'm so stupid.

I don't know how long I cried on the floor; it could've been minutes or it could've been hours, but when my tears finally ran dry, I was no longer upset. I was downright furious.

He wants to leave? Well, fine, I'm not going to sit around and wait for him.

Hefting myself off the floor, I stormed to the door, snatched my keys off the hook, and left.

How dare he accuse me of cheating? I'm pregnant with his son, for fuck's sake!

Tears resurfaced, streaming down my face as I went down the

stairs to my car. As I was about to open the door, a hand clamped down on my mouth and another came around my huge, bulging waist.

"I've been waiting for that meathead to leave you alone."

Bryce? What is he doing here?

I tried to pry his hands off of me but he tightened his grip. A feeling of dread permeated my stomach as I started to put two and two together.

Oh, God, no.

My words were muffled through Bryce's hand as he began to pull me away from my car. "What are you doing, Bryce?" My eyes darted around the empty parking lot, searching for anyone to help me.

"All those years, I was there for you. Every time you needed me, I was there. Then, you met him and threw everything we had away!"

His breath was hot against the side of my face, and it reeked of alcohol. "Bryce, please don't do this," I pleaded, even though I wasn't sure if he could make out my words since his hand was drowning them out. "I'm pregnant. I—"

He put more pressure on my stomach with his hand. "I see that! You barely know him, Ky. What were you thinking?" he spat.

More tears spilled from my eyes. I didn't know if they had even stopped from earlier. I struggled against Bryce as panic began to set in. He held me tighter to him and pressed me up against a car. His car.

I can't let him get me in the car.

I tried to scream, but with his hand over my mouth, I barely made a sound. I threw some back elbows into his ribs, but there wasn't much force in them because of how I was positioned. I managed to get a good hit in, forcing him to let me go briefly, but he pushed me by my chest against the car and held me there.

Bryce reared his fist back to punch me, but I turned and blocked it with both arms. Then, I gripped his forearm with my hands before throwing a back elbow into his chest. I used the momentum of the strike to force him to twist into the car, then pinned him there with my forearm on his throat.

Kneeing him in the groin, I caused him to clutch himself and drop to his knees. I screamed for help and turned to run away, but Bryce grabbed my ankle, sending me to smash my face on the hard asphalt.

Spots dotted my vision as the world spun around me. I felt Bryce pulling me into his arms as everything went black.

My eyes fluttered open to a ceiling. I was no longer outside. I was being carried inside somewhere.

Where am I? What is going on?

My head and nose throbbed with pain as I struggled to shake the disorientation clouding me. Then, I registered Bryce's face and everything came rushing back.

Oh my God!

"Help! Somebody help me!" I screamed as I squirmed in his arms.

Bryce clamped his hand over my mouth, muffling my cries. I bit down on his hand as hard as I could, causing him to pull his hand back and drop me. "You bitch!"

I fell to the floor and winced from the resulting pain. I glanced around, trying to take in my surroundings.

Shit.

I was in Bryce's apartment.

Out of the corner of my eye, I saw Bryce lunging toward me, so I turned on my side and kicked out, narrowly missing his knee and hitting his shin instead.

Get up. You can't let him pin you on the ground.

I rolled to the side and awkwardly stumbled to get up. I definitely wasn't as graceful as I used to be before I was pregnant. I got in my defensive stance as Bryce came at me again.

My techniques were limited since I was so large, and it was difficult for me to move fluidly like I needed to. I couldn't kick as well anymore, so I had to rely on my punching and hand techniques, which weren't my strong suit. I was at a huge disadvantage, but I wasn't going to give up. I had to protect my son.

Bryce threw punches as he advanced toward me. I backed up and blocked with my forearms, forgetting every thought except one:

Don't let him hit your stomach.

I kept retreating down the hallway as he advanced, blocking most of his punches, but not all. I was used to taking hits from all the sparring I had done, but each time he connected, the impact weakened me.

I backed through a doorway, then looked around to see where I was—Bryce had forced me into his bedroom.

Fuck, this isn't good.

I threw a palm strike toward his face, but he grabbed my wrist and jerked me forward. Wrenching my arm from his grasp, I stumbled backwards onto the bed.

I immediately sprung off and put my guard up. My eyes danced over Bryce as I tried to anticipate his movements.

In the brief time I had spent fighting him, I could already tell he preferred using his hands than kicking. Most men were like that, including Ryker, so I had experience against that style of fighting.

When I sparred Ryker, there was always one move that I got him with—a low high roundhouse attack. Unfortunately, I couldn't do the high kick anymore because of how big and off-balance I was, but I could still throw the low one.

Snapping my leg out, I caught Bryce in the thigh, but the hit didn't seem to faze him. He came in closer to me, causing panic to set in from his proximity. All I could think about was shielding my stomach from his hits.

I should've focused more on watching him and protecting my face. His hook caught me right on the jaw, causing fireworks to burst behind my eyelids before I crashed to the ground and darkness smothered me.

Chapter Twenty-Four

Ryker

I threw back another shot as I sat at the bar with Drew. Slamming the glass on the counter, I loudly ordered, "Another!"

Drew shook his head at the bartender, then looked at me. "Are you all right, bro? Shouldn't you be at home with Kaiya? The baby is due soon, right?"

Kaiya.

Hayden.

Home.

"Yeah. But I don't even know if he's mine," I lied. Deep down, I knew Hayden was mine. I was letting my stupid insecurities get the best of me.

"What are you talking about?" Drew looked at me skeptically, raising an eyebrow in question.

A glass of water was pushed in front of me, but I didn't take it. "They all cheat, you know. All of them."

Drew scoffed. "Are you serious? You really think Kaiya would cheat on you? Haven't you seen the way she looks at you? That girl has got it bad for you."

I didn't say anything for several seconds, trying to think of something to prove him wrong. My drunken mind came up with nothing. "I'm such an asshole."

Standing up, I wobbled slightly as I pulled out my wallet. I threw forty bucks down on the bar and rushed toward the door.

Drew quickly followed behind me. "What are you doing, bro?"

"Something I should have done hours ago. I need to get home to Kaiya." I pushed the door open before heading out into the warm summer night.

Drew stopped me by grabbing my arm. "You can't drive. You've had too much to drink."

I pulled my arm out of his grasp, and stumbled backwards. "I need to get home," I repeated more forcefully.

Drew tried to snatch my keys away, but I pushed him away. "Don't fuck with me, bro."

Drew put his hands up and took a step back. "All right, man. Be careful."

I walked away to my truck without a backwards glance, hoping I could fix the mistake I'd made.

I sped back to my complex, then sprinted up the stairs to our apartment. I fumbled to get the key in the lock as my eyes tried to focus on the knob.

Once I unlocked the door, I stumbled through and almost fell. "Kaiya," I called out into the dark room.

No response.

It's almost two in the morning. She's probably in bed by now, jackass.

"Warrior, I'm sorry," I apologized as I walked down the hall toward our bedroom.

The door was wide open. "Ky?"

Once I entered, I looked around the empty room, perplexed. Only Brownie lay sleeping in her bed in the corner.

Where is she?

I went into our bathroom and found the same thing. No Kaiya.

Damn it, where could she be?

I took my cell out and dialed her number. Her phone rang a couple of times, then went straight to voicemail.

Fuck.

Worry started to sink in. I tried to think of where Kaiya would go, especially since she was eight months pregnant. Then, the drunken fog lifted and the light bulb in my head went off.

I ran out of my apartment and didn't stop until I was banging on Kamden's door. "Hurry the fuck up, Kam! Open the goddamn door!"

The door abruptly opened, and I walked in, not waiting for an invitation. "Is Kaiya here?" I asked as I went down the hall toward her room.

I could hear Kamden's footsteps behind me. "No. I thought she was with you."

Shit.

Even though he just told me she wasn't there, I still went into her room. "What the fuck is going on, Ryker? Where's Kaiya?"

I turned around to face him and roughly ran my hands through my hair. "I don't know." I blew out a frustrated breath. "We got in an argument, and I left. She isn't answering her phone, and I have no clue where she is. I thought she'd be here."

Fuck.

Kamden's lip curled up angrily as he spat his words. "So, you're telling me that you got in a fight with my pregnant sister, then left her by herself, this late at night?"

"Look, I know I fucked up, but arguing about it isn't going to help us find her." I pushed past him to go back to the living room.

Where would she go?

Then, it hit me—Nori. "Maybe she went to Nori's," I said as I pulled out my phone and scrolled through my contacts.

Shit, I don't have her number.

I looked at Kam and asked, "Do you have her number?"

Kamden grabbed his phone from his back pocket and swiped the screen. He pressed it a few times before putting the phone to his ear.

I stuck my hand out. "Let me talk to her."

Kamden stared at me but didn't reply.

God, he's such an asshole,

I narrowed my eyes as anger simmered my blood. "Damn it, Kamden, give me the fucking phone!" I growled.

That motherfucker smirked at me, actually fucking smirked. He turned around as he greeted, "Hey, Nori. It's Kam. Is Kai—"

I ripped the phone from his hand, cutting off the rest of his sentence. He whirled around angrily as I put the phone to my ear. I gave him a warning glare as I spoke, "Nori, it's Ryker. Is Kaiya there?"

"No. Why would she be here?" She sounded confused.

"Fuck!" I yelled.

Where are you, Warrior?

"Ryker, what's going on? You're scaring me," Nori urgently replied.

I rubbed my hand over my face. "Kaiya and I got in a fight. I left the apartment, and when I came home she wasn't there. She's not with Kamden either. She isn't answering her phone."

I heard Nori gasp. "Oh my God, you don't think…"

"What?" I had no clue what she was talking about, but the fear and concern in her voice intensified mine.

When she didn't answer, I demanded, "Damn it, Nori, tell me!"

"You don't think the person who's been sending her those texts did something, do you?"

Now I was confused on top of being worried. "Wait, what?" I tried to make sense of what Nori was saying. "No, that was months ago, before Kaiya even found out she was pregnant. The texts stopped."

Nori sighed into the phone. "No, they didn't, Ryker. Kaiya just didn't want you to freak out and get yourself arrested over them, so she didn't tell you."

I slumped to the couch in shock. Those texts had been going on for over nine months and Kaiya had kept it to herself. No wonder she seemed so distant and off sometimes—she wasn't cheating, she was hiding the texts from me.

I wasn't sure if that revelation hurt more or less. I didn't fully believe that she'd been cheating on me, but keeping the texts from me was real. She didn't trust me enough to tell me what was going on.

Well, look how crazy you act.

I could hear Nori rambling through the phone, but I didn't care. All I cared about was finding Kaiya, and I had no idea where to start. And now I was terrified that whoever had been sending Kaiya the texts was somehow involved.

The phone fell from my hand to the couch. I bolted up and ran out the door, ignoring Kamden's shouts from behind me.

My apartment was still open since I'd left in such a hurry. I went inside and started looking around for anything that might tell me where Kaiya was. It was a long shot, but I was desperate.

I looked through our room first, but found nothing to help me so I went to the living room. I searched high and low, over every inch of the space, and still nothing.

Fuck.

Then, out of the corner of my eye, I could've sworn I saw a light flash. I jerked my head in the direction it came from, and then the small light flashed again from the couch.

Walking over to it, I found the source. There, barely sticking up out of the cushions, was Kaiya's phone.

I picked it and keyed in her passcode—Hayden's due date.

Why didn't you tell me what was going on, Warrior?

I went to her messages, hoping I could get some clues from the texts, and found the conversation with the unknown number.

The last text was sent at 10:33 PM, right after I had left.

Unknown: You're finally gonna be mine

My heart pounded with fear as my stomach clenched.

This is all my fault! Why did I act so stupid? Now Kaiya and our son are in danger, and I have no fucking clue where to find them.

I stared at the text, unable to take my eyes off it. Then, clutching the phone tightly in my hand, I reared back to chunk it across the room.

As I was about to let it fly, I stopped. I didn't want to destroy what little bit of a lead that I had.

"Find anything?" Kamden asked from the doorway.

I held up Kaiya's phone. "She left it here."

"Nori told me about the texts." He walked toward me with his arms crossed over his chest. "Any idea who sent them?"

"No," I sighed. "I didn't even know she was still getting them."

I scrolled through and read all the messages from the unknown number. Kamden was talking, but I zoned out everything he was saying, trying to pick out any detail that might point me in the direction of Kaiya.

Then, I stopped and zeroed in on one text.

No fucking way.

Kamden shoved me. "I'm talking to you, asshole!"

I clenched my jaw as I stared him down. "I found something," I gritted. I turned the screen to face him so that he could read it.

Unknown: Hope that meathead can protect you

Kamden's eyes met mine, then creased in confusion. He shrugged his shoulders. "What? I don't get it."

"You know who called me a meathead the last time Kaiya and I saw him?"

Kamden shook his head and raised an eyebrow. "No."

The rage coursing through me was evident in my voice. "Bryce."

After explaining to Kamden everything that had happened with Bryce, we got in my truck and took off toward Bryce's condo.

"I still don't think Bryce would do something like this. He and Kaiya have been friends for years."

I was almost positive that Bryce had something to do with Kaiya's disappearance. Not just because of the meathead text, but all of the messages combined. Especially the last one.

You're finally gonna be mine

Bryce had always wanted more than Kaiya was willing to give, and it seemed like he was going to take what he thought was his.

Too fucking bad—Kaiya is mine.

I was going to make him pay for taking her from me. Slowly and painfully.

Once Kamden navigated to Bryce's condo, I kicked down the door without even bothering to knock. Darkness blanketed the inside as I went in and switched on the light. "Kaiya!"

I surveyed the room, looking for any sign of Kaiya or Bryce. A chair was overturned and some picture frames lay broken on the ground. I searched the rest of Bryce's place and found more signs of a struggle, especially in the bedroom.

Pillows from the bed were on the floor, and the covers were bunched up at the foot of the bed. A lamp was turned over on the mattress and one of the nightstands was on its side.

I gripped the edge of the dresser as I fought to stay calm. I needed to be level-headed if I was going to find Kaiya, but the thought of Bryce hurting Kaiya, or worse, raping her, sent me over the edge.

I roared in fury as I swiped everything off the top of the dresser. Everything that was on top scattered to the floor as I turned and punched a hole through the wall.

Then, I saw something that made my heart sink—Kaiya's bracelet. It lay on the floor next to the bed. Kamden rushed in. "What? What happened?"

Ignoring him, I walked to the bracelet before bending over and picking it up. The link at the end of the chain was broken, probably during whatever happened. My eyes burned as I thought about Kaiya being hurt or worse, dead.

I closed my fist around the bracelet as a few tears fell down my face.

Not my Warrior. Please let her be okay.

A hand came down on my shoulder, and I turned and flung it

away, preparing to punch whoever touched me.

Kamden put his hands up. "Whoa, it's just me. As much as I want to kick your ass, we have other things to worry about. Like finding my sister."

He was right—I needed to focus on finding Kaiya and not get sucked into my emotions.

Where would he have taken her?

I put Kaiya's bracelet in my pocket before wiping my face. "Okay, let's search the house—maybe there's a clue as to where he would go."

We ripped the condo apart, looking for anything that would lead us to Kaiya. Bryce's office was where we had concentrated most of our efforts, but papers were strewn all over the floor and desk—it was like looking for a needle in a haystack.

Kamden sat in an office chair, going through papers on the desk. He huffed in frustration before throwing the papers down. "There's nothing here."

"Keep looking." I was searching through Bryce's filing cabinet when I came across a file of interest. It was labeled as "Real Estate Documents."

I pulled the file out and opened it. I began reading the papers, and finally found something that might help. I looked up at Kam, who had his elbows propped on the table as he held his head in his hands. "Hey, I think I found something."

His head jerked toward me, and he practically jumped out of the chair. "What?" he asked anxiously.

I scanned over the document one more time just to be sure before looking up at Kamden again. "Apparently Bryce has a house in Cape Cod."

"Do you think he might have taken her there?"

"I don't know." I took the paper and dropped the rest of the file on the ground. "But I'm gonna find out."

"Cape Cod is more than an hour away," Kamden pointed out as I started walking.

"Which means we better not waste any more time."

Chapter Twenty-Five

Kaiya

My eyes fluttered open slowly. Wincing from the pain swarming most of my body, I attempted to move, but couldn't. My hands were fastened to a chair behind my back and my ankles were tied together. Duct tape covered my mouth, stretching the skin around my lips uncomfortably.

My eyes darted around the room, attempting to take in my surroundings. I was in a bedroom, one that I'd never been in before. The walls were painted a light blue, resembling a springtime sky, and various beach décor adorned the room. The muted sound of waves barely registered, so I guessed that I was somewhere near a beach.

Where has he taken me?

Bryce didn't live near a beach, but I vaguely remembered him mentioning something about wanting to take me on a mini-vacation to a beach condo in Cape Cod. If he had brought me there, I was fucked. It was about an hour away from home.

Squirming, I tried to see if I could free myself and escape, but Bryce had firmly secured the knots restraining me.

Fuck.

I wasn't going to give up, though. The chances of someone coming out here to rescue me were slim, so I needed to figure out how to get out of here and back home.

Fumbling with the rope around my wrists, I attempted to loosen it but was interrupted.

"Ah, you're awake," Bryce spoke, drawing my eyes to the doorway where he stood.

I stilled as he approached me, not wanting him to see what I was doing. "Why are you doing this, Bryce?" My voice was muffled by the tape as I questioned him.

He circled around me. "Why am I doing this?" He responded rhetorically.

I tried to turn and follow his movement as he rounded my back, but I couldn't because of the way he had tied me to the chair.

His warm breath hit my neck, sending a chill over me as he spoke. "Because I'm finally taking what's mine."

Was he always this crazy?

No, you make people that way, just like Kaleb.

The pain of him ripping the tape off my mouth snapped me out of my thoughts. I screamed for help, but Bryce silenced me when he clutched my throat.

My heart started to pound as panic began to weave through me. I jerked my head back, but Bryce kept his grip on my skin. He wasn't applying enough pressure to block my air supply, but it was still uncomfortable.

"Bryce, please stop." I begged as tears formed at the corners of my eyes.

The pressure intensified for a few seconds before he let go and came around to face me. "I forgot that you hate to have your neck touched." His tone was mocking as he ran his finger over the scar on my throat.

My breaths were labored as panic ate at me and adrenaline rushed through my veins. Then, worry over Hayden's safety compounded my anxiety. I hadn't felt him move since back at the apartment. I knew the stress I was subjected to wasn't good for him, and I didn't want to go into early labor. I needed to calm down and find a way to get out of there.

I resumed messing with the ropes and locked eyes with Bryce. "Let me go, Bryce, please. I promise I won't tell anyone."

"Not even that meathead?" he replied snidely, his distaste for Ryker evident in his voice.

"I won't, I promise—he probably doesn't even know I'm gone. We had a fight and he left. He's probably not even home yet."

Bryce seemed to consider that for a moment as his eyes scanned my face. He looked like my old Bryce for a moment before his face shifted darkly, the way Kaleb's used to. His eyes narrowed menacingly at me. "I don't think so."

The tiny shred of hope I had evaporated. I knew that look—the one there was no reasoning with. I wasn't going to be able to convince Bryce to let me go.

The knots in the ropes loosened a little. I needed to keep Bryce distracted so I could finish untying the rope enough to escape. A few tears trickled down my cheeks as I held his gaze. "I'm sorry, Bryce. I never meant to hurt you."

He scoffed and shook his head. "I was there for you whenever you needed me. And how did you repay me?" He clenched his fists and raised his voice. "By kicking me to the curb for some asshole you had just met!"

"I'm sorry!" A sob broke through my throat as I looked into his wounded eyes. I felt bad for him for a split second, but pushed away the guilt and sadness, reminding myself of what he was doing to me. I tore my eyes away and steeled my voice. "I told you not to get involved with me, but you didn't listen."

"Oh, so it's my fault?" he replied incredulously. My eyes darted back to him as I heard his footsteps quickly approaching me, causing my body to tense in fear.

He lowered his face to my eye level. "You made me do this. I tried to make you see that I was the one for you. I tried to be patient. But after everything, I finally realized that when you want something, you have to take it."

I had almost unknotted the rope, but I didn't want to finish while Bryce was still in the room with me. I was in no shape to fight him off, and I wanted to escape with the least amount of confrontation as possible, preferably without him knowing.

He cupped my cheek, but I turned my face away, repulsed by his touch. Big mistake.

Out of the corner of my eye, I saw him rear his hand back. I flinched in anticipation before he backhanded me and bellowed in my face. "Look what you've done to us! I loved you!" His voice softened as he forced me to look at him by gripping my chin. His eyes were glazed with tears as he stared into mine. "I would've loved you forever, Ky."

I trembled as my gaze ran over his face. A face that used to be a source of comfort for me, but was now lost. He still looked the same, but the man I knew and loved was gone. I may not have loved him like he'd wanted, but I had loved him. And now I'd destroyed him, just like everyone else important in my life—Mom. Dad. Kaleb. Kamden… Ryker. Bryce had been one of my only friends, and I'd treated him like shit.

All I do is cause pain and ruin everything around me.

"You're right," I replied in a cracked whisper. "This is all my fault."

I hung my head as tears dripped from my eyes. My sight blurred as I looked down at my belly. I thought about the life inside me, something so perfect that I had helped create, something I'd finally done right. I wasn't going to let Hayden suffer from my destructive actions.

I kept my gaze downcast, hoping Bryce would think that I'd given up, then leave the room. Once he did, I could finish untying the ropes and get the fuck out of there.

"I'm sorry it had to come to this, Ky, but I can't live without you."

I felt him kiss the top of my head before the sound of his footsteps receding filled the room. The door closed and left me alone with just the dull murmur of the waves lapping up on the shore.

I waited a few minutes before straightening and working on the ropes around my wrists. My back was strained from the position I was in, making it harder for me to work on my task. Not to mention that I was utterly exhausted from everything that had happened.

My shoulders and arms burned after God knows how long. I was so close to untying the knots, but I just couldn't get them undone. I slumped in fatigue and sobbed, ready to give up.

I can't do this. I'm too weak.

Then, something amazing happened—Hayden kicked me, right when I needed it most. He reminded me of what I was fighting for, why I couldn't lose hope. Him.

I will get out of this. I have to

Sitting back up, I worked on the ropes again. I wasn't going to let Bryce win—I was going to escape and ensure my son's safety. Hayden was all that mattered.

After several minutes, the sound of a door crashing open halted my actions.

What was that?

Sounds of fighting, furniture breaking, and indistinct shouting followed. I strained to hear, but couldn't make out the voices through the closed door. All I could tell was that they were male.

What's going on? Who's here?

I started to get my hopes up that Ryker had come for me, but then I remembered our fight. He probably didn't even know I was gone. And if he did, he probably didn't care anymore.

His words replayed in my mind, making my heart sink back down into the pool of despair where my demons lay.

We're through.

The sting of tears assaulted my eyes as I thought about never seeing Ryker again, never feeling his skin against mine, or hearing him tell me he loves me.

The sound of doors opening roughly slamming into the walls broke through my thoughts.

"Kaiya! Kaiya!"

My breath hitched. I knew that voice.

Am I dreaming?

The voice became louder, sounding desperate and terrified. "Kaiya! Kaiya, where are you?"

The tears that had been pooling spilled over. "In here! I'm in here!"

Footsteps pounded down the hall, getting faster and louder as he neared. "Kaiya!"

I wriggled in the chair, trying to free my hands. "In here!" I screamed.

I didn't stop screaming until the doorknob jiggled seconds later. "I'm right here, baby. I'm gonna get you out of there."

Several thuds echoed off the door before it was kicked in. Ryker appeared in the doorway; his gaze immediately found mine, and in seconds, he was kneeling in front of me. Reaching behind me, he untied my wrists and slipped the rope off before unfastening my ankles from the bottom of the chair. He helped me stand, then wrapped his arms around me, holding me tightly to him. He expelled a breath of relief. "Thank God I found you."

My hands fisted the back of his shirt as tears ran down my face. "You came for me," I whispered in disbelief.

Ryker pulled back and framed my face in his hands. His eyes searched mine. "Of course I did, Warrior." He moved one of his hands to my belly. "I love you. You and Hayden are everything to me."

"But earlier you said th—"

"Fuck what I said. I was being a stupid asshole. I never should've said those things or left you. I'm so sorry, baby."

More tears flowed from my eyes. I should've been pissed as all hell, but all I felt was relief and my love for Ryker. He was, and always had been "it" for me. Nothing would ever change that.

I sobbed into his chest, my body shaking as reality sank in and overwhelmed me. The tears poured out of me and soaked Ryker's shirt as I held onto him for dear life.

Suddenly, my stomach was assaulted with the most intense pain I'd ever experienced. I couldn't stop the cry of agony that escaped me as my knees buckled, and I slumped against Ryker.

Ryker eased us down to the floor and cupped my face. "Ky, what's wrong, baby?" His eyes scanned over my face with concern.

Clenching my teeth, I gritted out my words. "I don't know." I clutched my stomach. "It just hurts."

Ryker draped my arm over his shoulders before lifting me up and into his arms. "I'm going to take you to the hospital."

Biting my lip, I buried my face back in his chest and fisted his shirt in my hands. Tears involuntarily streamed down my heated cheeks from the excruciating pain. "It hurts so bad," I whimpered.

"I know, baby. I'm sorry. I'll get you there as fast as I can." Ryker replied as he rushed through Bryce's condo.

"What happened?" Kamden urgently questioned. "Is she okay?"

"I don't know. She's having some stomach pain. I'm taking her to the hospital."

I cried out, unable to stifle the sound. The pain was too much. I felt like my insides were being shredded with a razor-sharp saw, and I worried for Hayden. I was still five weeks away from being full term, which wasn't that bad, but so much could go wrong, and I didn't want anything happening to him.

"Ryker, please," I whimpered. "Hayden."

We started moving again. "You coming or not?" Ryker gruffly asked my brother.

"What about him?" Kamden replied.

"Fuck him. All I care about is Kaiya and the baby. I'm leaving. You can stay if you want," Ryker abruptly retorted.

Even though my eyes were closed, I knew we were outside. The smell of the ocean wafted over me as the sea breeze cooled my fevered skin. I could hear the waves crashing against the sand as we continued walking.

Ryker laid me down in the backseat before climbing in next to me. He rested my head in his lap and another wave of pain slammed through me.

Fuck! It hurts so bad.

I arched my back as I writhed in the seat and screamed. Sweat beaded on my forehead and my body felt like it was on fire.

Ryker pushed some hair out of my face and yelled at Kamden in the front seat. "Drive! Fast!"

I closed my eyes again as Kamden and Ryker shouted back and forth about the closest hospital and what highway to take. Their voices faded out as darkness overtook me.

Chapter Twenty-Six

Ryker

Kamden drove to the nearest emergency room in Cape Cod. Kaiya had passed out when we started driving, and I hadn't been able to wake her.

Staring down at her, I was unable to take my eyes off her slowly rising and falling chest. I feared that if I looked away, she would stop breathing.

Stay with me, baby.

Kamden parked right in front of the emergency room doors. He had barely put the truck in park as I hurried to get Kaiya out of the truck and inside.

Cradling her in my arms, I rushed through the sliding glass doors and to the front desk. The nurse stood when I reached the counter. "What's your emergency?"

"My girlfriend started having stomach pains. She's thirty-five weeks pregnant."

"Okay, I need you to fill out this paperwork." The nurse handed me a clipboard.

Kaiya started to stir. She writhed in my arms and moaned.

Fuck I hate when she's in pain.

Tears flowed from her eyes, which were clenched shut in pain. Her cries became louder and her fingers dug into my arm and back. "Ryker!"

The agony in her voice sliced right through my heart. I directed my attention to the nurse. There was no mistaking the anxiousness in my tone. "Please get someone!"

"Sir, I nee-"

"Now!" My voice boomed through the room. "Can't you see how much pain she's in?"

Kamden reached for the clipboard. "I'm her brother. I promise I'll fill everything out, just please get my sister some help."

The nurse looked back and forth between both of us before handing Kamden the clipboard. Then, she grabbed the phone as Kaiya screamed out in pain again.

I pulled her closer against me. "It's going to be okay, Warrior. They're getting someone right now. Just hold on."

Sweat coated Kaiya's forehead as she buried her face into my chest. Kamden stood in front of me and stroked her hair. "Shhh, *sorella*. Everything's going to be okay."

Kamden began filling out the paperwork as I impatiently paced back and forth in the waiting area. After a few minutes, two medical personnel came through some double doors to our right. They wheeled a rolling hospital bed through and approached us. "Kaiya Marlow?"

I took a hurried step toward them. "Right here."

The male nurse quickly glanced up at me. "Lay her down gently."

I carefully lay Kaiya on the stretcher, but she wouldn't let go of my shirt. "Don't leave me," she pleaded.

I ran one of my hands through her hair. "I'm right here, baby. I'm not going anywhere."

She winced and squirmed on the bed as she pulled me closer to her. "Make it stop."

Fuck. Shit. Fuck.

I hated being helpless. Not being able to ease Kaiya's pain was killing me inside. I looked up at the female nurse across from me. "Please hurry. She's in a lot of pain."

She smiled sympathetically. "My name is Meredith, and that's Jake.

226

We're going to take care of her." She attached a medical bracelet to Kaiya's wrist and continued speaking, "We need to check the baby's heart rate. If he or she is in distress, then we'll need to do an emergency C-section."

I wasn't an expert on pregnancy, but I knew that Kaiya wasn't full term yet. "She's only thirty-five weeks," I replied with concern.

"I'm sorry, but if the baby is at risk, we have to deliver."

"No," Kaiya whimpered. "He's not ready."

I pried her hands from my shirt and held them in mine. "He's gonna be okay, Warrior."

Kaiya's eyes watered as she squeezed my hands. She gritted her teeth and groaned in pain again.

Jake and Meredith pushed the stretcher through the open double doors in front of us. Soon, we were wheeled down the hall into a room with an ultrasound machine.

After getting settled in the room, Meredith prepped Kaiya, attaching various wires to her chest to monitor her vitals while Jake grabbed a small machine from one of the cabinets—it looked similar to the one Kaiya's doctor had used when we listened to Hayden's heartbeat.

Meredith applied gel to Kaiya's stomach as Jake handed her the wand to the fetal doppler. Noise soon filled the room as Meredith moved the wand around Kaiya's abdomen. I immediately recognized the sound of Hayden's heartbeat, even though it was noticeably slower than the other times we'd heard it.

Meredith's forehead creased in concern as she stared at the handheld machine. "Eighty-five bpm. We need to get an OB in here stat."

"Wait, is that bad?" I questioned anxiously.

Kaiya moaned in pain as Meredith grabbed the phone. "I need an OB to room 103. I have a patient and fetal heart rate is 85 bpm."

Meredith hung up the phone, then grabbed some supplies from a drawer and swabbed Kaiya's inner elbow with an alcohol wipe. "Normal fetal heart rate is between one hundred twenty and one hundred eighty beats per minute. Anything over or under that puts the baby at risk."

My mind was all over the place, unable to register what either of them were saying. I finally was able to come up with a coherent thought. "Are they going to be okay?"

Meredith hesitated before answering, "They'll be fine. There are always risks when it comes to any surgery, but the sooner we act, the better. The doctor will probably want to get the baby out as soon as possible."

The doctor entered as Meredith wrapped a band around Kaiya's belly. Kaiya writhed in pain on the stretcher and moaned again. Meredith addressed the doctor. "Fetal heart rate is 85 bpm."

The doctor looked at the monitor that was hooked up to Kaiya. "Let's monitor for a few minutes. Start the IV and get some fluids in her."

Meredith inserted an IV into Kaiya's arm. She winced in pain. "Ryker."

Rushing to her side, I grabbed her hand. "I'm right here, baby."

"What's going on? Is Hayden okay?" She gritted out as she tightly squeezed my hand.

"He's going to be fine. His heart rate is a little slow so they may have to do an emergency C-section."

"What? No," She moaned. Suddenly, her grip on my hand loosened. "I don't feel good."

The monitor started beeping wildly. Meredith rushed to Kaiya's other side. "Blood pressure is dropping." Her voice was urgent.

Kaiya's skin went pale, and her eyes slowly closed. Her words were slurred and barely audible. "Ryker, I—"

Kaiya's head lolled to the side.

My heart dropped into my stomach.

Please, God, no.

I shook our joined hands, trying to wake her. "Kaiya! Kaiya!"

"Get her to surgery now. We have to perform an emergency C-section." The doctor said, then directed his attention to me. "Are you the father?"

I couldn't process what was happening. My eyes burned from tears as I stared down at Kaiya.

The doctor placed a hand on my shoulder. "Sir, we have to go now. Are you the father?"

I looked up at him, my sight blurred. "What?"

"Are you the father?

My voice cracked. "Yes."

"Do we have your consent for surgery? We need to get the baby out now."

I looked down at Kaiya, then back at the doctor, still trying to take in everything. "Do whatever you need to do. Please save them."

The doctor nodded, then walked toward the door. "Let's get her into surgery."

Jake pushed the stretcher as Meredith guided it out of the room behind the doctor jogged beside it, keeping Kaiya's hand in mine as we rushed down the hallway.

When we reached the set of double doors at the end of the hall, Meredith turned and looked at me. "There's a waiting area back down the hall, to the right. The doctor will come speak to you following the surgery."

My heart rate increased as anxiety set in. "I can't come with her?"

"I'm sorry, but due to the complications she's experiencing, no."

I reluctantly nodded my understanding before leaning down and kissing Kaiya on the forehead. I brushed the sweaty hair out of her face. "I love you, Warrior." My voice was strained by emotion.

"I'm sorry, we have to go now." The doctor stated impatiently as he went through the doors.

Meredith gave me a sympathetic look as she and Jake began to push Kaiya behind the doctor. "We'll take good care of her. Don't worry."

I nodded as tears fell down my face. I stared at Kaiya until the doors closed, taking her out of sight. I ran my hands over my face, then through my hair.

Fuck! This can't be happening.

I slammed my fist into the metal and pressed my forehead against the doors.

Calm down, everything is going to be fine. Think positive.

I let out a breath in an attempt to calm myself down. And then, for the first time since God knows when, I prayed.

I know I'm not one of your favorites, but please take care of them. I can't lose them.

I stayed there for a few seconds before I pushed off the doors and headed back to the lobby, unable to stop the anxiety that was overtaking me.

Ethan was talking to Kamden when I entered the waiting room. When he caught sight of me, he ran over, stopping right in front of me and meeting my gaze. "What happened? Are Kaiya and the baby okay?"

My vision blurred as tears stung my eyes. I took a deep breath and exhaled heavily. I hadn't explained the details over the phone when I called him; I just told him to get his ass to the hospital as fast as he could. "Kaiya was... attacked. The trauma sent the baby into distress, and as they were monitoring her, she passed out. They had to do an emergency C-section."

Ethan stared at me, apparently stunned by my words. He raked his hands over his face. "Oh my God, Ryker, I'm sorry."

I sat down next to Kamden. I held my head in my hands and bounced my leg anxiously. I was not prepared for this.

Please let them be okay. Don't take them from me.

Kamden placed a hand on my back. "They'll be okay. My sister's a fighter—always has been."

I couldn't speak because of the emotion threatening to choke me, so I nodded. I knew Kaiya was a fighter, but I still had a knot of worry balled deep in my gut that grew with each passing second they were in there.

Ethan sat on my other side and sighed. "I can't believe this is happening."

Me neither.

About twenty minutes passed before the surgeon came into the waiting area. He looked at the screen of an iPad. "Ryker Campbell?"

I stood up immediately and went toward him. "That's me—is Kaiya okay?"

Kamden and Ethan came up next to me as the doctor replied, "She's in recovery right now. The surgery went well—no complications."

I let out a heavy breath. "And the baby?"

The doctor smiled. "A healthy seven pound, three ounce boy. He's doing very well. You should be able see him soon."

Thank God.

I couldn't stop the smile that slowly spread over my face.

They're okay.

Ethan patted me on the back. "Congratulations, bro."

I looked at him, still in shock that both Kaiya and Hayden were okay after everything they'd been through in the last few hours. "Thanks."

Kamden started asking the doctor questions about Kaiya's surgery and recovery, but all I could think about was seeing her and Hayden. Images of what he looked like ran through my head.

"Are you ready to meet your son?" The doctor asked, breaking through my thoughts.

Son. My son.

I laughed. "Yes. Hell yes."

Chapter Twenty-Seven

Kaiya

"Wake up, my Warrior," a soft, deep voice spoke, sounding garbled as I teetered between awake and sleep.

My eyes fluttered open to a dimly lit room.

Where am I?

I tried to sit up, but I was too weak and everything hurt. I moaned in pain.

"Easy, baby. You just had surgery."

I gingerly turned my head toward the sound of the voice I loved so much. "Surgery?" I rasped, my mouth dry and cottony.

My eyes stung, and I was unable to focus on anything so I closed them as Ryker answered, "Hayden went into distress, and you passed out. The doctor had to do an emergency C-section."

"Is Hayden okay? Where is he?" I asked as my mind scrambled to make sense of everything. I strained to open my eyes, but the faint light hurt, forcing me to shut them again.

"He's fine, baby. He's right here. We've been waiting for you to wake up." He paused before talking again, this time in a gentler tone. "Ready to meet Mommy, Hayden?"

Tears leaked from my closed eyes. I fought to open them, anxious to see my baby and finally succeeded. My sight may have been blurred, but I knew I was looking at the most beautiful thing I'd ever seen as I laid eyes on my son.

Ryker stood next to the bed, cradling the tiny bundle in his huge, inked arms. So opposite, yet so perfect. He gazed down at Hayden lovingly before giving me the same look. "Wanna hold him, Momma?"

I weakly lifted my arms, but couldn't hold them up.

Damn anesthesia.

"More than anything," I whispered as more tears fell down my face.

"Relax." He shifted toward me and gently laid Hayden on my chest. I used every ounce of strength I had in me to bring my arms up to wrap around my baby.

My baby.

I softly kissed his fuzzy head as Ryker ran a hand through my hair. "You did amazing, Warrior. He's perfect."

He is, isn't he?

I stared down at my son, unable to take my eyes off of him. My eyes ran over every feature as my fingers traced over his velvety skin.

I can't believe I created something so perfect. I finally did something right.

I glanced up at Ryker, who was also gazing down at Hayden on my chest. I smiled as I continued to stare at the man I loved.

Our eyes met as one corner of his mouth curved up. "What?"

My lips spread wider. "Nothing."

He brushed his knuckles down my cheek. "Tell me."

"I just love you. I'm so lucky to have you."

"Nah, Warrior, you've got it all wrong." He looked down at Hayden and carefully rubbed him on his little back. "I'm the lucky one."

Chapter Twenty-Eight

Ryker

It felt amazing to finally bring Kaiya and our son home. The few days we had spent in the hospital seemed to drag, especially since Kaiya and I both hated hospitals. And to make matters worse, we had to deal with the police asking questions about Bryce. Bastards wouldn't even wait until Kaiya was discharged.

Kamden, Kaiya, and I had given our statements about the incident. The police had decided not to press any charges on Kamden or me for assaulting Bryce or breaking into either of his properties. The investigating officers had informed us that Bryce would be charged with assault and kidnapping and would face up to fifteen years in prison.

Kamden and I had done a number on Bryce, breaking four of his ribs, his jaw, and rupturing his spleen. I probably would've beat him to death if I hadn't been so desperate to find Kaiya.

Kaiya had broken down once the police finally left the hospital. Bryce had been one of her only friends, and what he had done hurt her deeply. But I knew she'd recover; my Warrior always did.

I carried Hayden in his car seat as I helped Kaiya inside the house. There were still stacks of boxes in every room that needed to be unpacked, and Hayden's room was filled with everything he needed and more.

I set down his carrier and all of Kaiya's bags, then led her to our bedroom. She was exhausted and had been fighting sleep to spend as much time with Hayden as possible, but now she was going to rest whether she liked it or not.

After carefully helping her get into bed, I covered her with the blankets before kissing her forehead. "You need to rest, Warrior."

"I don't want to rest—I need to take care of Hayden," she argued stubbornly, throwing the blankets and sitting up in bed.

I shook my head and chuckled. "I'll take care of Hayden—you sleep."

She yawned but still resisted. "But—"

"No buts. You've barely slept since he was born."

Sighing in defeat, she gingerly laid back on the bed. "Fine. But wake me up to feed him in two hours."

I wasn't planning to wake her up. Kaiya had already pumped some breast milk at the hospital, so I could feed Hayden myself. "Okay. Now get some sleep," I said as I backed toward the door.

She yawned again and closed her eyes. "I love you."

A smile tugged at my lips. I wish she knew how much I loved her, how much she and our son meant to me. They owned my whole fucking heart. "I love you, too."

I went back to the living room to check on Hayden. He was fast asleep in his car seat, so I decided to unpack some more of our things while he and Kaiya slept. We'd managed to get most of our large furniture in, but hadn't planned on Hayden coming early, so we weren't fully moved in yet.

After about an hour or so, Hayden started crying. Kaiya was still sleeping, so I grabbed a bottle of breast milk from the fridge and put it in some hot water to warm up before taking Hayden out of his carrier.

I was so fucking nervous holding him. He seemed so small and fragile, especially in my bulky arms. I was afraid I would break him, so I tried to be as gentle as possible whenever I handled him.

Laying him against my chest, I held his head steady as I went back to the kitchen to check if his bottle was ready. His cries had died down to a whimper now that I held him, but the sound still made me anxious, definitely something that would take getting used to.

I checked the temperature of the milk, but it was still too cold. I set it back in the water and patted Hayden on the back as I waited a few more minutes. I was thankful that the nurses in the maternity ward had shown us how to prepare Hayden's bottles and feed him because I would've been lost otherwise.

When the bottle was ready, I grabbed it and carefully carried Hayden to the bedroom. Kaiya had made me move the rocking chair from the nursery a couple of weeks ago because she planned to keep Hayden in our room for a few months.

I sat down with the speed of a turtle and cautiously positioned Hayden in my arms so that I could feed him. I started to rock him once he started eating, and I relaxed a little. Just like with his mom, I hated hearing him cry, and would do anything to fix what was causing it.

My eyes ran over his tiny form in my large, inked arms. So out of place, yet right where he belonged. He was perfect. His mom was perfect.

I looked up at Kaiya sleeping in our bed and smiled. I would've never guessed in a million years that we'd be where we are now. But I wouldn't change it for anything. Life had a way of sorting itself out, and every detour or obstacle was there for a purpose, getting us to where we needed to be. And I was exactly where I needed to be.

Epilogue

Kaiya

Four Years Later

Laying on the gym mat, propped up on my elbows, I watched Ryker and Hayden over by the punching bag. Ryker was trying to teach Hayden some basic punches, even though he had just turned four and had a short attention span.

Ryker lowered the bag all the way down so Hayden could reach it. He squatted next to our son and put his hands up in front of his face. "Put your hands up like this—always protect your face. Don't let anyone hit you."

Hayden put up his hands. They looked huge compared to his head with the gloves that Ryker had just bought him for his birthday. "Like this, Daddy?"

Ryker's mouth spread in a huge, proud grin, lighting up his whole face. "Yeah, just like that." He mussed Hayden's hair. "Now, hit the bag with your fist like this."

239

Ryker modeled a few punches that Hayden attempted to copy. I couldn't stop the smile that formed as I watched them. Hayden was the spitting image of Ryker, with the same brown hair and eyes. It was amazing how much they looked alike.

My two boys.

Ryker glanced over at me, giving me that look that still knotted my stomach. His love for me was evident all over his face, just like it was when he looked at our son.

After a few more punches, he scooped Hayden up and brought him over to me. "Mommy, did you see me?" Hayden squealed as he threw his arms around my neck.

I hugged him back. "Yes, baby, you did so great!"

Hayden pulled away and stood next to me before flexing his muscles. "I want to be big and strong, just like Daddy."

Ryker and I both laughed before Ryker said, "You will, buddy. And remember that you'll always need to protect Mommy and your little sister when she's born, okay?"

"I will, Daddy. I promise."

Ryker leaned over and pressed a kiss to my lips as he placed his tattooed hand on my bulging belly and softly rubbed it. "How's my little Warrior today?"

"She's been kicking a lot lately."

"Sounds like her mama—always fighting." He chuckled.

I set my hand on top of his and smiled. "I wouldn't want her any other way."

the End

Acknowledgements

Wow.

I've finished my fourth book.

This is the first series I've completed, and its bittersweet for me. Kaiya and Ryker got the happily ever after they both deserved, but I don't think I'm ready to say good-bye to them—I'm not sure I ever will be. They'll always have a special place in my heart, and I'll never forget their journey.

The pressure to create a sequel worthy to The Scars of Us was overwhelming. I really hope that you enjoyed the way Kaiya' and Ryker's story ended—it was definitely an emotional roller-coaster for me to write.

Thank you to my beta readers, Vanessa, Natasha, Nicki, Andrea, Jennifer, and Erin for their feedback. I don't know what I'd do without your support. I love you girls!

To my editor, Ana Zaun, for once again pushing me and helping my writing grow. There were times I wanted to chunk my laptop in frustration, but I know your criticism was only meant to help better myself. Thank you for spending your time making my work shine.

To Kari at Cover to Cover Designs, thank you for making another beautiful cover. The *Mending Scars* cover is a perfect follow-up to the one you made for *The Scars of Us*, and I know readers will love it as much as I do.

To Simon Barnes for taking another amazing photo. Your work always impresses me, and I appreciate everything that you do. Your hard work and dedication is evident in every photo you shoot, and I'm grateful for every time I get to work with you and Andrew.

And most importantly, to my readers. I know it took me longer than I originally planned to release this book, and I thank you for your patience. Seeing your excitement and interest while I dealt with my personal issues meant so much and helped lift my spirits. I'd be nothing without your support, and you will never understand how much you all mean to me.

Made in the USA
Charleston, SC
13 June 2016